Henry Lytton Bulwer

Historical characters: Talleyrand, Cobbet, Mackintosh, Canning

Henry Lytton Bulwer

Historical characters: Talleyrand, Cobbet, Mackintosh, Canning

ISBN/EAN: 9783742842060

Manufactured in Europe, USA, Canada, Australia, Japa

Cover: Foto ©Raphael Reischuk / pixelio.de

Manufactured and distributed by brebook publishing software
(www.brebook.com)

Henry Lytton Bulwer

Historical characters: Talleyrand, Cobbet, Mackintosh, Canning

HISTORICAL
CHARACTERS:

TALLEYRAND
COBBETT MACKINTOSH
CANNING

BY

SIR HENRY LYTTON BULWER, G.C.B.

COPYRIGHT EDITION.

IN TWO VOLUMES.

VOL. II.

L E I P Z I G

BERNHARD TAUCHNITZ

1868.

MACKINTOSH,

THE MAN OF PROMISE.

———

PART I.

Mackintosh's character. — Character of men of his type. — Birth and parentage. — Starts as a physician, fails, and becomes a newspaper writer, and author of a celebrated pamphlet in answer to Burke's "Thoughts on the French Revolution." — Studies for the bar. — Becomes noted as a public character, violent on the Liberal side. — Becomes acquainted with Mr. Burke. — Modifies his opinions. — Gives lectures on public law, remarkable for their eloquence and their Conservative opinions. — Becomes the advocate of Peltier; makes a great speech, and shortly afterwards accepts a place in India.

MACKINTOSH,

THE MAN OF PROMISE.

PART I.

FROM HIS YOUTH TO HIS APPOINTMENT IN INDIA.

I.

I STILL remember, amongst the memorable events
of my early youth, an invitation to meet Sir James
Mackintosh at dinner; and the eager and respectful
attention with which this honoured guest was received.
I still remember also my anxiety to learn the especial
talents, or remarkable works, for which Sir James was
distinguished, and the unsatisfactory replies which all
my questions elicited. He was a writer, but many had
written better; he was a speaker, but many had spoken
better; he was a philosopher, but many had done far
more for philosophy; and yet, though it was difficult
to fix on any one thing in which he was first-rate, it
was generally maintained that he was a first-rate man.
There is, indeed, a class amongst mankind, a body
numerous in all literary societies, who are far less
valued for any precise thing they have done than according to a vague notion of what they are capable of

doing. Mackintosh may be taken as a type of this class; not that he passed his life in the learned inactivity to which the resident members of our own universities sometimes consign their intellectual powers, but which more frequently characterizes the tranquil scholars, whose erudition is the boast of some small German or Italian city.

But though mixing in the action of a great and stirring community, a lawyer, an author, a member of parliament, Mackintosh never arrived at an eminence in law, in letters, or in politics, that satisfied the expectations of those who, living in his society, were impressed by his intellect and astonished at his acquirements.

If I were to sum up in a few words the characteristics of the persons who thus promise more than they ever perform, I should say that their powers of comprehension are greater than their powers either of creation or exposition; and that their energy, though capable of being roused occasionally to great exertions, can rarely be relied on for any continued effort.

They collect, sometimes in rather a sauntering manner, an immense store of varied information. But it is only by fits and starts that they are able to use it with effect, and at their happiest moments they rarely attain the simple grace or the natural vigour which give beauty and life to composition. Their deficiencies are inherent in their nature, and are never therefore entirely overcome. They have not in their minds the immortal spark of genius; but the faculty of comprehending genius may give them, in a certain degree, the power of imitating it; whilst ambition, interest, and necessity, will at times stimulate them to extraordinary exertions.

As writers, they usually want originality, ease, and power; as men of action, tact, firmness, and decision. The works in which they most succeed are usually short, and written under temporary excitement; as statesmen, they at times attract attention and win applause, but rarely obtain authority or take and keep the lead in public affairs. In society, however, the mere faculty of remembering and comprehending a variety of things is quite sufficient to obtain a considerable reputation; whilst the world, when indulgent, often estimates the power of a man's abilities by some transient and ephemeral display of them.

I will now turn from these general observations to see how far they are exemplified in the history of the person whose name is before me; a person who advanced to the very frontier of those lands which it was not given to him to enter; and who is not only a favourable specimen of his class, but who, as belonging to that class, represents in many respects a great portion of the public during that memorable period of our annals, which extends from the French Revolution of 1789 to the English Reform Bill in 1830.

II.

The father of Sir James was a Scotch country gentleman, who, having a small hereditary property, which he could neither part with nor live upon, entered the army early, and passed his life almost entirely with his regiment. Young Mackintosh was born on the 24th of October, 1765, in the county of Inverness, and was sent as soon as he could be to a school at Fort Rose;

where he fell in with two books which had a permanent influence on his future career. These books were "Plutarch's Lives" and the "Roman History," books which, by making him ambitious of public honours, rendered his existence a perpetual struggle between that which he desired to be and that for which he was best suited. At Aberdeen, then, where he was sent on quitting Fort Rose, he was alike remarkable for his zeal in politics, and his love for metaphysics — that is, for his alternate coquetry between an active and a meditative life. At Edinburgh, also, where he subsequently went to study medicine, it was the same thing. In the evening he would go now and then to a spouting club and make speeches, while the greater part of his mornings was spent in poetical lucubrations. To the medical profession he paid little attention, till all of a sudden the necessity aroused him. He then applied himself, with a start, to that which he was obliged to know; but his diligence was not of that resolute and steady kind which ensures success as the consequence of a certain period of application; and after rushing into the novelties of the Brunonian System, * which promised knowledge with little labour, and then, rushing back again, he resolved on taking his countrymen's

---

* *Brunonian System.* — Medical doctrines first broached by Dr. John Brown, in 1780. He imagined that the body was endowed with a certain quantity of *excitability,* and that every external agent acted as a *stimulant* on this property of excitability. Health consisted in a just proportion of stimulation, but when this was carried too far, *exhaustion,* or *direct debility,* was the consequence, and when not far enough, *indirect debility.* The diseases which he supposed to arise from one or other of those two states were classed into two orders, the *sthenic* and the *asthenic.* Brown was considered no great prophet in his own country, but he exercised considerable influence on the medical doctrines of the Italian schools, which to this day are somewhat tinctured with Brunonianism.

short road to fortune, and set out for England. His journey, however, did not answer. He got a wife, but no patients; and on the failure of his attempts to establish himself àt Salisbury and at Weymouth, retired to Brussels — ill, wearied, and disgusted. The Low Countries were at that time the theatre of a struggle between the Emperor Joseph and his subjects; the general convulsion which shortly afterwards took place throughout Europe was preparing, and the agitation of men's minds excessive. These exciting scenes called the disappointed physician back to the more alluring study of politics; and to this short visit to the Continent he owed a knowledge of its opinions and its public men, which first served him as the correspondent of a newspaper, *The Oracle;* and, subsequently, furnished him with materials for a pamphlet which in an instant placed him in the situation he so long occupied as one of *the most promising men of his day.* This celebrated pamphlet, published in 1791, and known under the name of "Vindiciæ Gallicæ," whether we consider the circumstances under which it appeared, the opponent which it combated, or the ability of the composition itself, merited all the attention it received, and was the more successful because it gave just the answer to Burke which Burke himself would have given to his own Reflections.

Thus, the club of Saint James's, the cloister of Trinity College, had a writer to quote, whose sentiments were in favour of liberty, and whose language, agreeable to the ear of the gentleman and the scholar, did not, in defending the patriots of France, advise their imitation or patronise their excesses.

"Burke," he says, "admires the Revolution of 1688;

but we, who conceive that we pay the purest homage to the authors of that Revolution, not in contending for what they then did, but for what they would now do, can feel no inconsistency in looking on France — not to model our conduct, but to invigorate the spirit of freedom. We permit ourselves to imagine how Lord Somers, in the light and knowledge of the eighteenth century, how the patriots of France, in the tranquillity and opulence of England, would have acted.

"We are not bound to copy the conduct to which the last were driven by a bankrupt exchequer, and a dissolved government; nor to maintain the establishments which were spared by the first in a prejudiced. and benighted age.

"Exact imitation is not necessary to reverence. We venerate the principles which presided in both, and we adapt to political admiration a maxim which has long been received in polite letters, that the only manly and liberal imitation is to speak as a great man would have spoken, had he lived in our times, and been placed in our circumstances."

There is much even in this passage to show that the adversary was still the imitator, imbued with the spirit and under the influence of the genius of the very writer whom he was bold enough to attack. Many, nevertheless, who, taken by surprise, had surrendered to the magisterial eloquence of the master, were rescued by the elegant pleading of the scholar. Everywhere, then, might be heard the loudest applause, and an applause well merited. On the greatest question of the times, the first man of the times had been answered by a young gentleman aged twenty-six, and who, hitherto unknown, was appreciated by his first success.

The leaders of the Whig party sought him out; they paid him every attention. His opinions went further than theirs; for he was an advocate of universal suffrage, an abolitionist of all titles, an enemy to a senate or second assembly. No persons practically contending for power could say they exactly sanctioned such notions as these; but all praised the style in which they were put forth, and, allowing for the youth, lauded the talent, of the author. Indeed, "the love to hatred turned" ever repudiates moderation, and the antagonist of Burke was certain of the rapturous cheers of those whom that great but passionate man had deserted. In this manner Mackintosh (who was now preparing for the bar) became necessarily a party man, and a violent party man. Mr. Fox praised his abilities in Parliament; the famous Reform Association, called the "Friends of the People," chose him for their honorary secretary. A great portion of the well-known declaration of this society was his composition; and in a letter to the Prime Minister of the day (Mr. Pitt), he abused that statesman with a fierceness and boldness of invective which even political controversy scarcely allowed.

Here was the great misfortune of his life. This fierceness and boldness were not in his nature; in becoming a man of action, he entered upon a part which was not suited to his character, and which it was certain therefore he would not sustain. The reaction soon followed. Amongst its first symptoms was a review of Mr. Burke's "Regicide Peace." The author of the review became known to the person whose writing was criticised: a correspondence ensued, very flattering to Mr. Mackintosh, who shortly afterwards spent a few days at Beaconsfield (1796).

It was usual for him to say, referring to this visit, that in half an hour Mr. Burke overturned the previous reflections of his whole life. There was some exaggeration, doubtless, in this assertion, but it is also likely that there was some truth in it. His opinions had begun to waver, and at that critical moment he came into personal contact with, and was flattered by, a man whom every one praised, and who praised few. Such flattery converted him: nor was he ashamed of his conversion; but, on the contrary, mounted with confidence a stage on which his change might be boldly justified.

The faults as well as the excellences of the English character arise from that great dislike to generalise which has made us the practical, and in many instances the prejudiced, people that we are. Abroad, a knowledge of general or natural law, of the foundations on which all laws are or ought to be based, enters as a matter of course into a liberal education. In England lawyers themselves disregard this study as useless or worse than useless. * They look, and they look diligently, into English law, such as it is, established by custom, precedent, or act of Parliament. They know all the nice points and proud formalities on which legal justice rests, or by which it may be eluded. The conflicting cases and opposing opinions, which may be brought to bear on an unsound horse, or a contested footpath, are cautiously pondered over, carefully investigated. But the great edifice of general jurisprudence, though standing on his wayside, is usually passed by the legal traveller with averted eyes: the antiquary and the philosopher, indeed, may linger

* It is fair to observe that this prejudice is gradually disappearing.

there; but the plodding man of business scorns to arrest his steps.

When, however, amidst the mighty crash of states and doctrines that followed the storm of 1791, when, amidst the birth of new empires and new legislatures, custom lost its sanctity, precedent its authority, and statute was made referable to common justice and common sense — then, indeed, there uprose a strong and earnest desire to become acquainted with those general principles so often cited by the opponents of the past; to visit that armoury in which such terrible weapons had been found, and to see whether it could not afford means as powerful for defending what remained as it had furnished for destroying what had already been swept away.

III.

A course of Lectures on Public Law — about which the public knew so little, and were yet so curious — offered a road to distinction, which the young lawyer, confident in his own abilities and researches, had every temptation to tread. Private interest procured him the Hall at Lincoln's Inn; but this was not sufficient; it was necessary that he should make the world aware of the talent, the knowledge, and the sentiments with which he undertook so great a task. He published his introductory essay — the only portion of the Lectures to which we are referring that now remains. The views contained in this essay may in many instances be erroneous; but its merits as a composition are of no common kind. Learned, eloquent, it excited nearly as much enthusiasm as the "Vindiciæ

Gallicæ," and deserved, upon the whole, a higher order of admiration.

But praise came this time from a different quarter. A few years before, and Mackintosh had spoken of Mr. Pitt as cold, stern, crafty, and ambitious; possessing "the parade without the restraint of morals;" the "most profound dissimulation with the utmost ardour of enterprise; prepared by one part of his character for the violence of a multitude, by another for the duplicity of a court." *

It was under the patronage of this same Mr. Pitt that the hardy innovator now turned back to "the old ways," proclaiming that "history was a vast museum, in which specimens of every variety of human nature might be studied. From these great occasions to knowledge," he said, "lawgivers and statesmen, but more especially moralists and political philosophers, may reap the most important instruction. There, they may plainly discover, amid all the useful and beautiful variety of governments and institutions, and under all the fantastic multitude of usages and rites which ever prevailed among men, the same fundamental, comprehensive truths — truths which have ever been the guardians of society, recognised and revered (with very few and slight exceptions) by every nation upon earth, and uniformly taught, with still fewer exceptions, by a succession of wise men, from the first dawn of speculation down to the latest times."

"See," he continued, "whether from the remotest periods any improvement, or even any change, has been made in the practical rules of human conduct. Look at the code of Moses. I speak of it now as a

* Letter to Mr. Pitt.

mere human composition, without considering its sacred origin. Considering it merely in that light, it is the most ancient and the most curious memorial of the early history of mankind. More than 3000 years have elapsed since the composition of the Pentateuch; and let any man, if he is able, tell me in what important respects the rule of life has varied since that distant period. Let the institutes of Menu be explored with the same view; we shall arrive at the same conclusion. Let the books of false religion be opened; it will be found that their moral system is, in all its good features, the same. The impostors who composed them were compelled to pay this homage to the uniform moral sentiments of the world. Examine the codes of nations, those authentic depositories of the moral judgments of men: you everywhere find the same rules prescribed, the same duties imposed. Even the boldest of these ingenious sceptics who have attacked every other opinion, have spared the sacred and immortal simplicity of the rules of life. In our common duties, Bayle and Hume agree with Bossuet and Barrow. Such as the rule was at the first dawn of history, such it continues at the present day. Ages roll over mankind; mighty nations pass away like a shadow; virtue alone remains the same, immutable and unchangeable."

The object of Mackintosh was to show, that the instinct of man was towards society; that society could not be kept together except on certain principles; that these principles, therefore, from the very nature of man — a nature predestined and fashioned by God — were at once universal and divine, and that societies would perish that ignored them; — a true and sublime theory; but with respect to which we must, if we desire to be practical, admit that variety of qualifications which different civilizations, different climates, accidental interests, and religious prescriptions interpose.

It may be said, for instance, that no society could exist if its institutions honoured theft as a virtue and instructed parents to murder their children; but a great and celebrated society did exist in ancient Greece, — a society which outlived its brilliant contemporaries, and which sanctioned robbery, if not detected; and allowed parents to kill their children, if sickly. It is perfectly true that the ten commandments of the Jewish legislator are applicable to all mankind, and are as much revered by the people of the civilized world at the present day, as by the semi-barbarous people of Israel 3000 years ago. They are admitted as integrally into the religion taught by Christ, as they were into the religion taught by Moses. But how different the morality founded on them! How different the doctrine of charity and forgiveness from the retributive prescription of vindicative justice! Nay, how different the precepts taught by the various followers of Christ themselves, who draw those precepts from the same book!

If there is anything on which it is necessary for the interest and happiness of mankind to constitute a fixed principle of custom or of law, it is the position of woman. The social relationship of man with woman rules the destiny of both from the cradle to the grave; and yet, on this same relationship, what various notions, customs, and laws!

I make these observations because it is well that we should see how much is left to the liberty of man, whilst we recognise the certain rules by which his

caprice is limited: how much is to be learned from the
past — how much is left open to the future!

But all argument at the time that Mackintosh
opened his lectures consisted in the opposition of extremes. As the one party decried history altogether,
so the other referred everything to history; as the
former sect declared that no reverence was due to
custom, so the latter announced that all upon which
we valued ourselves most was traditional. Because
those fanatics scoffed at the ideas and manners of the
century that had just elapsed, these referred with exultation to the manners and ideas that prevailed some
thousands of years before.

Mackintosh stood forth, confessedly, as History's
champion; and with the beautiful candour which
marked his modest and elevated frame of mind, confessed that the sight of those who surrounded his chair
— the opinions he knew them to entertain — the
longing after applause, for which every public speaker,
whatever his theme, naturally thirsts — and also, he
adds, "a proper repentance for former errors" — might
all have heightened the qualities of the orator to the
detriment of the lecturer, and carried him, "in the re-
bound from his original opinions, too far towards the
opposite extreme."*

* Letters to Mr. Sharp. See "Life of Sir James Mackintosh," by his
Son.

IV.

We shall soon have to inquire what were the real nature and character of the change which he confessed that his language at this time exaggerated. Suffice it here to say that, amidst the sighs of his old friends, the applauses of his new, and the sneering murmurs and scornful remarks of the stupid and the envious of all parties, his eloquence (for he was eloquent as a professor) produced generally the most flattering effects. Statesmen, lawyers, men of letters, idlers, crowded with equal admiration round the amusing moralist, whose glittering store of knowledge was collected from the philosopher, the poet, the writer of romance and history.

"In mixing up the sparkling julep," says an eloquent though somewhat affected writer, "that by its potent application was to scour away the drugs and feculence and peccant humours of the body politic, he (Mackintosh) seemed to stand with his back to the drawers in a metaphysical dispensary, and to take out of them whatever ingredients suited his purpose."*

In the meanwhile (having lost his first wife and married again) he pursued his professional course, though without doing anything as an advocate equal to his success as a professor.

M. Peltier's trial, however, now took place. M. Peltier was an *émigré*, whom the neighbouring revolution had driven to our shores; a gentleman possessing some ability, and ardently attached to the royal cause.

* Hazlitt.

He had not profited by the permission to return to France which had been given to all French exiles, but carried on a French journal, which, finding its way to the Continent, excited the remarkable susceptibility of the first consul. This was just after the peace of Amiens. Urged by the French government, our own undertook the prosecution of M. Peltier's paper. The occasion was an ode, in which the apotheosis of Bonaparte was referred to, and his assassination pretty plainly advocated. So atrocious a suggestion, however veiled, or however provoked, merited, no doubt, the reprobation of all worthy and high-minded men; but party spirit and national rancour ran high, and the defender of the prosecuted journalist was sure to stand before his country as the enemy of France and the advocate of freedom.

A variety of circumstances pointed out Mr. Mackintosh as the proper counsel to place in this position; and here, by a singular fortune, he was enabled to combine a hatred to revolutionary principles with an ardent admiration of that ancient spirit of liberty, which is embodied in the most popular institutions of England.

"Circumstanced as my client is," he exclaimed, in his rather studied but yet powerful declamation, "the most refreshing object his eye can rest upon is an English jury; and he feels with me gratitude to the Ruler of empires, that after the wreck of everything else ancient and venerable in Europe, of all established forms and acknowledged principles, of all long-subsisting laws and sacred institutions, we are met here, administering justice after the manner of our forefathers in this her ancient sanctuary. Here these parties come to judgment; one, the master of the greatest empire on the earth; the other, a weak, defenceless fugitive, who waives his privilege of having half his jury composed of foreigners, and puts himself with confidence on a jury entirely English. Gentlemen, there is another view in which this case is highly interesting, important, and momentous, and I confess I am animated to every exertion that I can make, not more by a sense of my duty to my client, than by a persuasion that this cause is the first of a series of contests with the 'freedom of the press.' My learned friend, Mr. Perceval, I am sure, will never disgrace his magistracy by being instrumental to a measure so calamitous. But viewing this as I do, as the first of a series of contests between the greatest power on earth and the only press that is now free, I cannot help calling upon him and you to pause, before the great earthquake swallows up all the freedom that remains among men; for though no indication has yet been made to attack the freedom of the press in this country, yet the many other countries that have been deprived of this benefit must forcibly impress us with the propriety of looking vigilantly to ourselves. Holland and Switzerland are now no more, and near fifty of the imperial crowns in Germany have vanished since the commencement of this prosecution. All these being gone, there is no longer any control but what this country affords. Every press on the Continent, from Palermo to Hamburgh, is enclaved; one place alone remains where the press is free, protected by our government and our patriotism. It is an awfully proud consideration that that venerable fabric, raised by our ancestors, still stands unshaken amidst the ruins that surround us. *You are the advanced guard of liberty*," &c.

After the delivery of this speech, which, being translated by Madame de Staël, was read with admiration not only in England, but on the Continent, Mr. Mackintosh, though he lost his cause, was considered no less promising as a pleader, than after the publication of the "Vindiciæ Gallicæ" he had been considered as a pamphleteer. In both instances, however, the sort of effort he had made seemed to have exhausted him, and three months had not elapsed, when, with the plaudits of the public, and the praise of Erskine, still ringing in his ears, he accepted the Recordership of Bombay from Mr. Addington, and retired with satisfaction to the well-paid and knighted indolence of India. His objects in so doing were, he said, — to make a fortune, and to write a work.

We shall thoroughly understand the man when we see what he achieved towards the attainment of these two objects. He did not make a fortune; he did not write a work. The greater part of his time seems to have been employed in a restless longing after society, and a perpetual dawdling over books; during the seven years he was absent, he speaks continually of his projected work as "always to be projected." "I observe," he says in one of his letters to Mr. Sharpe, "that you touch me once or twice with the spur about my books on Morals. I felt it gall me, for I have not begun."

MACKINTOSH,

THE MAN OF PROMISE.

PART II.

Goes to India. — Pursuits there. — Returns home dissatisfied with himself. — Enters Parliament on the Liberal side. — Reasons why he took it. — Fails in first speech. — Merits as an orator. — Extracts from his speeches. — Modern ideas. — Excessive punishments. — Mackintosh's success as a law reformer. — General parliamentary career.

PART II.

I.

SIR JAMES MACKINTOSH, in accepting a place in India, abdicated the chances of a brilliant and useful career in England; still his presence in one of our great dependencies was not without its use — for his literary reputation offered him facilities in the encouragement of learned and scientific pursuits — which, when they tend to explore and illustrate the history and resources of a new empire, are, in fact, political ones; while his attempts to obtain a statistical survey, as well as to form different societies, the objects of which were the acquirement and communication of knowledge, though not immediately successful, did not fail to arouse in Bombay, and to spread much farther, a different and a far more enlightened spirit than that which had hitherto prevailed amongst our speculating settlers, or rather sojourners in the East. The mildness of his judicial sway, moreover, and a wish to return, if possible, to Europe with a "bloodless ermine,"* contributed not only to extend the views, but to soften the manners of the merchant conquerors, and to lay thereby something like a practical foundation for subsequent legislative improvement.

To himself, however, this distant scene seems to

* He only sanctioned one execution.

have possessed no 'interest, to have procured no advantage. Worn by the climate, wearied by a series of those small duties and trifling exertions which, unattended by fame, offer none of that moral excitement which overcomes physical fatigue; but little wealthier than when he undertook his voyage, having accomplished none of those works, and enjoyed little of that ease the visions of which cheered him in undertaking it; a sick, a sad, and, so far as the acceptance of his judgeship was concerned, a repentant man (in 1810), he took his way homewards.

"It has happened," he observes in one of his letters — "it has happened by the merest accident that the 'trial of Peltier' is among the books in the cabin; and when I recollect the way in which you saw me opposed to Perceval on the 21st of February, 1803 (the day of the trial), and that I compare his present situation — whether at the head of an administration or an opposition — with mine, scanty as my stock is of fortune, health, and spirits, in a cabin nine feet square, on the Indian Ocean, I think it enough that I am free from the soreness of disappointment."

There is, indeed, something melancholy in the contrast thus offered between a man still young, hopeful, rising high in the most exciting profession, just crowned with the honours of forensic triumph, and the man prematurely old, who in seven short years had become broken, dispirited, and was now under the necessity of beginning life anew, with wasted energies and baffled aspirations.

But Sir James Mackintosh deceived himself in thinking that if the seven years to which he alludes had been passed in England, they would have placed him

in the position to which Mr. Percival had ascended
within the same period. Had he remained at the bar,
or entered Parliament instead of going to India, he
might, indeed, have made several better speeches than
Mr. Perceval, as he had already made one; but he
would not always have been speaking well, like Mr.
Perceval, nor have pushed himself forward in those
situations, and at those opportunities, when a good
speech would have been most wanted or most effective.
At all events, his talents for active life were about to
have a tardy trial; the object of his early dreams and
hopes was about to be attained — a seat in the House
of Commons. He took his place amongst the members
of the Liberal opposition; and many who remembered
the auspices under which he left England, were somewhat surprised at the banner under which he now
enlisted.

II.

Here is the place at which it may be most convenient to consider Sir James Mackintosh's former change;
as well as the circumstances which led him back to
his old connections. He had entered life violently
democratical, — a strong upholder of the French Revolution; he became, so to speak, violently moderate,
and a strong opponent of this same Revolution. He
altered his politics, and this alteration was followed by
his receiving an appointment.

Such is the outline which malignity might fill up
with the darkest colours; but it would be unjustly.
The machinery of human conduct is complex; and it
would be absurd to say that a man's interests are not

likely to have an influence on his actions. But they
who see more of our nature than the surface, know
that our interests are quite as frequently governed by
our character as our character is by our interests. The
true explanation, then, of Mackintosh's conduct is to
be found in his order of intellect. His mind was not
a mind led by its own inspirations, but rather a mind
reflecting the ideas of other men, and of that class of
men more especially to which he, as studious and speculative, belonged. The commencement of the French
Revolution, the long-prepared work of the Encyclo-
pedists, was hailed by such persons (I speak generally)
as a sort of individual success. Burke did much to
check this feeling; and subsequent events favoured
Burke. But by far the greater number of those ad-
dicted to literary pursuits sympathised with the popular
party in the States-General. Under this impulse the
"Vindiciæ Gallicæ" was written. The exclusion of
the eminent men of the National Assembly from power
modified, the execution of the Girondists subdued, this
impulse. At the fall of those eloquent Republicans
the lettered usurpation ceased; and now literature, instead of being opposed to royalty, owed, like it, a debt
of vengeance to that inexorable mob which had spared
neither.

It was at the time, then, when everybody was
recanting that Mackintosh made *his* recantation. Most
men of his order took the same part in the same
events; for such men were delighted with the theories
of freedom, but shocked at its excesses; and, indeed,
it is difficult to conceive anything more abhorrent to
the gentle dreams of a civilised philosophy than that
wild hurricane of liberty which carried ruin and deso-

lation over France in the same blast that spread the seeds of future prosperity.

We find, it is true, this beautiful passage in the "Vindiciæ Gallicæ": "The soil of Attica was remarked by antiquity as producing at once the most delicious fruits and the most violent poisons. It is thus 'with the human mind; and to the frequency of convulsions in the commonwealths we owe those examples of sanguinary tumult and virtuous heroism which distinguish their history from the monotonous tranquillity of modern states." But though these words were used by Mackintosh, they were merely transcribed by him; they belong to a deeper and more daring genius — they are almost literally the words of Machiavel, and were furnished by the reading, and not by the genuine reflections, of the youthful pamphleteer. He had not in rejoicing over the work of the Constituante anticipated the horrors of the Convention; the regret, therefore, that he expressed for what he condemned as his early want of judgment, was undoubtedly sincere; and no one can fairly blame him for accepting, under such circumstances, a post which was not political, and which removed him from the angry arena in which he would have had to combat with former friends, — whose rancour may be appreciated by Dr. Parr's brutal reply, — when Mackintosh asked him, how Quigley, an Irish priest executed for treason, could have been worse. "I'll tell you, Jemmy — Quigley was an Irishman, he might have been a Scotchman; he was a priest, he might have been a lawyer; he was a traitor, he might have been an apostate."

Thus much for the Bombay Recordership. But the feverish panic which the sanguinary government of

Robespierre had produced—calmed by his fall, soothed
by the feeble government which succeeded him, and
replaced at last by the stern domination of a warrior
who had at least the merit of restoring order and tranquillity to his country — died away.

A variety of circumstances — including the publication of the "Edinburgh Review," which, conducted
in a liberal and moderate spirit, made upon the better
educated class of the British population a considerable
impression — favoured and aided the reaction towards
a more temperate state of thought. A new era began,
in which the timid lost their fears, the factious their
hopes. All question of the overthrow of the constitution and of the confiscation of property was at an end;
and as politics thus fell back into more quiet channels,
parties adopted new watchwords and new devices.
The cry was no longer, "Shall there be a Monarchy
or a Republic?" but, "Shall the Catholics continue
proscribed as helots, or shall they be treated as free
men?"

During the seven years which Sir James had passed
in India, this was the turn that had been taking place
in affairs and opinions. Is is hardly possible to conceive any change more calculated to carry along with
it a mild and intelligent philosopher, to whom fanati-
cism of all kinds was hateful.

Those whom he had left, under the standard of
Mr. Pitt, contending against anarchical doctrines and
universal conquest, were now for disputing one of Mr.
Pitt's most sacred promises, and refusing to secure
peace to an empire, at the very crisis of its fortunes,
by the establishment of a system of civil equality between citizens who thought differently on the some-

what abstruse subject of transubstantiation.   Mr. Perceval, at the head of this section of politicians, was
separated from almost every statesman who possessed
any reputation as a scholar.   Mr. Canning did not belong to his administration; Lord Wellesley was on the
point of quitting it.   There never was a government
to which what may be called the thinking class of the
country stood so opposed.   Thus, the very same sort
of disposition which had detached Sir James Mackintosh, some years ago, from his early friends, was now
disposing him to rejoin them; and he moved backwards
and forwards, I must repeat, in both instances, when
he went to India a Tory,* and when he entered Parliament a Whig — with a considerable body of persons
who, though less remarked because less distinguished,
honestly pursued the same conduct.

All the circumstances, indeed, which marked his
conduct at this time do him honour.   Almost immediately on his return to England, the premier offered
him a seat in Parliament, and held out to him the
hopes of the high and lucrative situation of President
of the Board of Control.   A poor man, and an ambitious man, equally anxious for place and distinction,
he refused both; and this refusal, of which we have
now the surest proof, was a worthy answer to the
imputations which had attended the acceptance of his
former appointment.   It was Lord Abinger, who has
since recorded to us the refusal of a seat from Mr.
Perceval, who was himself the bearer of a similar offer
from Lord Cawdor;** and under the patronage of this

---

* He would perhaps have repudiated this name; but, as far as opinions
gave the title, it certainly at this time belonged to him.
** See "Life of Sir James Mackintosh," by his Son, pp. 246 and 279.

nobleman Sir James Mackintosh first entered Parliament (1813) as the Member for Nairnshire, a representation the more agreeable, since it was that of his
native county, wherein he had inherited the small property which some years before he had been compelled
to part with.*

III.

Any man entering the House of Commons for the
first time late in life possesses a small chance of attain-
ing considerable parliamentary eminence. It requires
some time to seize the spirit of that singular assembly,
of which most novices are at first inclined to over-rate
and then to under-rate the judgment.

A learned man is more likely to be wrong than
any other. He fancies himself amidst an assembly
of meditative and philosophic statesmen; he calls up all
his deepest thoughts and most refined speculations; he
is anxious to astonish by the profundity and extent of
his views, the novelty and sublimity of his conceptions;
as he commences, the listeners are convinced he is a
bore, and before he concludes, he is satisfied that they
are blockheads.

The orator, however, is far more out in his conjec-
tures than the audience. The House of Commons consists of a mob of gentlemen, the greater part of whom
are neither without talent nor information. But a mob
of well-informed gentlemen is still a mob, requiring to
be amused rather than instructed, and only touched by
those reasons and expressions which, clear to the dull-

* Subsequently he sat for Knaresborough, under the patronage of the
Duke of Devonshire.

est as the quickest intellect, vibrate through an assembly as if it had but one ear and one mind.

Besides, the House of Commons is a mob divided beneficially, though it requires some knowledge of the general genius and practical bearings of a representative government to see all the advantages of such a division, into parties. What such parties value is that which is done in their ranks, that which is useful to themselves, of advantage to a common cause; any mere personal exhibition is almost certain to be regarded by them with contempt or displeasure. Differing amongst themselves, indeed, in almost everything else — some being silent and fastidious, some bustling and loquacious, some indolent and looking after amusement, some incapable and desiring the appearance of men of business, some active, public-spirited and ambitious — all agree in detecting the philosophic rhetorician. Anything in the shape of subtle refinement, — anything that borders on learned generalities, is sure to be out of place. Even supposing that the new member, already distinguished elsewhere, although now at his maiden essay on this strange arena, has sufficient tact to see the errors into which he is likely to fall, he is still a suspected person, and will be narrowly watched as to any design of parading his own acquirements at the expense of other people's patience.

How did Sir J. Mackintosh first appear amongst auditors thus disposed? Lord Castlereagh moved, on the 20th of December, 1814, for an adjournment to the 1st of March. At that moment the whole of Europe was pouring, in the full tide of victory, into France. Every heart thrilled with recent triumph and the anticipation of more complete success. The min-

3*

istry had acquired popularity as the reflection of the talents of their general and the tardy good fortune of their allies. The demand for adjournment was the demand for a confidence which they had a right to expect, and which Mr. Whitbread and the leading Whigs saw it would be ungenerous and impolitic to refuse. They granted then what was asked; Mackintosh alone opposed it. His opposition was isolated, certain to be without any practical result, and could only be accounted for by the desire to make a speech!

Lord Castlereagh, who was by nature the man of action which Mackintosh was not, saw at once the error which the new Whig member had committed, and determined to add as much as possible to his difficulties. Instead, therefore, of making the statement which he knew was expected from him, and to which he presumed the orator opposite would affect to reply, he merely moved for the adjournment as a matter of course, which needed no justification. By this simple manœuvre all the formidable artillery which the profound reflector on foreign politics and the eloquent lecturer on the law of nations had brought into the field, was rendered useless. A fire against objects which were not in view, an answer to arguments which had never been employed, was necessarily a very tame exhibition, and indeed the new member was hardly able to get through the oration to which it was evident he had given no common care. In slang phrase, he "broke down." Why was this? Sir James Mackintosh was not ignorant of the nature of the assembly he addressed; he could have explained to another all that was necessary to catch its ear; but, as I have said a few pages back, the character of a person governs his interests far more frequently than his interests govern his character; and the man I am speaking of was not the man whom a sort of instinct hurries into the heat and fervour of a real contest. To brandish his glittering arms was to him the battle. He, therefore, persuaded himself that what he did with satisfaction he should do with success. It was just this which made his failure serious to him.

The runner who trips in a race and loses it may win races for the rest of his life; but if he stops in the middle of his course, because he is asthmatic and cannot keep his breath, few persons would bet on him again. Now, the failure of Mackintosh was of this kind; it was not an accidental but a constitutional one, arising from defects or peculiarities that were part of himself. He never, then, recovered from it. And yet it could not be said that he spoke ill; on the contrary, notwithstanding certain defects in manner, he spoke, after a little practice, well, and far above the ordinary speaking of learned men and lawyers. Some of his orations may be read with admiration, and were even received with applause.

IV.

Where shall we find a nobler tone of statesmanlike philosophy than in the following condemnation of that policy which attached Genoa to Piedmont,* a condemnation not the less remarkable for the orator's not unskilful attempt to connect his former opposition to

* 27th April, 1815.

the French Revolution with the war he was then waging against the Holy Alliance?

"One of the grand and patent errors of the French
Revolution was the fatal opinion, that it was possible
for human skill to make a government. It was an
error too generally prevalent not to be excusable. The
American Revolution had given it a fallacious semblance
of support, though no event in history more clearly
showed its falsehood. The system of laws and the
frame of society in North America remained after the
Revolution, and remain to this day, fundamentally the
same as they ever were.* The change in America,
like the change in 1688, was made in defence of legal
right, not in pursuit of political improvement; and it
was limited by the necessity of defence which produced
it. The whole internal order remained, which had always been Republican. The somewhat slender tie which
loosely joined these Republics to a monarchy, was easily
and without violence divided. But the error of the
French Revolutionists was, in 1789, the error of Europe. From that error we have been long reclaimed
by fatal experience.

"We now see, or rather we have seen and felt,
that a government is not like a machine or a building,
the work of man; that it is the work of nature, like
the nobler productions of the vegetable or animal world,
which man may improve and corrupt, and even destroy,
but which he cannot create. We have long learned to
despise the ignorance or the hypocrisy of those who
speak of giving a free constitution to a people, and to
exclaim, with a great living poet:

* This idea has lately been brought forward by M. de Tocqueville,
and treated by many as a novelty.

'A gift of that which never can be given
By all the blended powers of earth and heaven!'

"Indeed, we have gone, perhaps as usual, too near to the opposite error, and not made sufficient allowances for those dreadful cases, which I must call desperate, where, in long enslaved countries, it is necessary either humbly and cautiously to lay foundations from which liberty may slowly rise, or acquiesce in the doom of perpetual bondage on ourselves and our children.

"But though we no longer dream of making governments, the confederacy of kings seem to feel no doubt of their own power to make a nation. A government cannot be made, because its whole spirit and principles spring from the character of the nation. There would be no difficulty in framing a government, if the habits of a people could be changed by a lawgiver; if he could obliterate their recollections, transform their attachment and reverence, extinguish their animosities and correct those sentiments which, being at variance with his opinions of public interest, he calls prejudices. Now this is precisely the power which our statesmen at Vienna have arrogated to themselves. They not only form nations, but they compose them of elements apparently the most irreconcilable. They made one nation out of Norway and Sweden; they tried to make another out of Prussia and Saxony. They have, in the present case, forced together Piedmont and Genoa to form a nation which is to guard the avenues of Italy, and to be one of the main securities of Europe against universal monarchy.

"It was not the pretension of the ancient system to

form states, to divide territory according to speculations of military convenience.

"The great statesmen of former times did not speak of their measures as the noble lord (Lord Castlereagh) did about the incorporation of Belgium with Holland (about which I say nothing), as a great improvement in the system of Europe. That is the language of those who revolutionize that system by a partition like that of Poland, by the establishment of the Federation of the Rhine at Paris, or by the creation of new states at Vienna. The ancient principle was to preserve all those States which had been founded by Time and Nature, the character of which was often maintained, and the nationality of which was sometimes created by the very irregularities of frontier and inequalities of strength, of which a shallow policy complains; to preserve all such States down to the smallest, first by their own national spirit, and secondly by that mutual jealousy which makes every great power the opponent of the dangerous ambition of every other; to preserve nations, living bodies, produced by the hand of Nature — not to form artificial dead machines, called nations, by the words and parchment of a diplomatic act — was the ancient system of our wiser forefathers," &c. &c.

V.

There is also a noble strain of eloquence in the following short defence of the slave-treaty with Spain:

"I feel pride in the British flag being for this object subjected to foreign ships. I think it a great and striking proof of magnanimity that the darling point of honour of our country, the British flag itself, which for a thousand years has braved the battle and the breeze, which has defied confederacies of nations, to which we have clung closer and closer as the tempest roared around us, which has borne us through all perils and raised its head higher as the storm has assailed us more fearfully, should now bend voluntarily to the cause of justice and humanity — should now lower itself, never having been brought low by the mightiest, to the most feeble and defenceless — to those who, far from being able to return the benefits we would confer upon them, will never hear of those benefits, will never know, perhaps, even our name."

By far the most effective of Sir James Mackintosh's speeches in Parliament, however, was one that he delivered (June, 1819,) against "The Foreign Enlistment Bill," a measure which was intended to prevent British subjects from aiding the South American colonies in the struggle they were then making for independence. No good report of this oration remains, but even our parliamentary records are sufficient to show that it possessed many of the rarer attributes of eloquence, and moving with a rapidity and a vigour (not frequent in Sir James's efforts), prevented his language from seeming laboured or his learning tedious.

It contained, doubtless, other passages more striking in the delivery, but the one which follows is peculiarly pleasing to me — considering the argument it answered and the audience to which it was addressed:

"Much has been said of the motives by which the merchants of England are actuated as to this question. A noble lord, the other night, treated these persons with great and unjust severity, imputing the solicitude which they feel for the success of the South American cause to interested motives. Without indulging in commonplace declamations against party men, I must considerately say that it is a question with me whether the interest of merchants do not more frequently coincide with the best interests of mankind than do the transient and limited views of politicians. If British merchants look with eagerness to the event of the struggle in America, no doubt they do so with the hope of deriving advantage from that event. But on what is such hope founded? On the diffusion of beggary, on the maintenance of ignorance, on the confirmation, on the establishment of tyranny in America? No; these are the expectations of Ferdinand. The British merchant builds his hopes of trade and profit on the progress of civilisation and good government; on the successful assertion of freedom — of freedom, that parent of talent, that parent of heroism, that parent of every virtue. The fate of America can only be necessary to commerce as it becomes accessory to the dignity and the happiness of the race of man."

VI.

As a parliamentary orator, Sir James Mackintosh never before or afterwards rose to so great an height as in this debate; but he continued at intervals, and on great and national questions, to deliver what may be called very remarkable essays up to the end of his career. I myself was present at his last·effort of this description; and most interesting it was to hear the man who began his public life with the "Vindiciæ

Gallicæ," closing it with a speech in favour of the Reform Bill. During the interval, nearly half a century had run its course. The principles which, forty years before, had appeared amidst the storm and tempest of doubtful discussion, and which, since that period, had been at various times almost totally obscured, were now again on the horizon, bright in the steady sunshine of matured opinion. The distinguished person who was addressing his countrymen on a great historical question was himself a history, — a history of his own time, of which, with the flexibility of an intelligent but somewhat feeble nature, he had shared the enthusiasm, the doubt, the despair, the hope, the triumph.

The speech itself was remarkable. Overflowing with thought and knowledge, containing sound general principles as to government, undisfigured by the violence of party-spirit, it pleased and instructed those who took the pains to listen to it attentively; but it wanted the qualities which attract or command attention.

It was vain to seek for the playful fancy of Canning, the withering invective of Brougham, the deep earnestness of Plunkett. The speaker's person, moreover, was gaunt and ungainly, his accent Scotch, his voice monotonous, his action (the regular and graceless vibration of two long arms) sometimes vehement, without passion, and sometimes almost cringing, through good nature and civility. In short, his manner, wanting altogether the quiet concentration of self-possession, was peculiarly opposed to that dignified, simple, and straightforward way of addressing an audience which may be called "English."

Still, it must be remembered that he was then at an advanced age, and deprived, in some degree, of

that mental, and yet more of that physical, energy,
which at an earlier period might possibly have concealed these defects. I have heard, indeed, that on
previous occasions there had been moments when a
temporary excitement gave a natural animation to his
voice and gestures, and that then the excellence of his
arguments was made strikingly manifest by an effective
delivery.

His chief reputation in Parliament, nevertheless,
is not as an orator, but as a person successfully connected with one of those great movements of opinion
which are so long running their course, and which it
is the fortune of a man's life to encounter and be borne
up upon when they are near their goal.

VII.

Sir Thomas More, in his "Utopia" (1520), says
of thieving, that, "as the severity of the remedy is too
great, so it is ineffectual." In Erasmus, Raleigh, Bacon,
are to be found almost precisely the same phrases and
maxims that a few years ago startled the House of
Commons as novelties. "What a lamentable case it
is," observes Sir Edward Coke, in the "Epilogue to the
Third Institutes" (1620), "to see so many Christian
men and women strangled on that cursed tree of the
gallows, the prevention of which consisteth in three
things:

'Good education,
'Good laws,
'Rare pardons.'"

Evelyn, in his preface to "State Trials" (1730),

observes, "that our legislation is very liberal of the
lives of offenders, making no distinction between the
most atrocious crimes and those of a less degree."

"Experience," says Montesquieu, "shows that in
countries remarkable for the lenity of their laws, the
spirit of its inhabitants is as much affected by slight
penalties as in other countries by severe punishments."[*]

This feeling became general amongst reflecting men
in the middle and towards the end of the eighteenth
century.

Johnson displays it in the "Rambler" (1751).
Blackstone expressly declares that "every humane legislator should be extremely cautious of establishing laws
which inflict the penalty of death, especially for slight
offences." Mr. Grose, in writing on the Criminal Laws
of England (1769), observes: "The sanguinary disposition of our laws, besides being a national reproach,
is, as it may appear, an encouragement instead of a
terror to delinquents."

At this time also appeared the pamphlet of "Bec-
caria" (1767), which was followed by an almost general
movement in favour of milder laws throughout Europe.
The Duke of Modena (1780) abolished the Inquisition
in his states; the King of France, in 1781, the torture;
in Russia, capital punishment — never used but in
cases of treason — may be said, for all ordinary
crimes, to have been done away with.

In England, where every doctrine is sure to find
two parties, there was a contest between one set of
men who wished our rigorous laws to be still more
rigorously executed, and another that considered the
rigour of those laws to be the main cause of their in-

* "On the Power of Punishments," ch. xII.

efficiency. A pamphlet, called "Thoughts on Executive Justice," which produced some sensation at the moment, represented the first class of malcontents, and the author declaimed vehemently against those juries who acquitted capital offenders, because it went against their conscience to take away men's lives. Sir Samuel Romilly, then a very young man, replied to this pamphlet with its own facts, and contended that the way of insuring the punishment of criminals was to make that punishment more proportionate to their offences.

From this pamphlet dates the modern battle which the great lawyer, whose public career commenced with it, carried subsequently to the floor of the House of Commons.

His exertions, however, were less fortunate than they deserved to be. To him, indeed, we owe, in a great measure, the spreading of truths amongst the many which had previously been confined to the few; but he never enjoyed the substantial triumph of these truths, for the one or two small successes which he obtained are scarcely worth mentioning.

His melancholy death took place in 1819, and Sir James Mackintosh, who had just previously called the attention of Parliament to the barbarous extent to which executions for forgery had been carried, now came forward as the successor of Romilly in the general work of criminal law reformation.

In March, 1819, accordingly, he moved for a committee to inquire into the subject, and obtained, in a great measure the result of his own able and temperate manner, a majority of nineteen. Again, in 1822, though opposed by the ministers and law-officers of the Crown, he carried a motion which pledged the House *to increase the efficiency by diminishing the rigour of our criminal jurisprudence;* and, in 1823, he followed up this triumph by Nine Resolutions, which, had they been adopted, would have taken away the punishment of death in the case of larceny from shops, dwelling-houses, and on navigable rivers, and also in those of forgery, sheep-stealing, and other felonies, made capital by the *"Marriage* and Black Act;" in short, he proposed that sentences of death should only be pronounced when it was intended to carry them into execution. Mr. Peel, then home secretary, opposed these resolutions, and obtained a majority against them; but he pledged himself at the same time to undertake, in behalf of the government, a plan of law reform, which, although less comprehensive than that which Sir James Mackintosh contended for, was a great measure in itself, and an immense step towards further improvement.

Mackintosh's success, throughout these efforts, was mainly due to the plain unpretending manner in which he stated his case. "I don't mean," he said, "to frame a new criminal code; God forbid I should have such an idle and extravagant pretension. I do not mean to abolish the punishment of death; I believe that societies and individuals may use it as a legitimate mode of defence. Neither do I mean to usurp on the right of pardon now held by the Crown, which, on the contrary, I wish, practically speaking, to restore. I do not even hope that I shall be able to point out a manner in which the penalty of the law should always be inflicted and never remitted. But I find things in this condition — that the infliction of the law is the exception, and I desire to make it the rule. I find

two hundred cases in which capital punishment is
awarded by the statute-book, and only twenty-five in
which, for seventy years, such punishment has been
executed. Why is this? Because the code says one
thing, and the moral feeling of your society another.
All I desire is that the two should be analogous, and
that our laws should award such punishments as our
consciences permit us to inflict."

It was this kind of tone which reassured the House
that it was not periling property by respecting life, and
brought about more quickly than less prudent management would have done that reform to which the general
spirit of the time was tending, and which must necessarily, a few years sooner or later, have arrived.

VIII.

' Thus, Sir James Mackintosh not only delivered
some remarkable speeches in Parliament, but he connected his name with a great and memorable parliamentary triumph; nor is this all, he was true to his
party, opposing the government, though with some internal scruples, in 1820; supporting Mr. Canning in
1827; and going again into opposition, to the Duke of
Wellington, in 1828. And yet, notwithstanding the
ability usually displayed in his speeches, notwithstanding the result of his efforts in criminal law reform,
and, more than all, notwithstanding the constancy
during late years of his politics, he held but a third-
rate place with the Whigs, and when they came into
office in 1830, was only made secretary at that board
over which, when untried, he had been offered, twenty

years before, to preside. It is easy to say that this was because he had not aristocratical connections. Mr. Poulett Thompson was not more highly connected, and yet, though thirty years his junior, and far his inferior in knowledge and mental capacity, received at the time a higher office, and rose in ten years to the first places and honours of the State. The one had much the higher order of intelligence, the other the more resolute practical character. What you expected from the first, he did not perform; the other went beyond your expectations. For this is to be remarked: a man's career is formed of the number of little things he is always doing, whereas your opinion of him is frequently derived, as I have already said, from something which, under a particular stimulus, he has done once or twice, and may do now and then.

The fact is that Mackintosh was not fit for the daily toil and struggle of Parliament; he had not the quickness, the energy, the hard and active nature of those who rise by constant exertions in popular assemblies. He did very well to come out like the State steed, on great and solemn occasions, with gorgeous caparison and prancing action, but he did not do as the every-day hack on a plain road. He was, moreover, inclined by his nature rather to repose than to strife; and that which we do by effort we cannot be doing for ever — nor even do frequently well. His reason, which was acute, told him what he should be; but he had not the energy to be it. For instance, on returning to England, he exclaimed: "It is time to be something decided, and I am resolved to exert myself to the utmost in public life, if I have a seat in Parliament, or to condemn myself to profound retirement if the doors of St. Stephen's are barred to me.*

He had not, however, been many years a member before he accepted a professorship (year 1818) at Hailesbury College, because it left him in the House of Commons; and refused the chair of moral philosophy at Edinburgh (1818) because it would have withdrawn him from it. The great stream of public life thus passed for ever by him; he could neither commit himself to its waves nor yet avoid lingering on its shores. Now and then, in a moment of excitement, he would rush into it, but it was soon again to retire to some sunny reverie, or some shady regret, where he could quietly plot for the future, or mourn over the past, or indulge the scheme of lettered indolence which wooed him at the moment.

* See "Life of Sir James Mackintosh," by his Son, vol. n. p. 2.

MACKINTOSH,

THE MAN OF PROMISE.

PART III.

History of England. — Reviews in Edinburgh. — Treatise on Ethical Philosophy. — Revolution, 1688. — Bentham's system of morals and politics. — His own death. — Comparison with Montaigne.

PART III.

I.

I HAVE said that Sir James Mackintosh allowed
himself to be lured from the strife of politics by the
love of letters. And what was the species of learned
labour on which his intervals of musing leisure were
employed? He read at times; this he was always able
and willing to do, for the future composition of a great
historical work — the "History of England" — which
his friends and the public, with a total ignorance of his
sort of character and ability, always sighed that he
should undertake, and considered that he would worthily
accomplish. But while he read for the future composition of this work, he actually wrote little or nothing
for it. The little he did write was undertaken at the
call of some particular impulse, and capable of being
finished before that impulse was passed away. In such
writings he followed the bent of his nature, and in
them accordingly he best succeeded, as they who refer
to his contributions to the "Edinburgh Review" * may

---

* Principal Papers of Sir James Mackintosh in the "Edinburgh
Review":
   Vol. 20. Account of Boy born Blind and Deaf.
   Ib. Wakefield's Account of Ireland.
   21. Madame de Staël: On Suicide.
   22. *Ib.* L'Allemagne.
   Ib. On Rogers' Poems.

be well disposed to acknowledge. At last, within a few yards of his grave, he made a start. Life was drawing to a close, the season for action was almost passed, and of all he had mused and read and planned for it, there existed nothing. This thought galled him to a species of exertion, and he is one of the very few men who, at an advanced age, crowded the most considerable and ambitious of their works into the last years of their life.

The volumes on "English History" brought out in Dr. Lardner's "Encyclopædia," the "Life of Sir Thomas More," which appeared in the same publication, a "Treatise on Ethical Philosophy," and a commencement of the "History of the Revolution of 1688,"

Vol. 24. On the French Restoration.
    26. Life of James II. (Stuart's Papers.)
·   27. Stuart's Preliminary Essay (Metaphysics) to Encyclopædia Britannica.
    36. *Ib.*
    34. Parliamentary Reform.
    35. Sismondi: Histoire des Français.
    36. Sir George Mackenzie's "Scotland."
    44. Who wrote "Eikon Basilicos?"
    Ib. Danish Revolution. (Struensee.)
November, 1822. The Partition of Poland.
  No. 89. Portugal — Don Miguel.

The following articles were also published by Sir James in the "Monthly Review":

Year 1795. Vol. 19. Burke's Letter to a Noble Lord.
           Ib. A Letter to Mr. Miles, occasioned by his late scurrilous attack on Mr. Burke.
           20. Miscellaneous Works of Gibbon (Part).
1796.   *Ib.* Roscoe's "Life of Lorenzo de Medici."
           Ib. Moore's "View of the Causes of the French Revolution."
           21. Burke's Two Letters.
           Ib. Thoughts on Regicide Peace.
           Ib. O'Brien's "Utrum Florium."
           Ib. Burke's Two Letters (concluded).

delivered to the world after his death, are these works.

They all exhibit the author's defects and merits; third-rate in themselves, and yet at various times persuading us that he who wrote them was a first-rate man. Let us take up for instance the volumes on "English History." The narrative is languid, and interrupted by disquisitions: the style is in general prolix, cumbrous, cold, profuse; nevertheless, these volumes are full of thought and knowledge; they contain many curious anecdotes, many scattered observations of profound wisdom, while here and there burst upon us, by surprise it must be confessed, passages which, written under a temporary excitement, display remarkable spirit and power. Such is the description of Beckct's murder:

II.

"Provoked by these acts of extraordinary imprudence, Henry is said to have called out before an audience of lords, knights, and gentlemen, 'To what a miserable state am I reduced, when I cannot be at rest in my own realm, by reason of only one priest; is there no one to deliver me from my troubles?' Four knights of distinguished rank, William de Tracy, Hugh de Moreville, Richard Briths, and Reginald Fitz-Urse (December 28), interpreted the King's complaints as commands. They repaired to Canterbury, confirmed in their purpose by finding that Becket had recommenced his excommunications by that of Robert de Broe, and that he had altered his course homeward to avoid the royalist bishops on their way to court, in Normandy;

they instantly went to his house, and required him,
not very mildly, to withdraw the censures of the pre-
lates, and take the oath to his lord-paramount. He
refused. John of Salisbury, his faithful and learned
secretary, ventured at this alarming moment to counsel
peace. The primate thought that nothing was left to
him but a becoming death.

"The knights retired to put on their armour, and
there seems to have been sufficient interval either for
negotiation or escape. At that moment indeed, measures were preparing for legal proceedings against
him.

"But the visible approach of peril awakened his
sense of dignity, and breathed an unusual decorum
over his language and deportment. He went through
the cloisters into the church, whither he was followed
by his enemies, attended by a band of soldiers, whom
they had hastily gathered together. They rushed into
the church with drawn swords. Tracy cried out,
'Where is the traitor? Where is the archbishop?'
Becket, who stood before the altar of St. Bennet, answered gravely, 'Here am I, no traitor, but the archbishop.' Tracy pulled him by the sleeve, saying:
'Come hither, thou art a prisoner.' He pulled back
his arm with such force, as to make Tracy stagger, and
said: 'What meaneth this, William? I have done *thee*
many pleasures; comest thou with armed men into my
church?' 'It is not possible that thou shouldst live
any longer,' called out Fitz-Urse. The intrepid primate
replied: 'I am ready to die for my God, in defence of
the liberties of the Church.'

"At that moment, either by a relapse into his old
disorders, or to show that his non-resistance sprung not

from weakness, but from duty, he took hold of Tracy by the habergeon, or gorget, and flung him with such violence as had nearly thrown him to the ground. He then bowed his head, as if he would pray, and uttered his last words: "To God and St. Mary I commend my soul, and the cause of the Church!' Tracy aimed a heavy blow at him which fell on a by-stander. The assassins fell on him with many strokes, and though the second brought him to the ground, they did not cease till his brains were scattered over the pavement."*

III.

The characters of Alfred, of William I., of Henry VII., are superior to any sketches of the same persons with which I am acquainted. The summing up of events into pictures of certain epochs is frequently done with much skill, and I particularly remember a short description of the commencement of the Crusaders, concluding with the capture of Jerusalem; — the state of Europe in the thirteenth century, comprising a large portion of history in two pages; and the death of Simon de Montfort, with the establishment of the English Constitution. In a true spirit of historical philosophy, Sir James Mackintosh says:

"The introduction of knights, citizens, and burgesses into the Legislature, by its continuance in circumstances so apparently inauspicious, showed how exactly it suited the necessities and demands of society at that moment. No sooner had events brought forward the measure, than its fitness to the state of the community

* The death of Rizzio is an almost equally vivid description.

became apparent. It is often thus that in the clamours
of men for a succession of objects, society selects from
among them the one that has an affinity with itself,
and which most easily combines with its state at the
time."

The condition of Europe, also, just prior to the wars
of the Roses, is rapidly, picturesquely, and comprehen-
sively sketched.

"'The historian who rests for a little space between
the termination of the Plantagenet wars in France and
the commencement of the civil wars of the two branches
of that family in England, may naturally look around
him, reviewing some of the more important events
which had passed, and casting his eye onward to the
preparations for the mighty changes which were to
produce an influence on the character and lot of the
human race. A very few particulars only can be
selected as specimens from so vast a mass. The foundations of the political system of the European com-
monwealth were now laid. A glance over the map
of Europe, in 1453, will satisfy an observer that the
territories of different nations were then fast approaching to the shape and extent which they retain at this
day. The English islanders had only one town of the
continent remaining in their hands. The Mahometans
of Spain were on the eve of being reduced under the
Christian authority. Italy had, indeed, lost her liberty,
but had yet escaped the ignominy of a foreign yoke.
Moscovy was emerging from the long domination of
the Tartars. Venice, Hungary, and Poland, three
states now placed under foreign masters, guarded the
eastern frontier of Christendom against the Ottoman
barbarians, whom the absence of foresight, of mutual

confidence, and a disregard of general safety and honour, disgraceful to the western governments, had just
suffered to master Constantinople and to subjugate the
eastern Christians. France had consolidated the greater
part of her central and commanding territories. In the
transfer of the Netherlands to the house of Austria
originated the French jealousy of that power, then
rising in South-Eastern Germany. The empire was
daily becoming a looser confederacy under a nominal
ruler, whose small remains of authority every day continued to lessen. The internal or constitutional history
of the European nations threatened, in almost every
continental country, the fatál establishment of an absolute monarchy, from which the free and generous
spirit of the northern barbarians did not protect their
degenerate posterity. In the Netherlands an ancient
gentry, and burghers, enriched by traffic, held their
still limited princes in check. In Switzerland, the
patricians of a few towns, together with the gallant
peasantry of the Alpine valleys, escaped a master.
But Parliaments and Diets, States-General and Cortes,
were gradually disappearing from view, or reduced
from august assemblies to insignificant formalities, and
Europe s eemed on the eve of exhibiting nothing to
the disgusted eye but the dead uniformity of imbecile
despotism, dissolute courts, and cruelly oppressed
nations.

"In the meantime the unobserved advancement and
diffusion of knowledge were preparing the way for discoveries, of which the high result will be contemplated
only by unborn ages. The mariner's compass had conducted the Portuguese to distant points on the coast of
Africa, and was about to lead them through the un-

ploughed ocean to the famous regions of the East.
Civilized men, hitherto cooped up on the shores of the
Mediterranean and the Atlantic, now visited the whole
of their subject planet and became its undisputed sovereigns. The great adventurer * was then born, who,
with two undecked boats and one frail sloop, containing with difficulty a hundred and twenty persons, dared
to stretch across an untraversed ocean, which had
hitherto bounded the imaginations as well as the enter-
prises of men; and who, instead of that India renowned
in legend and in story, of which he was in quest,
laid open a new world which, under the hands of the
European race, was one day to produce governments,
laws, manners, modes of civilization and states of society
almost as different as its native plants and animals from
those of ancient Europe.

"Who could then — who can even now — foresee
all the prodigious effects of these discoveries on the
fortunes of mankind?"

IV.

No one will deny that what I have just quoted
might have been written by a great historian? Yet no
one will say that the work I quote from is a great
history.

It is a series of parts, some excellent, some indifferent, but which, altogether do not form a whole.
The fragment of the Revolution, though a fragment,
presents the same qualities and defects. The narrative is poor; some of the characters, such as those of
Rochester, Sunderland, and Halifax — and some of

* Columbus, born 1441, or earlier, according to Mr. W. Irving.

the passages (that with which the work opens for instance) — are excellent; but then, these fine figures of gold embroidery are worked here and there with care and toil, on an ordinary sort of canvas.

The "Life of Sir Thomas More" is the only complete performance; and this because it was a portrait which might have been taken at one sitting.

The "Treatise on Ethics," first published in the supplement of the seventh edition of the "Encyclopædia Britannica," and which has since appeared in a separate form under the auspices of Professor Whewell, is still more remarkable, both in its design and execution, as characterising the author. He seems here, indeed, to have been aware of his own capabilities, and to have accommodated his labours to them; for his work is conceived in separate and distinct portions, and he undertakes to write the course and progress of philosophy by descriptions of its most illustrious masters and professors; a plan gracefully imagined, as diffusing the charm of personal narrative over dry and speculative disquisition.

Nothing, accordingly, can be better executed than some of these pictures. It would be difficult to paint Hobbes, Leibnitz, Shaftesbury, more faithfully, or in more suitable colours; the contrast between the haughty Bossuet and the gentle Fénelon is perfectly sustained; while Berkeley the virtuous, the benevolent, the imaginative, is drawn with a pencil which would even have satisfied the admiration of his contemporaries:

V.

"*Berkeley.*—Ancient learning, exact science, polished society, modern literature, and the fine arts, contributed to adorn and enrich the mind of this accomplished man. All his contemporaries agreed with the satirist in ascribing

"'To Berkeley every virtue under heaven!'

"Adverse factions and hostile wits concurred only in loving, admiring, and contributing to advance him. The severe sense of Swift endured his visions; the modest Addison endeavoured to reconcile Clarke to his ambitious speculations. His character converted the satire of Pope into fervid praise. Even the fastidious and turbulent Atterbury said, after an interview with him, 'So much understanding, so much knowledge, so much innocence, and such humility, I did not think had been the portion of any but angels, till I saw this gentleman.' * 'Lord Bathurst told me,' says Warton, 'that the members of the Scribblers' Club being met at his house at dinner, they agreed to rally Berkeley, who was also his guest, on his scheme at Bermudas. Berkeley, having listened to the many lively things they had to say, begged to be heard in his turn, and displayed his plan with such an astonishing and animating force of eloquence and enthusiasm that they were struck dumb, and, after some pause, rose all up together, with earnestness exclaiming, "Let us set out with him immediately!"' ** It was when thus beloved and cele-

* Duncombe's Letters, pp. 106, 107.
** Warton on "Pope."

brated that he conceived, at the age of forty-five, the design of devoting his life to reclaim and convert the natives of North America; and he employed as much influence and solicitation as common men do for their most prized objects, in obtaining leave to resign his dignities and revenues, to quit his accomplished and affectionate friends, and to bury himself in what must have seemed an intellectual desert. After four years' residence at Newport, in Rhode Island, he was compelled, by the refusal of government to furnish him with funds for his college, to forego his work of heroic, or rather god-like benevolence, though not without some consoling forethought of the fortune of a country where he had sojourned:

"'Westward the course of empire takes its way:
The first four acts already past,
A fifth shall close the drama with the day,
Time's noblest offspring is its last.'

"Thus disappointed in his ambition of keeping a school for savage children, at a salary of a hundred pounds a year, he was received on his return with open arms by the philosophical Queen, at whose metaphysical parties he made one, with Sherlock, who, as well as Smallridge, was his supporter, and with Hoadley, who, following Clarke, was his antagonist. By her influence he was made Bishop of Cloyne. It is one of his greatest merits, that though of English extraction, he was a true Irishman, and the first eminent Protestant, after the unhappy contest at the Revolution, who avowed his love for all his countrymen;* and contributed, by a truly Christian address to the Roman Catholics of his diocese, to their perfect quiet during

* See his "Querist," p. 858, published in 1787.

the rebellion of 1745. From the writings of his advanced years, when he chose a medical tract * to be
the vehicle of philosophical reflections, though it cannot
be said that he relinquished his early opinions, it is at
least apparent that his mind had received a new bent,
and was habitually turned from reasoning towards contemplation. His immaterialism, indeed, modestly appears, but only to purify and elevate our thoughts, and
to fix them on mind, the paramount and primeval
principle of all things. 'Perhaps,' says he, 'the truth
about innate ideas may be, that there are properly no
ideas on passive objects in the mind but what are
derived from sense, but that there are also, besides
these, her own acts and operations — such are notions;'
a statement which seems once more to admit general
conceptions, and which might have served, as well as
the parallel passage of Leibnitz, as the basis of modern
philosophy in Germany. From these compositions of
his old age, he then appears to have recurred with
fondness to Plato, and the later Platonists: writers
from whose mere reasonings an intellect so acute could
hardly hope for an argumentative satisfaction of all its
difficulties, and whom he probably either studied as
a means of inuring his mind to objects beyond the
visible diurnal sphere, and of attaching it, through
frequent meditation, to that perfect and transcendent
goodness, to which his moral feelings always pointed,
and which they incessantly strove to grasp. His mind,
enlarging as it rose, at length receives every theist,
however imperfect his belief, to a communion in its
philosophic piety. 'Truth,' he beautifully concludes,
'is the cry of all, but the game of few. Certainly,

* "Siris; or, Reflections on Tar Water."

where it is the chief passion, it does not give way to vulgar cares, nor is it contented with a little ardour in the early time of life; active perhaps to pursue, but not so fit to weigh and revise. He that would make a real progress in knowledge, must dedicate his age as well as youth, the latter growth as well as first fruits, at the altar of truth.' So did Berkeley, and such were almost his latest words.

"His general principles of ethics may be shortly stated by himself: 'As God is a being of infinite goodness, His end is the good of His creatures. The general well-being of all men of all nations, of all ages of the world, is that which He designs should be procured by the concurring actions of each individual.' Having stated that this end can be pursued only in one of two ways — either by computing the consequences of each action, or by obeying the rules which generally tend to happiness; and having shown the first to be impossible, he rightly infers, 'That the end to which God requires the concurrence of human actions, must be carried on by the observation of certain determinate and universal rules, or moral precepts, which in their own nature have a necessary tendency to promote the well-being of mankind, taking in all nations and ages, from the beginning to the end of the world.'[*] A romance, of which a journey to an Utopia in the centre of Africa forms the chief part, called, 'The adventures of Signor Gaudentio di Lucca,' has been commonly ascribed to him; probably on no other ground than its union of pleasing invention with benevolence and elegance."[**]

[*] Sermon in Trinity College Chapel on "Passive Obedience," 1712.
[**] "Gentleman's Magazine," 1777.

VI.

The following short description of the practical
Paley comes aptly after that of this charming Utopian:
"*Paley.* — The natural frame of Paley's understanding fitted it more for business and the world than
for philosophy; and he accordingly enjoyed with considerable relish the few opportunities which the latter
part of his life afforded, of taking a part in the affairs
of his country, as a magistrate. Penetration and
shrewdness, firmness and coolness, a vein of pleasantry,
fruitful, though somewhat unrefined, with an original
homeliness and significancy of expression, were perhaps
more remarkable in his conversation than the restraints
of authorship and profession allowed them to be in his
'writings. His taste for the common business and ordinary amusements of life, fortunately gave a zest to the
company which his neighbourhood chanced to yield,
without rendering him insensible to the pleasures of
intercourse with more enlightened society. The practical bent of his nature is visible in the language of
his writings, which, on practical matters, is as precise
as the nature of the subject requires; but, in his rare
and reluctant efforts to rise to first principles, becomes
undeterminate and unsatisfactory, though no man's
composition was more free from the impediments which
hinder a writer's meaning from being quickly and
clearly seen. He possessed that chastised acuteness of
discrimination, exercised on the affairs of men, and
habitually looking to a purpose beyond the mere increase of knowledge, which forms the character of a
lawyer's understanding, and which is apt to render a

mere lawyer too subtle for the management of affairs, and yet too gross for the pursuit of general truths. His style is as near perfection, in its kind, as any in our language. Perhaps no words were ever more expressive and illustrative than those in which he represents the art of life to be that of rightly setting our habits." — "Ethical Philosophy," p. 274.

Such are the portraits in this work; the history of ancient ethics, and the vindication of the scholiasts also, are in themselves and as separate compositions of great merit; but when, after admiring these different fragments, we look at the plan, at the system which is to result from them, or endeavour to follow out the line of reasoning which is to bring them together — we quit the land of realities for that of shadows, and are obliged to confess that the author has barely sufficient vigour to make his meaning intelligible.

VII.

To give the history intended to be given by Sir James's treatise, would be without the scope of the present sketch; but it may not be amiss to say something of the state of the philosophical opinions which existed at the time of its publication, and which, in fact, called it forth. Helvetius, the friend of Voltaire and Diderot — Helvetius, whose works have been considered as merely the record of those opinions which circulated around him — the most amusing, if not the most logical of metaphysicians, wrote that everything proceeded from the senses, and that man (for this was one of his favourite hypotheses) differed from a mon-

5*

key mainly because his hands were tenderer and more soft.

The doctrine of sensation led necessarily to that of selfishness, since, owing what we think to what we feel, every idea is the consequence of some pain or pleasure, and our own pains and pleasures are thus the parents of all our emotions.

A strong reaction, however, took place in the beginning of the nineteenth against the eighteenth century; the original existence of certain sentiments or affections implanted by nature, was contended for, in Germany and in Scotland, under a variety of qualifications. The school, which said that the affections arose from this primary source, called them disinterested, as that which contended that they more or less directly proceeded from some cause which had reference to ourselves, called them interested. There was but one step easily made by both parties in carrying out their doctrines.

The philosophers who thought that self-interest, "through some certain strainers well refined," was the cause of all our actions and ideas, maintained that utility was the only measure of virtue, or of greatness. The philosophers of the opposite faction argued on the contrary, that as many of our emotions were natural and involuntary, so there was also a sense of wrong and right, natural and involuntary, and connected with those emotions implanted in us.

Living in a retired part of London, visited only by his adorers and disciples, looking rarely beyond the confines of his early knowledge, and on the train of thinking it had inspired, an old and singular gentleman, with great native powers of mind, almost alone resisted the new impulse, and, classifying and extending the doctrines of the French philosophy, established a reputation and a school of his own. The charm of Mr. Bentham's philosophy, however obscured by fanciful names and unnecessary subdivisions, is its apparent clearness and simplicity.

He considers with the Helvetians — 1, that our ideas do come from our sensations, and that consequently we are selfish; 2, that man in doing what is most useful to himself does what is right.

Very strange and fantastical notions have been propagated against the philosopher by persons so egregiously mistaking him as to imagine that what he thus says of mankind generally — of man, meaning every man — is said of *a* man, of man separately; so that a murderer, pretend these commentators, has only to be sure that a second murder is useful to him by preventing the detection of the first, in order to be justified in committing it. It were useless to dwell upon this ridiculous construction. But in urging men to pursue the general interest of society at large, in telling them that to do what is most for that interest is to act usefully and thereby virtuously, Mr. Bentham found it necessary to explain how such interest was to be discovered.

Accordingly he has propounded that the general interest of a society must be considered to be the interest of the greatest number in that society, and that the greatest number in any society is the best judge of its interest. Moreover, in the further development of his doctrine, he contends that a majority would always, under natural circumstances, govern a minority, and that, therefore, there is a natural tendency, if not thwarted, towards the happiness and good government of mankind. This system of philosophy gained the

more attention from its being also a system of politics.
According to Mr. Bentham, that which was most important to men depended on maintaining what he considered the natural law, viz., governing the minority
by the majority.

VIII.

Unfortunately for the destiny of mankind, and the
soundness of the Benthamite doctrine, it is by no means
certain that the majority in any community is the best
judge of its interests; whilst it is even less certain, that
if it did know these interests, it would necessarily and
invariably follow them. In almost every collection of
men the intelligent few know better what is for the
common interest than the ignorant many; and it is rare
indeed to see communities or individuals pursuing their
interest steadily even when they perceive it clearly.
It would, perhaps, be more reconcilable to reason to
say that the intellect of a community should govern a
community; but this is also subject to objection, since
a small number of intelligent men might govern for
their own interest, and not for the interest of the society
they represented. In short, though it is easy to see
that the science of government does not consist in giving power to the greatest number, but in giving it to
the most intelligent, and making it for their interest to
govern for the interest of the greatest number; still,
every day teaches us that good government is rather a
thing relative than a thing absolute; that all governments have good mixed with evil, and evil mixed with
good; and that the statesman's task, as is beautifully
demonstrated by Montesquieu, is, not to destroy an

evil combined with a greater good, nor to create a good
accompanied with a greater evil; but to calculate how
the greatest amount of good and the least amount of
evil can be combined together. Hence it is, that the
best governments with which we are acquainted seem
rather to have been fashioned by the working hand of
daily experience, than by the artistic fingers of philosophical speculation.

Nevertheless, the theory, that the good of the
greatest number in any community ought to be the
object which its government should strive to attain,
and the maxim, that the interest and happiness of every
unit in a community is to be treated as a portion of
the interest and happiness of the whole community, are
humanizing precepts, and have, through the influence
of Mr. Bentham and of his disciples, produced, within
my own memory, a considerable change in the public
opinion of England.

Mr. Bentham's name, then, is far more above the
scoff of his antagonists than below the enthusiasm of
his disciples; and it is in this spirit, and with a becoming respect, that Sir James Mackintosh treats the philosopher while he combats his philosophy.

IX.

In regard to the theory of Sir James himself, if I
understand it rightly (and it is rather, as I have said,
indistinctly expressed), he accepts neither the doctrine
of innate ideas disinterestedly producing or ordering
our actions, nor that of sense-derived ideas by which,
with a concentrated regard to self, some suppose men
to be governed — but imagines an association of ideas,

naturally suggested by our human condition, which, according to a pre-ordinated state of the mind, produces, as in chemical processes, some emotion different from any of the combined elements or causes from which it springs.

This emotion, once existing, requires, without con-, sideration or reflection, its gratification. In this manner the satisfaction of benevolence and pity is as much a spontaneous desire as hunger, and man is unconsciously taught, through feelings necessary to him as man, to wish involuntarily for that which, on reflection and ex· perience, he would find, such is the beautiful dispensa- tion of Providence, most for his happiness and advan- tage.

The union, assemblage, or incorporation, if one may so speak, of these involuntary desires, affecting and affected by them all, becomes our universal moral sense or conscience, which in each of its propensities is gratified or mortified, according to our conduct.

X.

Here end my criticisms. They have passed rapidly in review the principal works and events of Sir James Mackintosh's life; * and what have they illustrated? That, which I commenced by observing: that he had made several excellent speeches, that he had taken an

---

* He published the "Vindiciæ Gallicæ" in 1791; he gave his lectures in 1799; he appeared as Peltier's advocate in the same year; he entered Parliament in 1813; he delivered his celebrated speech against the Foreign Enlistment Bill in 1819, and carried his motion pledging the House of Commons to an improvement in the criminal law in 1822; his work on "Ethics" was published in 1830; his "History of England" in 1830—31.

active part in politics, that he had written ably upon
history, that he had manifested a profound knowledge
of philosophy; but that he had not been pre-eminent as
an orator, as a politician, as an historian, as a philosopher.* It may be doubted whether any speech or
book of his will long survive his time; but a very
valuable work might be compiled from his writings
and speeches. Indeed, there are hardly any books in
our language more interesting or more instructive than
the two volumes published by his son, and which display in every page the best qualities of an excellent
heart and an excellent understanding, set off by the
most amiable and remarkable simplicity and amiability
of character. His striking, peculiar, and unrivalled
merit, however, was that of a conversationalist. Great
good-nature, great and yet gentle animation, much
learning, and a sound, discriminating, and comprehensive judgment, made him this. He had little of the
wit of words — brilliant repartées, caustic sayings,
concentrated and epigrammatic turns of expression. But
he knew everything and could talk of everything without being tedious. A Lady of great wit and intellect
in describing his soft Scotch voice said to me — "Mackintosh played on your understanding with a flageolet,
Macaulay with a trumpet." Having lived much by
himself and with books, and much also in the world
and with men, he had the light anecdote and easy

---

* B. Constant was another instance of this kind, and it is singular to
see Mackintosh himself thus judging him: — "Few men have turned talent
to less account than Constant. His powers of mind are very great, but as
they have always been exerted on the events of the moment, and as his
works want that laboured perfection which is more necessary but more
difficult in such writings than in any others, they have left us a vague or
faint reputation which will scarcely survive the speaker or writer."

manner of society, and the grave and serious gatherings
in of lonely hours. .He added also to much knowledge
considerable powers of observation; and there are few
persons of whom he speaks, even at the dawn of their
career, whom he has not judged with discrimination.
His agreeableness, moreover, being that of a full mind
expressed with facility, was the most translatable of
any man's, and he succeeded with foreigners, and in
France which he visited three times — once at the
peace of Amiens, again in 1814, and again in 1824
— quite as much as in his own country, and with his
own countrymen. Madame de Staël and Benjamin
Constant prized him not less than Lord Dudley or
Lord Byron. It was not only in England, then, but
also on the Continent, where his early pamphlet and
distinguished friendships had made him equally known
— that he ever remained the *man of promise;* until,
amidst hopes which his vast and various information,
his wonderful memory, his copious elocution, and his
transitory fits of energy, still nourished, he died, in the
sixty-seventh year of his age, universally admired and
regretted, though without a high reputation for any
one thing, or the ardent attachment of any particular
set of persons. His death, which took place the 30th
of May, 1832, was occasioned by a small fragment of
chicken-bone, which, having, in swallowing, lacerated
the trachea, created a wound, that ultimately proved
fatal. He met his end with calmness and resignation,
expressing his belief in the Christian faith, and placing
his trust in it.

XI.

No man doing so little ever went through a long life, continually creating the belief that he would ultimately do so much. A want of earnestness, a want of passion, a want of genius, prevented him from playing a first-rate part amongst men during his day, and from leaving any of those monuments behind him which command the attention of posterity. A love of knowledge, an acute and capacious intelligence, an early and noble ambition, led him into literary and active life, and furnished him with the materials and at moments with the energy by which success in both is obtained. An amiable disposition, a lively flow of spirits, an extraordinary and various stock of information made his society agreeable to the most distinguished persons of his age, and induced them to expect greater things from him than he could ever perform.

"What have you done," he relates that a French lady once said to him, "that people should think you so superior?" "I was obliged," he adds, "as usual to refer to my projects." For active life he was too much of the academic school. Believing nearly all great distinctions to be less than they were, and remaining irresolute between small ones. He passed, as he himself said, from Burke to Fox in half an hour, and remained weeks, as we learn from a friend (Lord Nugent), in determining whether he should employ "usefulness" or "utility" in some particular composition. Such is not the stuff out of which great leaders or statesmen are formed. His main error as a writer and as a speaker was his painstaking and struggle with that easy idle way of delivering himself, which made his charm when he did not think of what he was saying. "The great fault of my manner," he himself observes somewhere, "is that I overload." And to many of his more finished compositions we might, indeed, apply the old saying of the critic, who on being asked whether he admired a certain tragedy of Dionysius, replied: "I have not seen it; it is obscured with language." His early compositions had a sharper and terser style than his later ones, the activity of the author's mind being greater, and his doubts and toils after perfection less; but even these were over-prepared. Can he be considered a failure? No; if you compare him with other men. Yes; if you compare him with the general idea entertained as to himself. The reputation he attained, however vague and uncertain, the writings that he left, though inferior to the prevalent notion as to his powers, — all placed him on a pedestal of conspicuous, though not of gigantic elevation amongst his contemporaries. The results of his life only disappointed, when you measured them by the anticipations which his merits had excited — then he became "the man of promise." Could he have arrived at greater eminence than that which he attained? if so, it must have been by a different road. I cannot repeat too often that no man struggles perpetually and victoriously against his own character; and one of the first principles of success in life, is so to regulate our career as rather to turn our physical constitution and natural inclinations to good account, than to endeavour to counteract the one or oppose the other.

There can be no general comparison between Montaigne and Mackintosh. The first was an original thinker, and the latter a combiner and retailer of the thoughts of others. But I have often pictured to myself the French philosopher lounging away the greatest portion of his life in the old square turret of his château, yielding to his laziness all that it exacted from him, and becoming, almost in spite of himself, the first magistrate of his town, and, though carelessly and discursively, the greatest writer of his time. He gave the rein to the idleness of his nature, and had reason to be satisfied with the employment of his life.

On the other hand, let us look at the accomplished Scotchman, constantly agitated by his aspirations after fame and his inclinations for repose; formed for literary ease, forcing himself into political conflict — dreaming of a long-laboured history, and writing a hasty article in a review; earnest about nothing, because the objects to which he momentarily directed his efforts were not likely to give the permanent distinction for which he pined; and thus, with a doubtful mind and a broken career, achieving little that was worthy of his abilities, or equal to the expectations of his friends. I have said there can be no general comparison between men whose particular faculties were no doubt of a very different order; yet, had the one mixed in contest with the bold and factious spirits of his day, he would have been but a poor "*ligueur;*" and had the other abstained from politics and renounced long and laborious compositions, merely writing under the stimulus of some accidental inspiration, it is probable that his name would have gone down to posterity as that of the most agreeable and

instructive essayist of his remarkable epoch. But at
all events that name is graven on the monument
which commemorates more Christian manners and more
mild legislation: and "Blessed shall he be," as said
our great lawyer, "who layeth the first stone of this
building; more blessed he that proceeds in it; most of
all he that finisheth it in the glory of God, and the
honour of our king and nation."

COBBETT,

THE CONTENTIOUS MAN.

PART I.

Son of a small farmer. — Boyhood spent in the country. — Runs away from home. — Becomes a lawyer's clerk. — Enlists as a soldier, 1784. — Learns grammar and studies Swift. — Goes to Canada. — Remarked for good conduct. — Rises to rank of sergeant-major. — Gets discharge, 1791. — Marries. — Quits Europe for United States. — Starts as a bookseller in Pennsylvania. — Becomes a political writer of great power. — Takes a violent anti-republican tone. — Has to suffer different prosecutions, and at last sets sail for England.

COBBETT,

THE CONTENTIOUS MAN.

PART I.

FROM HIS BIRTH, IN MARCH, 1766, TO HIS QUITTING THE UNITED
STATES, JUNE 1ST, 1800.

I.

THE character which I am now tempted to delineate is just the reverse of that which I rise from
describing. Mackintosh was a man of great powers of
reasoning, of accomplished learning, but of little or no
sustained energy. His vision took a wide and calm
range; he saw all things coolly, dispassionately, and,
except at his first entry into life, was never so lost in
his admiration of one object as to overlook the rest.
His fault lay in rather the opposite extreme; his perception of the universal weakened that of the particular, and the variety of colours which appeared at
once before him became too blent in his sight for the
adequate appreciation of each.

The subject of this memoir, on the contrary,
though he could argue well in favour of any opinion
he adopted, had not that elevated and philosophic cast
of mind which makes men inquire after truth for the

Historical Characters. II.   6 sake of truth, regarding its pursuit as a delight, its attainment as a duty. Neither could he take that comprehensive view of affairs which affords to the judgment an ample scope for the comparison and selection of opinions. But he possessed a rapid power of concentration; a will that scorned opposition; he saw clearly that one side of a question which caught his attention; and pursued the object he had momentarily in view with an energy that never recoiled before a danger, and was rarely arrested by a scruple. The sense of his force gave him the passion for action; but he encouraged this passion until it became restlessness, a desire to fight rather for the pleasure of fighting than for devotion to any cause for which he fought.

While Mackintosh always struggled against his character, and thereby never gave himself fair play, the person of whom I am now about to speak — borne away in a perfectly opposite extreme — allowed his character to usurp and govern his abilities, frequently without either usefulness or aim. Thus, the one changed sides two or three times in his life, from that want of natural ardour which creates strong attachments; the other attacked and defended various parties with a furious zeal, upon which no one could rely, because it proceeded from the temporary caprice of a whimsical imagination, and not from the steadfast enthusiasm of any well-meditated conviction. With two or three qualities more, Cobbett would have been a very great man in the world; as it was, he made a great noise in it. But I pass from criticism to narrative.

II.

William Cobbett was born in the neighbourhood of Farnham, on the 9th of March, 1766. The remotest ancestor he had ever heard of was his grandfather, who had been a day labourer, and, according to the rustic habits of old times, worked with the same farmer from the day of his marriage to that of his death. The son, Cobbett's parent, was a man superior to the generality of persons in his station of life. He not only knew reading and writing, but a little mathematics; understood land surveying, was honest and industrious, and had thus risen from the position of labourer, in which he was born, to that of having labourers under him.

Cobbett's boyhood, I may say his childhood, was passed in the fields: first frightening the birds from the turnips, then weeding wheat, then leading a horse at harrowing barley, finally joining the reapers at harvest, driving the team, and holding the plough. His literary instruction was small, and only such as he could learn at home. It was shrewdly asked by Dr. Johnson, "What becomes of all the clever schoolboys?" In fact many of the boys clever at school are not heard of afterwards, because if they are docile they are also timid, and attend to the routine of education less from the love of learning than the want of animal spirits. Cobbett would not have been a boy of this kind. At the age of sixteen he determined to go to sea, but could not get a captain to take him. At the age of seventeen (having already, when much younger, made a similar absence in search of adventures) he quitted his home without communicating his design to

6*

any one, and started, dressed in his Sunday clothes, for the great city of London. Here, owing to the kind exertions of a passenger in the coach in which this his first journey was made, he got engaged after some time and trouble as under-clerk to an attorney (Mr. Holland), in Gray's Inn Lane.

It is natural enough that to a lad accustomed to fresh air, green fields, and out-of-door exercise, the close atmosphere, dull aspect, and sedentary position awaiting an attorney's under-clerk at Gray's Inn must have been hateful. But William Cobbett never once thought of escaping from what he called "an earthly hell" by a return to his home and friends. This would have been to confess himself beaten, which he never meant to be. On the contrary, rushing from one bold step to another still more so, he enlisted himself (1784) as a soldier in a regiment intended to serve in Nova Scotia. His father, though somewhat of his own stern and surly nature, begged, prayed, and remonstrated. But it was useless. The recruit, however, had some months to pass in England, since, peace having taken place, there was no hurry in sending off the troops. These months he spent in Chatham, storing his brains with the lore of a circulating library, and his heart with love-dreams of the librarian's daughter.

To this period he owed what he always considered his most valuable acquisition, a knowledge of his native language; the assiduity with which he gave himself up to study, on this occasion, ensured his success and evinced his character. He wrote out the whole of an English grammar two or three times; he got it by heart; he repeated it every morning and evening, and he imposed on himself the task of saying it over once every time that he mounted guard. "I learned grammar," he himself says, "when I was a private soldier on the pay of sixpence a day. The edge of my berth, or that of the guard-bed, was my seat to study on; my knapsack was my book-case, a bit of bread lying on my lap was my writing-table, and the task did not demand anything like a year of my life." Such is will. In America, Cobbett remained as a soldier till the month of September, 1791, when his regiment was relieved and sent home. On the 19th of November, he obtained his discharge, after having served nearly eight years, never having once been disgraced, confined, or reprimanded, and having attained, owing to his zeal and intelligence, the rank of sergeant-major without having passed through the intermediate rank of sergeant.

The following were the orders issued at Portsmouth on the day of his discharge:

"Portsmouth, 19th Dec. 1791.

"Sergeant-Major Cobbett having most pressingly applied for his discharge, at Major Lord Edward Fitzgerald's request, General Frederick has ordered Major Lord Edward Fitzgerald to return the Sergeant-Major thanks for his behaviour and conduct during the time of his being in the regiment, and Major Lord Edward adds his most hearty thanks to those of the General."

III.

At this period Cobbett married. Nobody has left us wiser sentiments or pithier sentences on the choice of a wife. His own, the daughter of a sergeant of

artillery, stationed like himself at New Brunswick, had
been selected at once. He had met her two or three
times, and found her pretty; beauty, indeed, he considered indispensable, but beauty alone would never
have suited him. Industry, activity, energy, the qualities which he possessed, were those which he most admired, and the partner of his life was fixed upon when
he found her, one morning before it was distinctly
light, "scrubbing out a washing-tub before her father's
door." "That's the girl for me," he said, and he kept
to this resolution with a fortitude which the object of
his attachment deserved and imitated.

The courtship was continued, and the assurance of
reciprocated affection given; but before the union of
hands could sanctify that of hearts, the artillery were
ordered home for England. Cobbett, whose regiment
was then at some distance from the spot where his be-
trothed was still residing, could not have even the satisfaction of a personal farewell, but he sent her 150
guineas, the whole amount of his savings, and begged
her to use this sum — as he feared her residence with
her father at Woolwich might expose her to bad company — in making herself comfortable in a small lodging with respectable people until his arrival. It was
not until four years afterwards that he himself was
able to quit America, and he then found the damsel he
had so judiciously chosen not with her father, it is true,
nor yet lodging in idleness, but as servant-of-all-work
for five pounds a year, and at their first interview she
put into his hands the 150 guineas which had been
confided to her — untouched. Such a woman had no
ordinary force of mind; and it has been frequently asserted that he who, once beyond his own threshold,

was ready to contend with every government in the world, was, when at home, under what has been appropriately called the government of the petticoat.

Cobbett's marriage took place on the 3rd of February, 1792; that is, about ten weeks after his discharge; but having in March brought a very grave charge against some of the officers of his regiment, which, when a court-martial was summoned, he did not appear to support, he was forced to quit England for France, where he remained till September, 1792, when he determined on trying his fortune in the United States.

IV.

On his arrival he settled in Philadelphia, and was soon joined by Mrs. Cobbett, who had not accompanied him out. His livelihood was at first procured by giving English lessons to French emigrants; and it is a fact not without interest that a celebrated person who figures amongst these sketches — M. de Talleyrand — wished to be one of his pupils. He refused he says to go to the ci-devant bishop's house, but adds in his usual style, that the lame fiend hopped over this difficulty at once by offering to come to his (Cobbett's) house—an offer that was not accepted. About this time Doctor Priestley came to America; the enthusiasm with which the Doctor was received roused the resentment of the British soldier, who morover panted for a battle. He published then — though with some difficulty, booksellers objecting to the unpopularity of the subject, an objection at which the author was most indignant — a pamphlet called "Observations on Priestley's Emigration." This pamphlet, on account both of its ability and scurrility, made a sensation, and thus commenced the writer's fortunes, though it only added 1s. 7½d. to his riches. But he was abusing, he was abused: this was to be in his element, and he rose at once, so far as the power and peculiarity of his style were concerned, to a foremost place amongst political writers. This style had been formed at an early period of life, and perhaps unconsciously to himself.

"At eleven years of age," he says in an article in the *Evening Post*, calling upon the reformers to pay for returning him to Parliament, "my employment was clipping of box-edgings and weeding beds of flowers in the garden of the Bishop of Winchester at the castle of Farnham, my native town. I had always been fond of beautiful gardens, and a gardener who had just come from the King's gardens at Kew gave me such a description of them as made me instantly resolve to work in those gardens. The next morning" (this is the early adventure I have previously spoken of), "without saying a word to any one, off I set, with no clothes except those upon my back, and with thirteen halfpence in my pocket. I found that I must go to Richmond, and I accordingly went on from place to place inquiring my way thither. A long day (it was in June) brought me to Richmond in the afternoon. Two pennyworth of bread and cheese and a pennyworth of small beer which I had on the road, and one halfpenny that I had lost somehow or other, left threepence in my pocket. With this for my whole fortune, I was trudging through Richmond in my blue smock-frock, and my red garters tied under my knees, when, staring about me, my eye fell upon a little book in a book-

seller's window, on the outside of which was written
''The Tale of a Tub, price 3*d*.' The title was so odd
that my curiosity was excited. I had the threepence;
but then I could not have any supper. In I went and
got the little book, which I was so impatient to read,
that I got over into a field at the upper corner of Kew
Gardens, where there stood a haystack. On the shady
side of this I sat down to read. The book was so
different from anything that I had ever read before, it
was something so new to my mind, that, though I
could not understand some parts of it, it delighted me
beyond description, and produced what I have always
considered a sort of birth of intellect.

"I read on until it was dark without any thought
of supper or bed. When I could see no longer, I put
my little book in my pocket and tumbled down by the
side of the stack, where I slept till the birds in the
Kew Gardens awakened me in the morning, when off
I started to Kew, reading my little book. The singu-
larity of my dress, the simplicity of my manner, my
lively and confident air, and doubtless his own compassion besides, induced the gardener, who was a
Scotchman, I remember, to give me victuals, find me
lodging, and set me to work; and it was during the
period that I was at Kew that George IV. and two of
his brothers laughed at the oddness of my dress while
I was sweeping the grass-plot round the foot of the
Pagoda. The gardener, seeing me fond of books, lent
me some gardening books to read; but these I could
not relish after my 'Tale of a Tub,' which I carried
about with me wherever I went, and when I — at
about twenty years old — lost it in a box that fell
overboard in the Bay of Fundy, in North America, the

loss gave me greater pain than I have since felt at losing thousands of pounds."

V.

Many had cause to remember this evening passed under a haystack at Kew. The genius of Swift engrafted itself naturally on an intellect so clear and a disposition so inclined to satire as that of the gardener's boy.

Cobbett's earliest writings are more especially tinged with the colouring of his master. Take for instance the following fable, which will at all times find a ready application:

"In a pot-shop, well stocked with wares of all sorts, a discontented, ill-formed pitcher unluckily bore the sway. One day, after the mortifying neglect of several customers, 'Gentlemen,' said he, addressing himself to his brown brethren in general — 'gentlemen, with your permission, we are a set of tame fools, without ambition, without courage, condemned to the vilest uses; we suffer all without murmuring; let us dare to declare ourselves, and we shall soon see the difference. That superb ewer, which, like us, is but earth — these gilden jars, vases, china, and, in short, all those elegant nonsenses whose colour and beauty have neither weight nor solidity — must yield to our strength and give place to our superior merit.' This civic harangue was received with applause, and the pitcher, chosen president, became the organ of the assembly. Some, however, more moderate than the rest, attempted to calm the minds of the multitude; but all the vulgar utensils, which shall be nameless, were become intractable. Eager to vie with the bowls and the cups, they were impatient, almost to madness, to quit their obscure abodes to shine upon the table, kiss the lip, and ornament the cupboard.

"In vain did a wise water-jug — some say it was a platter — make them a long and serious discourse upon the utility of their vocation. 'Those,' said he, 'who are destined to great employments are rarely the most happy. We are all of the same clay, 'tis true, but He who made us formed us for different functions; one is for ornament, another for use. The posts the least important are often the most necessary. Our employments are extremely different, and so are our talents.'

"This had a most wonderful effect; the most stupid began to open their ears; perhaps it would have succeeded, if a grease-pot had not cried out in a decisive tone: 'You reason like an ass — to the devil with you and your silly lessons.' Now the scale was turned again; all the horde of pans, and pitchers, applauded the superior eloquence and reasoning of the grease-pot. In short, they determined on an enterprise; but a dispute arose — who should be the chief? Every one would command, but no one obey. It was then you might have heard a clatter; all put themselves in motion at once, and so wisely and with so much vigour were their operations conducted, that the whole was soon changed — not into china, but into rubbish."

VI.

The tendency of this tale is manifest. It was addressed to the democratic spirit mainly because such

was the ruling spirit of the country in which the author
had come to reside — a democratic spirit which has
since developed itself more fully, but which then,
though predominant, had a powerful and respectable
party to contend against.

The constitution of the· United States had indeed
perfectly satisfied none of its framers. Franklin had
declared that he consented to it, not as the best, but
as the best that he could then hope for. Washington
expressed the same opinion. It necessarily gave birth
to two parties, which for a time were held together by
the position, the abilities, and the reputation of the
first president of the new Republic. They existed,
however, in his government itself, where Jefferson represented the Democratic faction, and Hamilton the
Federal or Conservative one. To the latter the president — though holding the balance with apparent im-
partiality — belonged; for he was an English gentleman, of a firm and moderate character, and, moreover,
wished that the government of which he was the head
should be possessed of an adequate force. The great
movement, however, in France — which he was almost
the only person to judge from the first with calm dis-
cernment — overbore his views and complicated his
situation. Determined that the United States should
take only a neutral position in the European contest,
he was assailed on all sides — as a tyrant, because he
wished for order — as a partisan of Great Britain, because he wished for peace. To those among the native
Americans, who dreamt impossible theories, or desired
inextricable confusion, were joined all the foreign in-
triguers, who, banished from their own countries, had
no hopes of returning there but as enemies and in-

vaders. "I am called everything," said Washington, "even a Nero."* His continuance in the presidency, to which he was incited by some persons to pretend for a third time, had indeed become incompatible with his character and honour.

The respect which he had so worthily merited and so long inspired was on the wane. The cabinet with which he had commenced his government was broken up; his taxes, in some provinces, were refused; a treaty he had concluded with England was pretty generally condemned; and as he retired to Mount Vernon, the democratic party saw that approaching triumph which the election of their leader to the presidency was soon about to achieve. The cry against Great Britain was fiercer; the shout for Jefferson was louder than it had ever been before.

VII.

At this time Cobbett, then better known as Peter Porcupine, a name which on becoming an author he had assumed, and which had at least the merit of representing his character appropriately, having quarrelled with a legion of booksellers, determined to set up in the bookselling line for himself; and, in the spring of 1796, he took a house in Second Street for that purpose.

Though he was not so universally obnoxious then as he subsequently became, his enemies were already many and violent—his friends warm, but few. These last feared for him in the course he was entering upon; they advised him, therefore, to be prudent — to do

* Letter to Mr. Taylor. "Writings," vol. XII. s. 212.

nothing, at all events on commencing business, that might attract public indignation; and, above all, not to put up any aristocratic portraits in his windows.

Cobbett's plan was decided. His shop opened on a Monday, and he spent all the previous Sunday in so preparing it that, when he. took down his shutters on the morning following, the people of Philadelphia were actually aghast at the collection of prints, arrayed in their defiance, including the effigies of George III., which had never been shown at any window since the rebellion. From that moment the newspapers were filled, and the shops placarded, with "A Blue Pill for Peter Porcupine," "A Pill for Peter Porcupine," "A Roaster for Peter Porcupine," "A Picture of Peter Porcupine." Peter Porcupine had become a person of first-rate consideration and importance.

"Dear father," says the writer who had assumed this name, in one of his letters home, "when you used to set me off to work in the morning, dressed in my blue smock-frock and woollen spatterdashes, with a bag of bread and cheese and a bottle of small beer over my shoulder, on the little crook that my godfather gave me, little did you imagine that I should one day become so great a man."

VIII.

Paine's arrival in America soon furnished fresh matter for invective. Paine, like Priestley, was a Republican; and was, like Priestley, hailed with popular enthusiasm by the Republicans. Cobbett attacked this new idol, therefore, as he had done the preceding one, and even with still greater virulence. This carried him

to the highest pitch of unpopularity which it was possible to attain in the United States, and it was now
certain that no opportunity would be lost of calming his
violence or breaking his pen. In August, 1797, accordingly, he was indicted for a libel against the Spanish minister and his court;. but the bill was ignored
by a majority of one; and, indeed, it would have been
difficult for an American jury to have punished an
Englishman for declaring the Spanish king at that time
"the tool of France." A question was now raised as
to whether the obnoxious writer should not be turned
out of the United States, under the Alien Act.

This having been objected to by the Attorney-General, a new course of prosecution was adopted. Nearly
all Cobbett's writings were brought together into one
mass, and he was charged with having published
throughout them libels against almost every liberal man
of note in America, France, and England. Under such
a charge he was obliged to find recognisances for his
good behaviour to the amount of 4000 dollars, and it was
hoped by a diligent search into his subsequent writings
to convict him of having forfeited these recognisances.

His enemies, indeed, might safely count on his get-
ting into further troubles; nor had they long to wait.
A Doctor Rush having at this time risen into great re-
pute by a system of purging and bleeding, with which
he had attempted to stop the yellow fever, Cobbett,
who could ill tolerate another's reputation, even in medicine, darted forth against this new candidate for public
favour with his usual vigour of abuse. "Can the Rush
grow up without mire, or the flag without water?" was
his exclamation, and down went his ruthless and never-
pausing flail on poor Dr. Rush's birth, parentage, man-

ner, character, medicine, and everything that was his by nature, chance, or education. This could not long continue; Cobbett was again indicted for a libel.

In tyrannies justice is administered unscrupulously in the case of a political enemy; in democracies also law must frequently be controlled by vulgar prejudice and popular passion. This was seen in the present case. The defendant pleaded, in the first place, that his trial should be removed from the Court of the State of Pennsylvania to that of the United States. It seems fair that as an alien he should have had his cause thus transferred. The claim, however, was refused by the chief justice, whom he had recklessly affronted; and the trial coming on when a jury was pretty certain to be hostile, Cobbett was assessed in damages to the amount of 5000 dollars; nor was much consolation to be derived from the fact that on the 14th of December, the day on which he was condemned for libelling Rush, General Washington died, in some degree the victim of that treatment which the libelled doctor had prescribed.

The costs of the suit he had lost, added to the fine which the adverse sentence had imposed, made altogether a considerable sum. Cobbett was nearly ruined, but he bore himself up with a stout heart; and for a moment turning round at bay faced his enemies, and determined yet to remain in the United States. But on second thoughts, without despairing of his fortunes, he resolved to seek them elsewhere; and set sail for England. This he did on the 1st of June, 1800; shaking the dust from his feet on what he then stigmatised as "that infamous land, where judges become felons, and felons judges."

COBBETT,

THE CONTENTIOUS MAN.

PART II.

Starts a paper, by a title *The Porcupine*, which he had made famous in America. — Begins as a Tory. — Soon verges towards opposition. — Abandons *Porcupine* and commences *Register*. — Prosecuted for libel. — Changes politics, and becomes radical. — Prosecuted again for libel. — Convicted and imprisoned. — Industry and activity though confined in Newgate. — Sentence expires. — Released. — Power as a writer increases. — Government determined to put him down. — Creditors pressing. — He returns to the United States.

PART II.

I.

THE space Cobbett filled in the public mind of his native land was at this time, 1800, considerable. Few, in fact, have within so brief a period achieved so remarkable a career, or gained under similar circumstances an equal reputation. The boy from the plough had become the soldier, and distinguished himself, so far as his birth and term of service at that time admitted, in the military profession; the uneducated soldier had become the writer; and, as the advocate of monarchical principles in a Republican state, had shown a power and a resolution which had raised him to the position of an antagonist to the whole people amongst whom he had been residing. There was Cobbett on one side of the arena, and all the democracy of democratic America on the other!

He now returned to the Old World and the land for which he had been fighting the battle. His fame had preceded him. George III. admired him as his champion; Lord North hailed him as the greatest political reasoner of his time (Burke being amongst his contemporaries); Mr. Windham — the elegant, refined, classical, manly, but whimsical Mr. Windham — was in raptures at his genius; and though the English

7*

people at this time were beginning to be a little less violent than they had been in their hatred of France and America, the English writer who despised Frenchmen and insulted Americans, was still a popular character in England.

Numerous plans of life were open to him; that which he chose was the one for which he was most fitting, and into which he could most easily and naturally adopt himself. He again became editor of a public paper, designated by the name he had rendered famous, and called *The Porcupine.*

The principles on which this paper was to be conducted were announced with spirit and vigour. "The subjects of a British king," said Cobbett, "like the sons of every provident and tender father, never know his value till they feel the want of his protection. In the days of youth and ignorance I was led to believe that comfort, freedom, and virtue were exclusively the lot of Republicans. A very short trial convinced me of my error, admonished me to repent of my· folly, and urged me to compensate for the injustice of the opinion which I had conceived. During an eight years' absence from my country, I was not an unconcerned spectator of her perils, nor did I listen in silence to the slander of her enemies.

"Though divided from England by the ocean, though her gay fields were hidden probably for ever from my view, still her happiness and her glory were the objects of my constant solicitude. I rejoiced at her victories, I mourned at her defeats; her friends were my friends, her foes were my foes. Once more returned, once more under the safeguard of that sovereign who watched over me in my infancy, and the want of whose protecting arm I have so long had reason to lament, I feel an irresistible desire to communicate to my countrymen the fruit of my experience; to show them the injurious and degrading consequences of discontent, disloyalty, and innovation; to convince them that they are the first as well as happiest of the human race, and above all to warn them against the arts of those ambitious and perfidious demagogues who could willingly reduce them to a level with the cheated slaves, in the bearing of whose yoke I had the mortification to share."

II.

The events even at this time were preparing,.which in their series of eddies whirled the writer we have been quoting into the midst of those very ambitious and perfidious demagogues whom he here denounces. Nor was this notable change, under all the circumstances which surrounded it, very astonishing. In the first place, the party in power, after greeting him on his arrival with a welcome which, perhaps, was more marked by curiosity than courtesy, did little to gratify their champion's vanity, or to advance his interests. With that indifference usually shown by official men in our country to genius, if it is unaccompanied by aristocratical or social influence, they allowed the great writer to seek his fortunes as he had sought them hitherto, pen in hand, without aid or patronage.

In the second place, the part which Mr. Pitt took on the side of Catholic emancipation was contrary to all Cobbett's antecedent prejudices: and then Mr. Pitt had treated Cobbett with coolness one day when they met at Mr. Windham's. Thus a private grievance was added to a public one.

The peace with France — a peace for which he would not illuminate, having his windows smashed by the mob in consequence — disgusted him yet more with Mr. Addington, whose moderate character he heartily despised; and not the less so for that temporising statesman's inclination rather to catch wavering Whigs than to satisfy discontented Tories. These reasons partly suggested his giving up the daily journal he had started (called, as I have said, *The Porcupine*), and commencing the *Weekly Political Register*, which he conducted with singular ability against every party in the country. I say against every party in the country; for, though he was still, no doubt, a stout advocate of kingly government, he did not sufficiently admit, for the purposes of his personal safety, that the king's government was the king's ministers. Thus, no doubt to his great surprise, he found that he, George III.'s most devoted servant, was summoned one morning to answer before the law for maliciously intending to move and incite the liege subjects of his Majesty to hatred and contempt of his royal authority.

· The libel made to bear this forced interpretation was taken from letters in November and December, 1803, signed "Juverna," that appeared in the *Register*, and were not flattering to the government of Ireland.

III.

If we turn to the state of that country at this time, we shall find that the resignation of Mr. Pitt, and the hopeless situation of the Catholics, had naturally created much discontent. Mr. Addington, it is true, was anything but a severe minister; he did nothing to rouse the passions of the Irish, but he did nothing to win the heart, excite the imagination, or gain the affection of that sensitive people. The person he had nominated to the post of Lord Lieutenant was a fair type of his own ministry, that person being a sensible good-natured man, with nothing brilliant or striking in his manner or abilities, but carrying into his high office the honest intention to make the course he was enjoined to pursue as little obnoxious as possible to those whom he could not expect to please. In this manner his government, though mild and inoffensive, neither captivated the wavering nor overawed the disaffected; and under it was hatched, by a young and visionary enthusiast (Mr. Emmett), a conspiracy, which, though contemptible as the means of overturning the established authority, was accompanied at its explosion by the murder of the Lord Chief Justice, and the exposure of Dublin to pillage and flames. The enemies of ministers naturally seized on so fair an occasion for assailing them, and Cobbett, who held a want of energy to be at all times worse than the want of all other qualities, put his paper at their disposal.

In the present instance, the writer of "Juverna's" letters, calling to his aid the old story of the wooden horse which carried the Greeks within the walls of Troy, and exclaiming, "Equo ne credite Teucri!" compared the Irish administration, so simple and innocuous in its outward appearance, but containing within its bosom, as he said, all the elements of mischief, to that famous and fatal prodigy of wood; and after complimenting the Lord Lieutenant on having a head made

of the same harmless material as the wooden horse itself, thus flatteringly proceeded: "But who is this Lord
Hardwicke? I have discovered him to be in rank an
earl, in manners a gentleman, in morals a good father
and a kind husband, and that, moreover, he has a good
library in St. James's Square. Here I should have
been for ever stopped, if I had not by accident met
with one Mr. Lindsay, a Scotch parson, since become
(and I am sure it must be by Divine Providence, for
it would be impossible to account for it by secondary
causes) Bishop of Killaloe. From this Mr. Lindsay I
further learned that my Lord Hardwicke was celebrated
for understanding the mode and method of fattening
sheep as well as any man in Cambridgeshire."

The general character of the attack on Lord Hardwicke may be judged of by the above quotation, and
was certainly not of a very malignant nature. It sufficed, however, to procure a hostile verdict; and the
Editor of the *Political Register* was declared "Guilty
of having attempted to subvert the King's authority."

This, however, was not all. Mr. Plunkett, then
Solicitor General for Ireland, had pleaded against Mr.
Emmett, whose father he had known, with more bitterness than perhaps was necessary, since the culprit
brought forward no evidence in his favour, and did not
even attempt a defence. Mr. Plunkett, moreover, had
himself but a short time previously expressed rather
violent opinions, and, when speaking of the Union,
had gone so far as to say that, if it passed into a law,
no Irishman would be bound to obey it. In short, the
position in which he stood was one which required
great delicacy and forbearance, and delicacy and for-

bearance he had not shown. "Juverna" thus speaks of him:

"If any one man could be found of whom a young but unhappy victim of the justly offended laws of his country had, in the moment of his conviction and sentence, uttered the following apostrophe: 'That viper, whom my father nourished, he it is whose principles and doctrines now drag me to my grave; and he it is who is now brought forward as my prosecutor, and who, by an unheard-of exercise of the royal prerogative, has wantonly lashed with a speech to evidence the dying son of his former friend, when that dying son had produced no evidence, had made no defence, but, on the contrary, acknowledged the charge and submitted to his fate' — Lord Kenyon would have turned with horror from such a scene, in which, if guilt were in one part punished, justice in the whole drama was confounded, humanity outraged, and loyalty insulted."

These observations, made in a far more rancorous spirit than those relating to Lord Hardwicke, could not fail to be bitterly felt by the Solicitor General, who was probably obliged, in deference to Irish opinion, to prosecute the editor of the paper they appeared in.

He did so, and obtained 500*l.* damages.

Luckily for Cobbett, however, he escaped punishment in both suits; for the real author of these attacks, Mr. Johnson, subsequently Judge Johnson, having been discovered, or having discovered himself, Cobbett was left without further molestation. But an impression had been created in his mind. He had fought the battle of loyalty in America against a host of enemies to the loss of his property, and even at the hazard of his life. Shouts of triumph had hailed him from the

British shores. The virulence of his invectives, the
coarseness of his epithets, the exaggeration of his
opinions, were all forgotten and forgiven when he
wrote the English language out of England. He came
to his native country; he advocated the same doctrines,
and wrote in the same style; his heart was still as
devoted to his king, and his wishes as warm for the
welfare of his country; but, because it was stated in
his journal that Lord Hardwicke was an excellent
sheep-feeder, and Mr. Plunkett a viper — (a disagreeable appellation, certainly, but one soft and gentle in
comparison with many which he had bestowed, fifty
times over, on the most distinguished writers, members
of Congress, judges and lawyers in the United States
— without the regard and esteem of his British patrons
being one jot abated) — he had been stigmatised as a
traitor and condemned to pay five hundred pounds as
a libeller.

He did not recognise, in these proceedings, the
beauties of the British Constitution, nor the impartial
justice which, he had always maintained when in
America, was to be found in loyal old England. He
did not see why his respect for his sovereign prevented
him from saying or letting it be said that a Lord
Lieutenant of Ireland was a very ordinary man, nor
that a Solicitor General of Ireland had made a very
cruel and ungenerous speech, when the facts thus stated
were perfectly true. The Tory leaders had done nothing to gain him as a partisan, they had done much
that jarred with his general notions on politics, and
finally they treated him as a political foe. The insult,
for such he deemed it, was received with a grim smile
of defiance, and grievous was the loss which Conser-

vative opinions sustained when those who represented them drove the most powerful controversialist of his day into the opposite ranks.

· Nor can the value of his support be estimated merely by the injury inflicted by his hostility. When Cobbett departed from his consistency, he forfeited a great portion of his influence. With his marvellous skill in exciting the popular passions in favour of the ideas he espoused; with his nicknames, with his simple, sterling, and at all times powerful eloquence, it is difficult to limit the effect he might have produced amongst the classes to which he belonged, and which with an improved education were beginning to acquire greater power, if acquainted with their habits and warmed by their passions, he had devoted his self-taught intellect to the defence of ancient institutions and the depreciation of modern ideas.

But official gentlemen then were even more official than they are now; and fancying that every man in office was a great man, every one out of it a small one, their especial contempt was reserved for a public writer. If, however, such persons, the scarecrows of genius, were indifferent to Cobbett's defection, they whose standard he joined hailed with enthusiasm his conversion.

These were not the Whigs. Cobbett's was one of those natures which never did things by halves. Sir Francis Burdett, Mr. Hunt, Major Cartwright, and a set of men who propounded theories of parliamentary reform, — which no one, who was at that time considered a practical statesman, deemed capable of realization, — were his new associates and admirers.

Nor was his change a mere change in political

opinion. It was, unfortunately, a change in political morality. The farmer's son had not been educated at a learned university — having his youthful mind nourished and strengthened by great examples of patriotism and consistency, drawn from Greece and Rome: — he was educating himself by modern examples from the world in which he was living, and there he found statesmen slow to reward the advocacy of their public opinions, but quick to avenge any attack on their personal vanity, or individual interests. It struck him then that their principles were like the signs which inn-keepers stick over their tap-rooms, intended to catch the traveller's attention, and induce him to buy their liquors; but having no more real signification than "St. George and the Dragon," or the "Blue Boar," or the "Flying Serpent;" hence concluding that one sign might be pulled down and the other put up, to suit the taste of the customers, or the speculation of the landlord.

And now begins a perfectly new period in his life. Up to this date he had always been one and the same individual. Every corner of his being had been apparently filled with the same loyal hatred to Frenchmen and Democrats. He had loved, in every inch of him, the king and the church, and the wooden walls of Old England. "Who will say," he exclaims in America, "that an Englishman ought not to despise all the nations in the world? For my part I do, and that most heartily." What he here says of every one of a different nation from his own, he had said, and said constantly, of every one of a different political creed from his own, and his own political creed had as yet never varied. But consistency and Cobbett here

separated. Not only was his new self a complete and
constant contradiction with his old self — this was to
be expected: but whereas his old self was one solid
block, his new self was a piece of tesselated workmanship, in which were patched together all sorts of materials of all sorts of colours. I do not mean to say that,
having taken to the liberal side in politics, he ever
turned round again and became violent on the opposite
side. But his liberalism had no code. He recognised
no fixed friends — no definite opinions. The notions
he advocated were such as he selected for the particular
day of the week on which he was writing, and which
he considered himself free on the following day to dispute with those who adopted them. As to his alliances,
they were no more closely woven into his existence
than his doctrines; and he stood forth distinguished for
being dissatisfied with everything, and quarrelling with
every one.

IV.

The first tilt which he made from the new side of
the ring where he had now taken his stand was against
Mr. Pitt — whom it was not difficult towards the close
of his life to condemn, for the worst fault which a
minister can commit—being unfortunate. Cobbett's next
assault (on the demand of the Whigs for an increase of
allowance to the king's younger sons) was against Royalty
itself, its pensions, governorships, and rangerships, which
he called "its cheeseparings and candle-ends!" Some
republicans on the other side of the Atlantic must have
rubbed their spectacles when they read these effusions;
but the editor of the *Register* was indifferent to pro-

voking censure, and satisfied with exciting astonishment. Besides, we may fairly admit, that, when the
King demanded that his private property in the funds
should be free from taxation (showing he had such
property), and at the same time called upon the country
to increase the allowances of his children, he did much
to try the loyalty of the nation, and gave Cobbett occasion to observe that a rich man did not ask the
parish to provide for his offspring. "I am," said he,
"against these things, not because I am a Republican,
but because I am for monarchical government, and
consequently adverse to all that gives Republicans a
fair occasion for sneering at it."

In the meantime his periodical labours did not prevent his undertaking works of a more solid description;
and in 1806 he announced the "Parliamentary Register," which was to contain all the recorded proceedings
of Parliament from the earliest times; and was in the
highest degree useful, since the reader had previously
to wade through a hundred volumes of journals in
order to know anything of the history of the two Houses
of Parliament. These more serious labours did not,
however, interfere with his weekly paper, which had a
large circulation, and, though without any party influence (for Cobbett attacked all parties), gave him a
great deal of personal power and importance. "It
came up," says the author, proudly, "like a grain of
mustard-seed, and like a grain of mustard-seed it has
spread over the whole civilised world." Meanwhile,
this peasant-born politician was uniting rural pursuits
with literary labours, and becoming, in the occupation
of a farm at Botley, a prominent agriculturalist and a
sort of intellectual authority in his neighbourhood.

From this life, which no one has described with a pen more pregnant with the charm and freshness of green fields and woods, he was wrested by another prosecution for libel.

V.

The following paragraph had appeared in the *Courier* paper:

"London, Saturday, July 1st, 1809.

"Motto. — The mutiny amongst the Local Militia, which broke out at Ely, was *fortunately* suppressed on Wednesday by the arrival of four squadrons of the German Legion Cavalry from Bury, under the command of General Auckland.

"Five of the ringleaders were tried by a court-martial, and sentenced to receive *five hundred lashes each*, part of which punishment they received on Wednesday, and a part was remitted. A stoppage for their knapsacks was the ground of complaint which excited this mutinous spirit, and occasioned the men to surround their officers and demand what they deemed their arrears. The first division of the German Legion halted yesterday at Newmarket on their return to Bury."

On this paragraph Cobbett made the subjoining observations:

" 'Summary of politics. Local Militia and German Legion.' See the motto, English reader, see the motto, and then do, pray, recollect all that has been said about the way in which Bonaparte raises his soldiers. Well done, Lord Castlereagh! This is just what it was thought that your plan would produce. Well said,

Mr. Huskisson   It was really not without reason you dwelt with so much earnestness upon the great utility of the foreign troops, whom Mr. Wardle appeared to think of no utility at all.   Poor gentleman! he little thought how great a genius might find employment for such troops; he little imagined they might be made the means of compelling Englishmen to submit to that sort of discipline which is so conducive to producing in them a disposition to defend the country at the risk of their lives.   Let Mr. Wardle look at my motto, and then say whether the German soldiers are of no use. *Five hundred lashes each!*   Aye, that is right; flog them! flog them! flog them! they deserve it, and a great deal more!   They deserve a flogging at every meal time. Lash them daily!   Lash them daily!   What! shall the rascals dare to *mutiny*, and that, too, when the *German* Legion is so near at hand.   Lash them!   Lash them! Lash them! they deserve it.   Oh! yes, they deserve a double-tailed cat.   Base dogs, what mutiny for the sake of the price of a knapsack! Lash them! flog them! base rascals! mutiny for the price of a goat-skin, and then upon the appearance of the German soldiers they take a flogging as quietly as so many trunks of trees."

VI.

The attack on the Hanoverian troops, who had nothing to do with the question as to whether the militiamen were flogged justly or not, was doubtless most illiberal and unfair.   Those troops simply did their duty, as any other disciplined troops would have done, in seeing a superior's order executed.   It was not their fault if they were employed on this service; neither were they in our country or our army under ordinary circumstances. They had lost their own land for fighting our battles; they were in our army because they would not serve in the army of the enemy.

But we can hardly expect newspaper writers to be more logical and just than forensic advocates. A free press is not a good unmixed with evil; there are arguments against it, as there are arguments for it; but where it is admitted as an important part of a nation's institutions, this admission includes, as I conceive, the permission to state one side of a question in the most telling manner, the corrective being the juxtaposition of the other side of the question, stated with an equal intent to captivate, and perhaps to mislead.

Two years' imprisonment, and a fine of £1000 only wanted the gentle accompaniment of ear-cropping to have done honour to the Star Chamber; for, to a man who had a newspaper and a farm to carry on, imprisonment threatened to consummate the ruin which an exorbitant fine was well calculated to commence.

Cobbett was accused of yielding to the heaviness of the blow, and of offering the abandonment of his journal as the price of his forgiveness. I cannot agree with those who said that such an offer would have been an unparalleled act of baseness. In giving up his journal, Cobbett was not necessarily giving up his opinions. Every one who wages war unsuccessfully retains the right of capitulation. A writer is no more obliged to rot uselessly in a gaol for the sake of his cause, than a general is obliged to fight a battle without a chance of victory for the sake of his country.

A man, even if a hero, is not obliged to be a martyr. Cobbett's disgraceful act was not in making the proposal of which he was accused, but in denying most positively and repeatedly that he had ever made it; for it certainly seems pretty clear, amidst a good deal of contradictory evidence, that he did authorize Mr. Reeves, of the Alien Office, to promise that the *Register* should drop if he was not brought up for judgment; and if a Mr. Wright, who was a sort of factotum to Cobbett at the time, can be believed, the farewell was actually written, and only withdrawn when the negotiation was known to have failed. At all events, no indulgence being granted to the offender, he turned round and faced fortune with his usual hardihood. In no portion of his life, indeed, did he show greater courage — in none does the better side of his character come out in brighter relief than when, within the gloomy and stifling walls of Newgate, he carried on his farming, conducted his paper, educated his children, and waged war (his most natural and favourite pursuit) against his enemies with as gay a courage as could have been expected from him in sight of the yellow cornfields, and breathing the pure air, he loved so well.

"Now, then," he says, in describing this period of his life, "the book-learning was forced upon us. I had a farm in hand; it was necessary that I should be constantly informed of what was doing. I gave all the orders, whether as to purchases, sales, ploughing, sowing, breeding — in short, with regard to everything, and the things were in endless number and variety, and always full of interest. My eldest son and daughter could now write well and fast. One or the other of

these was always at Botley, and I had with me —
having hired the best part of the keeper's house —
one or two besides, either their brother or sister. We
had a hamper, with a lock and two keys, which came
up once a week or oftener, bringing me fruit and all
sorts of country fare. This hamper, which was always
at both ends of the line looked for with the most lively
interest, became our school. It brought me a journal
of labours, proceedings, and occurrences, written on
paper of shape and size uniform, and so contrived as
to margins as to admit of binding. The journal used,
when my eldest son was the writer, to be interspersed
with drawings of our dogs, colts, or anything that he
wanted me to have a correct idea of. The hamper
brought me plants, herbs, and the like, that I might
see the size of them; and almost every one sent his or
her most beautiful flowers, the earliest violets and primroses and cowslips and bluebells, the earliest twigs of
trees, and, in short, everything that they thought calculated to delight me. The moment the hamper arrived,
I — casting aside everything else — set to work to
answer every question, to give new directions, and to
add anything likely to give pleasure at Botley.

"Every hamper brought one letter, as they called
it, if not more, from every child, and to every letter
I wrote an answer, sealed up and sent to the party,
being sure that that was the way to produce other and
better letters; for though they could not read what I
wrote, and though their own consisted at first of mere
scratches, and afterwards, for awhile, of a few words
written down for them to imitate, I always thanked
them for their pretty letter, and never expressed any
wish to see them write better, but took care to write

8*

in a very neat and plain hand myself, and to do up my letter in a very neat manner.

"Thus, while the ferocious tigers thought I was doomed to incessant mortification, and to rage that must extinguish my mental powers, I found in my children, and in their spotless and courageous and affectionate mother, delights to which the callous hearts of those tigers were strangers. 'Heaven first taught letters for some wretch's aid.' How often did this line of Pope occur to me when I opened the little fuddling letters from Botley. This correspondence occupied a good part of my time. I had all the children with me, turn and turn about; and in order to give the boys exercise, and to give the two eldest an opportunity of beginning to learn French, I used for a part of the two years to send them for a few hours a day to an abbé, who lived in Castle Street, Holborn. All this was a great relaxation to my mind; and when I had to return to my literary labours, I returned fresh and cheerful, full of vigour, and full of hope of finally seeing my unjust and merciless foes at my feet, and that, too, without caring a straw on whom their fall might bring calamity, so that my own family were safe, because — say what any one might — the community, taken as a whole, had suffered this thing to be done unto us.

"The paying of the workpeople, the keeping of the accounts, the referring to books, the writing and reading of letters, this everlasting mixture of amusement with book-learning, made me, almost to my own surprise, find at the end of two years that I had a parcel of scholars growing up about me, and, long before the end of the time, I had dictated my *Register* to my two eldest children. Then there was copying out of books, which taught spelling correctly. The calculations about the farming affairs forced arithmetic upon us; the *use*, the *necessity* of the thing, led to the study.

"By and by we had to look into the laws, to know what to do about the highways, about the game, about the poor, and all rural and parochial affairs.

"I was, indeed, by the fangs of government defeated in my fondly-cherished project of making my sons farmers on their own land, and keeping them from all temptation to seek vicious and enervating enjoyments; but those fangs — merciless as they had been — had not been able to prevent me from laying in for their lives, a store of useful information, habits of industry, care, and sobriety, and a taste for innocent, healthful, and manly pleasures. The fiends had made me and them penniless, but had not been able to take from us our health, or our mental possessions, and these were ready for application as circumstances might ordain."

VII.

At length, however, Cobbett's punishment was over; and his talents still conferred on him sufficient consideration to have the event celebrated by a dinner, at which Sir Francis Burdett presided. This compliment paid, Cobbett returned to Botley and his old pursuits, literary and agricultural. The idea of publishing cheap newspapers, under the title of "Twopenny Trash," and which, not appearing as periodicals, escaped the

Stamp Tax, now added considerably to his power; and by extending the circulation of his writings to a new class, the mechanic and artisan, in urban populations, made that power dangerous at a period when great distress produced general discontent — a discontent of which the government rather tried to suppress the exhibition, than to remove the causes. Nor did Cobbett speak untruly when he said, that the suspension of the Habeas Corpus, and the passing of the celebrated "Six Acts," in the year 1817, were more directed against himself than against all the other writers of sedition put together. But notwithstanding the exultation which this position gave him for a moment, he soon saw that it was one which he should not be able to maintain, and that the importance he had temporarily acquired had no durable foundation. He had no heart, moreover, for another mid-summer's dream in Newgate. Nor was this all. Though he had not wanted friends or partisans, who had furnished him with pecuniary aid, his expenses had gone far beyond his means; and I may mention as one of the most extraordinary instances of this singular person's influence, that the debts he had at this time been allowed to contract amounted to no less than £34,000, a sum he could not hope to repay.

For the first time his ingenuity furnished him with no resource, or his usual audacity failed him; and with a secrecy, for which the state of his circumstances accounted, he made a sudden bolt (the 28th of March, 1817) for the United States, informing his countrymen that they were too lukewarm in their own behalf to justify the perils he incurred for their sakes; and observing to his creditors that, as they had not resisted the persecutions from which his losses had arisen, they must be prepared to share with his family the consequences of his ruin.

Sir Francis Burdett had been for many years, as we have seen, his friend and protector, and had but recently presided at the festival which commemorated his release from confinement; but Sir Francis Burdett was amongst those from whom Cobbett had borrowed pretty largely; and though the wealthy baronet could scarcely have expected this money to be repaid, yet, having advanced it to a political partisan, he was not altogether pleased at seeing his money and his partisan slip through his fingers at the same time; and made some remarks which, on reaching Cobbett's ears, aroused a vanity that never slept, and was only too ready to avenge itself by abuse equally ungrateful and unwise.

COBBETT,

THE CONTENTIOUS MAN.

PART III.

Settles on Long Island. — Professes at first great satisfaction. — Takes a farm. — Writes his Grammar. — Gets discontented. — His premises burnt. — He returns to England, and carries Paine's bones with him. — The bones do not succeed. — Tries twice to be returned to Parliament. — Is not elected. — Becomes a butcher at Kensington. — Fails there and is a bankrupt. — Works from 1820 to 1826. — Extracts. — New prosecution. — Acquitted. — Comes at last into Parliament for Oldham. — Character as a speaker. — Dies. — General summing up.

PART III.

I.

THE epoch of Cobbett's flight from England was decidedly the one most fatal to his character. So long as a man pays his bills, or sticks to his party, he has some one to speak in his favour; but a runaway from his party and his debts, whatever the circumstances that lead to his doing either, must give up the idea of leaving behind him any one disposed to say a word in his defence. Cobbett probably did give up this idea, and, having satisfied himself by declaring that the overthrow of the regular laws and constitution of England had rendered his person as a public writer insecure, and his talents unprofitable, in his native country, seemed disposed to a divorce from the old world, and to a reconciliation with the new. At all events, he viewed America with very different eyes from those with which he had formerly looked at it. The weather was the finest he had ever seen; the ground had no dirt; the air had no flies; the people were civil, not servile; there were none of the poor and wretched habitations which sicken the sight at the outskirts of cities and towns in England; the progress of wealth, ease, and enjoyment evinced by the regular increase of the size of the farmers' buildings, spoke in praise of the system of government under which it had taken place;

and, to crown all, four Yankee mowers weighed down eight English ones! During the greater part of the time that these encomiums were written, Cobbett was living at a farm he had taken on Hampstead Plains, Long Island, where he wrote his grammar, the only amusing grammar in the world, and which, being sent to his son in England, sold 10,000 copies in one month.

A year, however, after his arrival at Long Island, a fire broke out on his premises and destroyed them. The misfortune was not, perhaps, an untimely one.

Whatever Cobbett might have been able to do in the United States, as a farmer he did not seem to have a chance there of playing any part as a politician. He was not even taken up as a "lion," for his sudden preference for Republican institutions created no sensation amongst men who were now all heart and soul Republicans. He was not a hero; and he could not, consistently with his present doctrines, attempt to become a martyr. He had, to be sure, the satisfaction of saying bitter things about the tyranny established in his native land, but these produced no effect in America, where abuse of monarchical government was thought quite natural, and he did not see the effect they produced at home. Moreover, they did not after all produce much effect even there. His periodical writings were like wine meant to be drunk on the spot, and lost a great deal of their flavour when sent across the wide waters of the ocean. They were, indeed, essentially written for the day, and for the passions and purposes of the day. Arriving after the cause which had produced them had ceased to excite the public mind, their sound and fury were like the smoke and smell of an explosion without its noise or its powers of destruction. Cobbett saw this clearly, though to his own children he would never confess it.

II.

The condition of England, moreover, at this moment excited his attention, perhaps his hopes. A violent policy can never be a lasting one. The government was beginning to wear out the over-stretched authority that had been confided to it, and the community was beginning to feel that you should not make (to use the words of Mr. Burke) "the extreme remedies of the State its daily bread." On the other hand, the general distress, which had created the discontent that these extreme remedies had been employed to suppress, was in no wise diminished. The sovereign and the administration were unpopular, the people generally ignorant and undisciplined, neither the one nor the other understanding the causes of the prevalent disaffection, nor having any idea as to how it should be dealt with.

Such is the moment undoubtedly for rash or designing men to propagate wild theories; and such is also the moment when bold men, guided by better motives, will find, in a country where constitutional liberty cannot be entirely destroyed, the means of turning the oppressive measures of an unscrupulous minister against himself. With the one there was a chance of war against all government, with the other a chance of resistance against bad government. The revolutionist and the patriot were both stirring, whilst a vague idea prevailed amongst many, neither patriots nor revolutionists, that our society was about to be exposed to one of those great convulsions which overturn thrones and change the destiny of empires.

Cobbett was probably too shrewd to look on such a crisis as a certainty; but he was very probably sanguine enough to build schemes on it as a possibility. Besides, there were strife and contention in the great towns, and murmurings in the smaller hamlets; and, where there were strife and contention and murmurings, he could not fail to find a place and to produce an effect. This was sufficient to make him feel restlessly anxious to reappear on the stage he had so abruptly quitted. But he was essentially an actor, and disposed to study the dramatic in all his proceedings. To slink back unperceived to his old haunts, and recommence quietly his old habits, would neither suit his tastes, nor, as he thought, his interests. It was necessary that his return should be a sensation. Too vain and too quarrelsome to pay court to any one, he had through life made friends by making enemies. His plan now was to raise a howl against the returning exile as an atheist and a demagogue amongst one portion of society, not doubting that in such case he would be taken up as the champion of civil and religious liberty by another.

III.

The device he adopted for this object was disinterring, or saying he had disinterred, the bones of Thomas Paine, whom he had formerly assailed as "the greatest disgrace of mankind," and now declared to be "the great enlightener of the human race," and carrying these bones over to England as the relics of a patron saint, under whose auspices he was to carry on his future political career.

Now, Paine had been considered the enemy of kingly government and the Christian religion in his time, and had greatly occupied the attention of Cobbett, who had styled him "an infamous and atrocious miscreant," but he had never been a man of great weight or note in our country; many of the existing generation scarcely knew his name, and those who did felt but a very vague retrospective interest in his career. In vain Cobbett celebrated him as "an unflinching advocate for the curtailment of aristocratical power," and "the boldest champion of popular rights." In vain he gave it clearly to be understood that Paine did not believe a word of the Old Testament or the New; nobody, in spite of Cobbett's damning encomiums, would care about Paine, or consider a box of old bones as anything but a bad joke. So that after vainly offering locks of hair or any particle of the defunct and exhumed atheist and Republican at a low price, considering the value of the relics, he let the matter drop; and, rubbing his hands and chuckling with that peculiar sardonic smile which I well remember, began to treat the affair as the world did, and the inestimable fragments of the disinterred Quaker suddenly disappeared, and were never heard of more.

But though his stage trick had failed to give him importance, his sterling unmistakable talent and unflagging energy were sufficient to secure him from insignificance. Cobbett in England, carrying on his *Register*, charlatan as he might be, unreliable as he

had become, was still a personage and a power. He
supplied a sort of writing which every one read, and
which no one else wrote or could write. People had
no confidence in him as a politician, but, in spite of
themselves, they were under his charm as an author.
He was not, however, satisfied with this; he now pretended to play a higher part than he had hitherto attempted. In his own estimate of his abilities — and
perhaps he did not over-rate them — his eloquence as
an orator might, under cultivation and practice, become
equal to the talent which he never failed to display as
a pamphleteer.

A seat in the House of Commons had become then
the great object of his ambition, and with his usual
coolness, which might, perhaps, not unadvisedly be
termed impudence, he told his admirers that the first
thing they had to do, if they wanted reform, was to
subscribe £5000, and place the sum in his hands, to
be spent as he might think proper, and without giving
an account of it to any person. "One meeting," he
says, arguing this question — "one meeting sub-
scribing £5000 will be worth fifty meetings of 50,000
men."

On the dissolution of Parliament, at the demise of
George III., he pursues the subject. "To you" — he
is speaking to his partisans — "I do and must look for
support in my public efforts. As far as the press can
go, I want no assistance. Aided by my sons, I have
already made the ferocious cowards of the London press
sneak into silence. But there is a larger range — a
more advantageous ground to stand on, and that is
the House of Commons. A great effect on the public
mind I have already produced, but that is nothing to

what I should produce in only the next session of June in the House of Commons; yet there I cannot be without your assistance."

Coventry was the place fixed on as that which should have the honour of returning Cobbett to the House of Commons. Nor was the place badly chosen. In no town in England is the class of operatives more powerful, and by this class it was not unnatural to expect that he might be elected. The leading men, however, amongst the operatives, whilst admiring Cobbett, did not respect him. The Goodes and the Pooles — men whom I remember in my time — said in his day, "He is a man who will assuredly make good speeches, but nobody can tell what he will speak in favour of, or what he will speak about. That he will say and prove that Cobbett is a very clever fellow, we may be pretty sure; but with respect to every other subject there is no knowing what he will say or prove."

Nor did the story of Paine and his bones do Cobbett any service with the Coventry electors. Some considered his conduct in this affair impious, others ludicrous. "I say, Cobbett, where are the old Quaker's bones?" was a question which his most enthusiastic admirer heard put with an uncomfortable sensation.

He puffed himself in vain. His attempt to enter the great national council was this time a dead failure, and clearly indicated that though he might boast of enthusiastic partisans, he had not as yet obtained the esteem of an intelligent public. This, however, did not prevent his announcing not very long afterwards that bronze medals, which judges thought did justice to his physiognomy, might be had for a pound apiece — a price which he thought low, considering the article. The medals, however, in spite of their artistic value, and the intrinsic merit of the person they represented, were not considered a bargain; and some of Mr. Cobbett's most devoted friends observed that they had had already enough of his bronze. This was preparatory to his starting to contest Preston (1826). But he was no better treated there than at Coventry, being the last on the poll, though as usual perfectly satisfied with himself, notwithstanding a rather remarkable pamphlet got up by a rival candidate, Mr. Wood, which placed side by side his many inconsistencies. But though again unsuccessful in his attempt to astonish the world as a Member of Parliament, Mr. Huish in a work called "Memoirs of Cobbett" published in 1836, states that he now appeared in a character, equally remarkable, and that required no constituents; coming forth, "as a vendor of meat, and weekly assuring his readers, that there never was such mutton, such beef, or such veal, as that which might be seen in his windows; an assurance which continued uninterrupted," says this author, "until one inauspicious day, when it was replaced by the announcement of William Cobbett, butcher of Kensington, having become a bankrupt."* This story thus circumstantially told, (I have not, for the sake of brevity, copied the exact words but in all respects their meaning) though generally repeated, and apparently confirmed by other contemporaneous writers, is incorrect; and we are not to count amongst Cobbett's eccentricities that of cutting up carcases as well as characters.

* Page 393.

IV.

But whatever the pursuits Cobbett had indulged in since his return to England, none had interfered with those which his literary talents suggested to him.

"A Work on Cottage Economy," a Volume of Sermons, "The Woodlands," "Paper against Gold," "The Rural Rides," "The Protestant Reformation," were all published between the years 1820 and 1826. His "Rural Rides," indeed, are amongst his best compositions. No one ever described the country as he did. Everything he says about it is real. You see the dew on the grass, the fragrance comes fresh to you from the flowers; you fancy yourself jogging down the green lane, with the gipsy camp under the hedge, as the sun is rising; you learn the pursuits and pleasures of the country from a man who has been all his life practically engaged in the one, and keenly enjoying the other, and who sees everything he talks to you of with the eye of the poet and the farmer. I cannot resist the pleasure of quoting the following passage in the rural ride from Buttle to Kensington. "Woodland countries are interesting on many accounts; not so much on account of their masses of green leaves, as on account of the variety of sights, sounds and incidents that they offer. Even in winter the coppices are beautiful to the eye, while they comfort the mind with the idea of shelter and warmth. In spring, they change their hue from day to day during two whole months, which is about the time from the first appearance of the leaves of the birch to the full expansion

9*

of those of the ash; and even before the leaves come
at all to intercept the view. What in the vegetable
creation is so delightful to behold as the bed of a
coppice bespangled with primroses and blue bells.
The opening of the birch leaves is the signal for the
pheasant to begin to crow, for the blackbird to whistle
and the thrush to sing; and just when the oak-buds
begin to look reddish, and not a day before, the whole
tribe of finches burst forth in song from every bough,
while the lark, imitating them all, carries the joyous
sounds to the sky. These are among the means which
Providence has benignantly appointed to sweeten the
toils by which food and raiment are produced."

"The History of the Protestant Reformation" turned
out a more important production that was intended by
the author, whose chief aim seems to have been to
volunteer a contemptuous defiance to all the religious
and popular feelings in England. The work, however,
was taken up by the Catholics, translated into various
languages, and widely circulated throughout Europe.
The author's great satisfaction seems to consist in calling Queen Elizabeth, "Bloody Queen Bess," and Mary,
"Good Queen Mary," and he, doubtless, brought forward much that could be said against the one, and in
favour of the other, which Protestant writers had kept
back; but his two volumes still are not to be regarded
as a serious history, but rather as a party pamphlet,
and no more racy and eloquent party pamphlet was
ever written. I quote a passage of which those who
do not accept the argument may admire the composition:

"Nor must we by any means overlook the effects
of these institutions (monastic) on the mere face of the

country. That man must be low and mean of soul who is insensible to all feeling of pride in the noble edifices of his country. Love of country, that variety of feelings which altogether constitute what we properly call patriotism, consist in part of the admiration of, and veneration for, ancient and magnificent proofs of skill and opulence. The monastics built as well as wrote for posterity. The never-dying nature of their institutions set aside in all their undertakings every calculation as to time and age. Whether they built or planted, they set the generous example of providing for the pleasure, the honour, the wealth, and greatness of generations upon generations yet unborn. They executed everything in the very best manner: their gardens, fishponds, farms, were as near perfection as they could make them; in the whole of their economy they set an example tending to make the country beautiful, to make it an object of pride with the people, and to make the nation truly and permanently great.

"Go into any county and survey, even at this day, the ruins of its, perhaps, twenty abbeys and priories, and then ask yourself 'What have we in exchange for these?' Go to the site of some once opulent convent. Look at the cloister, now become in the hands of some rack-renter the receptacle for dung, fodder, and fagot-wood. See the hall, where for ages the widow, the orphan, the aged, and the stranger found a table ready spread. See a bit of its walls now helping to make a cattle-shed, the rest having been hauled away to build a workhouse. Recognize on the side of a barn, a part of the once magnificent chapel; and, if chained to the spot by your melancholy musings, you be admonished

of the approach of night by the voice of the screech-
owl issuing from those arches which once at the same
hour resounded with the vespers of the monk, and
which have for seven hundred years been assailed by
storms and tempests in vain; if thus admonished of the
necessity of seeking food, shelter, and a bed, lift up
your eyes and look at the white-washed and dry-rotten
shed on the hill called the 'Gentleman's House,' and
apprised of the 'board wages' and 'spring guns,' which
are the signs of his hospitality, turn your head, jog
away from the scene of former comfort and grandeur;
and with old-English welcoming in your mind, reach
the nearest inn, and there, in a room, half-warmed
and half-lighted, with a reception precisely proportioned
to the presumed length of your purse, sit down and
listen to an account of the hypocritical pretences, the
base motives, the tyrannical and bloody means, under
which, from which, and by which, the ruin you
have been witnessing was effected, and the hospitality you have lost was for ever banished from the
land."

V.

The popularity of Mr. Canning had now become
a grievous thorn in Cobbett's side. That of Mr. Robinson (afterwards Lord Goderich), had at one time sorely
galled him. But Mr. Robinson's reputation was on the
wane; the reputation of Mr. Canning, on the contrary,
rose higher every day; and when that statesman, after
being deserted by his colleagues, stood forward as
premier of a new government, being taken up by Sir
Francis Burdett, and many of the Whig leaders, Mr.

Cobbett set no bounds to his choler; and, in company with Mr. Hunt, made at a Westminster dinner (in 1827) a foolish and ill-timed display of his usual hostility to the popular feeling.

His character, in truth, was never so low as about this period, and in 1828, when he offered himself as a candidate for the place of common councilman (for Farringdon Without), he did not even find one person who would propose him for the office.

It is needless to add that he was now an utterly soured and disappointed man, and in this state the year 1830 found him. The close of that year was more full of melancholy presage for England than perhaps any which the oldest man then alive could remember. The success of the insurrection at Paris had shaken the political foundations of every state in Europe. Scarcely a courier arrived without the bulletin of a revolution. The minds of the intelligent classes were excited; they expected, and perhaps wished for, some great movement at home, analogous to those which a general enthusiasm was producing on the Continent. The minds of the lower classes were brutalized by the effects of a Poor Law which had taught them that idleness was more profitable than labour, prostitution than chastity, bad conduct, in short, than good. Consequently there was a widely-spread cry for parliamentary reform on the one hand, and a general rural insurrection on the other. Amidst this state of things the ministry of the Duke of Wellington retired, and Lord Grey's, composed of somewhat discordant materials, and with a doubtful parliamentary majority, took its place. Fires blazed throughout the country; rumours of plots and insurrections were rife, and the

Register appeared with an article remarkable for its power, and which indirectly excited to incendiarism and rebellion. The Attorney General prosecuted it. I had then just entered Parliament, and ventured to condemn the prosecution, not because the article in question was blameless, but because I thought that the period for newspaper prosecutions by government was gone by, and only excited sympathy for the offender. I was not wrong in that opinion; for the jury being unable to agree as to a verdict, Cobbett walked triumphantly out of court, and having gained some credit by his trial, was shortly afterwards returned to Parliament for Oldham.

The election, however, was less the effect of public esteem than of private admiration, since the veteran journalist owed his success mainly to the influence of a gentleman (Mr. Fielden) who had the borough of Oldham pretty nearly under his control. Still, it was a success, and not an inconsiderable one. The youthful plough-boy, the private of the 54th, after a variety of vicissitudes, had become a Member of the British Legislature. Nor for this had he bowed his knee to any minister, nor served any party, nor administered with ambitious interest to any popular feeling. His pen had been made to serve as a double-edged sword, which smote alike Whig and Tory, Pitt and Fox, Castlereagh and Tierney, Canning and Brougham, Wellington and Grey, even Hunt and Waithman. He had sneered at education, at philosophy, and at negro emancipation. He had assailed alike Catholicism and Protestantism; he had respected few feelings that Englishmen respect. Nevertheless, by force of character, by abilities to which he had allowed the full swing of their inclination, he had at last cut his way, unpatronized and poor, through conflicting opinions into the great council chamber of the British nation. He was there, as he had been through life, an isolated man. He owned no followers, and he was owned by none. His years surpassed those of any member who ever came into Parliament for the first time expecting to take an active part in it. He was stout and hale for his time of life, but over sixty, and fast advancing towards three score years and ten.

It was an interesting thing to most men who saw him enter the House to have palpably before them the real, living William Cobbett. The generation amongst which he yet moved had grown up in awe of his name, but few had ever seen the man who bore it.

The world had gone for years to the clubs, on Saturday evening, to find itself lectured by him, abused by him; it had the greatest admiration for his vigorous eloquence, the greatest dread of his scar-inflicting lash; it had been living with him, intimate with him, as it were, but it had not seen him.

I speak of the world's majority; for a few persons had met him at county and public meetings, at elections, and also in courts of justice. But to most members of Parliament the elderly, respectable-looking, red-faced gentleman, in a dust-coloured coat and drab breeches with gaiters, was a strange and almost historical curiosity. Tall and strongly built, but stooping, with sharp eyes, a round and ruddy countenance, smallish features, and a peculiarly cynical mouth, he realized pretty nearly the idea that might have been formed about him. The manner of his speaking might also have been anticipated. His style in writing was cynical and easy — such it was not unnatural to suppose it might also be in addressing an assembly; and this to a certain extent was the case. He was still colloquial, bitter, with a dry, caustic, and rather drawling delivery, and a rare manner of arguing with facts. To say that he spoke as well as he wrote, would be to place him where he was not — among the most effective orators of his time. He had not, as a speaker, the raciness of diction, nor the happiness of illustration, by which he excels as a writer. He wanted also some physical qualifications unnecessary to the author, but necessary to the orator, and which he might as a younger man have naturally possessed or easily acquired. In short, he could not be at that time the powerful personage that he might have been had he taken his seat on the benches where he was then sitting, when many surrounding him were unknown — even unborn. Still, I know no other instance of a man entering the House of Commons at his age, and becoming at once an effective debater in it. Looking carelessly round the assembly so new to him, with his usual self-confidence he spoke on the first occasion that presented itself, proposing an amendment to the Address; but this was not his happiest effort, and consequently created disappointment. He soon, however, obliterated the failure, and became rather a favourite with an audience which is only unforgiving when bored.

It was still seen, moreover, that nothing daunted him; the murmurs, the "Oh!" or more serious repre hension and censure, found him shaking his head with his hands in his pockets, as cool and as sarcastic as when he first stuck up the picture of King George in his shop-window at Philadelphia. He exhibited in Parliament, too, the same want of tact, prudence, and truth; the same egotism, the same combativeness, and the same reckless desire to struggle with received opinions, that had marked him previously through life, and shattered his career into glittering fragments, from which the world could never collect the image, nor the practical utility of a whole.

A foolish and out-of-the-way motion, praying his Majesty to strike Sir Robert Peel's name out of the Privy Council, for having proposed a return to cash payments in 1819, was his wildest effort and most signal defeat, the House receiving Sir Robert, when he stood up in his defence, with a loud burst of cheers, and voting in a majority of 298 to 4 in his favour.

Cobbett, however, was nothing abashed; for this motion was rather a piece of fun, in his own way, than anything serious; and in reality he was less angry with Sir Robert Peel, on account of his financial measures in 1819, than on account of his being the most able speaker in Parliament in 1833.

VI.

At the dissolution which took place in June, 1834, Cobbett was again elected member for Oldham. But his health was already much broken by the change of habits, the want of air, and the confinement which weighs on a parliamentary life. He did not, however, perceive this; it was not, indeed, his habit to perceive anything to his own disadvantage. He continued his attendance, therefore, and was in his usual place during the whole of the debate on the Marquis of Chandos's motion for a repeal of the Malt Tax, and would have spoken in favour of the repeal but for a sudden attack of the throat, to which it is said that he was subject. On the voting of Supplies, which followed almost immediately afterwards, he again, notwithstanding his indisposition, exerted himself, and on the 25th of May persisted in voting and speaking in support of a motion on Agricultural Distress. At last, he confessed he was knocked up, and retired to the country, where for some little time he seemed restored. But on the night of the 11th of June, 1835, he was seized with a violent illness, and on the two following days was considered in extreme danger by his medical attendant. He then again rallied, and on Monday, the 15th, talked (says his son in an account of his death, published on the 20th of June), in a collected and sprightly manner, upon politics and farming, "wishing for four days' rain for the Cobbett's corn and root crops," and on Wednesday could remain no longer shut up from the fields, but desired to be carried round the farm, and criticised the work which had been done in his absence. In the night, however, he grew more and more feeble, until it was evident (though he continued till within the last half hour to answer every question that was put to him) that his agitated career was drawing to a close. At ten minutes after one P.M. he shut his eyes as if to sleep, leant back, and was no more — an end singularly peaceful for one whose life had been so full of toil and turmoil.

The immediate cause of his death was water on

the chest. He was buried, according to his own desire, in a simple manner in the churchyard of Farnham, in the same mould as that in which his father and grand-father had been laid before him. His death struck people with surprise, for few could remember the com-mencement of his course, and there had seemed in it no middle and no decline; for though he went down to the grave an old man, he was young in the path he had lately started upon. He left a gap in the public mind which no one else could fill or attempt to fill up, for his loss was not merely that of a man, but of a habit — of a dose of strong drink which all of us had been taking for years, most of us during our lives, and which it was impossible for any one again to con-coct so strongly, so strangely, with so much spice and flavour, or with such a variety of ingredients. And there was this peculiarity in the general regret — it extended to all persons. Whatever a man's talents, whatever a man's opinions, he sought the *Register* on the day of its appearance with eagerness, and read it with amusement, partly, perhaps, if De la Rochefoucault is right, because, whatever his party, he was sure to see his friends abused. But partly also because he was certain to find, amidst a great many fictions and abundance of impudence, some felicitous nickname, some excellent piece of practical-looking argument, some capital expressions, and very often some marvel-lously-fine writing,* all the finer for being carelessly

---

* People are often at this day disputing as to whether a particular picture is by the master it is attributed to, or by one of his scholars. A peculiarity of genius in an artist is to create first-rate imitators in those who live in his society; and it is not unworthy of notice that one of the best pieces of writing in Cobbett's best style is "The Rat Hunt"

fine, and exhibiting whatever figure or sentiment it set forth, in the simplest as well as the most striking dress. Cobbett himself, indeed, said that *"his popularity was owing to his giving truth in clear language;"* and his language always did leave his meaning as visible as the most limpid stream leaves its bed. But as to its displaying truth, that is a different matter, and would be utterly impossible unless truth has, at least, as many heads as the Hydra of fable; in which case our author may claim the merit of having portrayed them all.

This, however, is to be remarked — he rarely abused that which was falling or fallen, but generally that which was rising or uppermost. He disinterred Paine when his memory was interred, and attacked him as an impostor amongst those who hailed him as a prophet. In the heat of the contest and cry against the Catholics — whom, when Mr. Pitt was for emancipating them, he was for grinding into the dust — he calls the Reformation a devastation, and pronounces the Protestant religion to have been established by gibbets, racks, and ripping-knives. When all London was yet rejoicing in Wellington hats and Wellington boots, he asserts "that the celebrated victory of Waterloo had caused to England more real shame, more real and substantial disgrace, more debt, more distress amongst the middle class, and more misery amongst the working class, more injuries of all kinds, than the kingdom could have ever experienced by a hundred defeats, whether by sea or by land." He had a sort

---

(*Political Register*, vol. XCI. p. 380), and was by the pen of Mr. J. M. Cobbett, Mr. Cobbett's son.

of itch for bespattering with mud everything that was popular, and gilding everything that was odious. Mary Tudor was with him "Merciful Queen Mary;" Elizabeth, as I have already observed, "Bloody Queen Bess;" our Navy, "the swaggering Navy;" Napoleon, "a French coxcomb;" Brougham, "a talking lawyer;" Canning, "a brazen defender of corruptions."

His praise or censure afforded a sort of test to be taken in an inverse sense of the world's opinion. He could not bear superiority of any kind, or reconcile himself to its presence. He declined to insert quack puffs in his journal, merely, I believe, because he could not bear to spread anybody's notoriety but his own; while he told his correspondents never to write under the name of subscriber — it sounded too much like *master*. As for absurdity, nothing was too absurd for him coolly and deliberately to assert: "The English government most anxiously wished for Napoleon's return to France." "There would have been no national debt and no paupers, if there had been no Reformation." "The population of England had not increased one single soul since he was born." Such are a few of the many paradoxes one could cite from his writings, and which are now before me.

Neither did his coarseness know any bounds. He called a newspaper a "cut and thrust weapon," to be used without mercy or delicacy, and never thought of anything but how he could strike the hardest. "'There's a fine Congress-man for you! If any d——d rascally rotten borough in the universe ever made such a choice as this (a Mr. Blair MacClenachan), you'll be bound to cut my throat, and suffer the *sans culottes* sovereigns of Philadelphia — the hob-snob snigger-snee-ers of

Germanstown — to kick me about in my blood till
my corpse is as ugly and disgusting as their living
carcases are." "Bark away, hell-hounds, till you are
suffocated in your own foam." "This hatter turned
painter (Samuel F. Bradford), whose heart is as black
and as foul as the liquid in which he dabbles."

"It is fair, also, to observe that this State (Pennsylvania) labours under disadvantages in one respect
that no other State does. Here is precisely that climate
which suits the vagabonds of Europe; here they bask
in summer, and lie curled up in winter, without fear
of scorching in one season, or freezing in the other.
Accordingly, hither they come in shoals, just roll themselves ashore, and begin to swear and poll away as if
they had been bred to the business from their infancy.
She has too unhappily acquired a reputation for the
mildness or rather the feebleness of her laws. There's
no gallows in Pennsylvania. These glad tidings have
rung through all the democratic club-rooms, all the
dark assemblies of traitors, all the dungeons and cells
of England, Scotland, and Ireland. Hence it is that
we are overwhelmed with the refuse, the sweeping, of
these kingdoms, the offal of the jail and the gibbet.
Hence it is that we see so many faces that never
looked comely but in the pillory, limbs that are awk-
ward out of chains, and necks that seem made to be
stretched."

It would be difficult to put together more pithy
sentences, or more picturesque abuse than is set forth
in the scurrilous extracts I have been citing; yet Cobbett's virulence could be conveyed in a more delicate
way whenever he thought proper:

"Since then, Citizen Barney is become a French

commodore of two frigates, and will rise probably to the rank of admiral, if contrary winds do not blow him in the way of an enemy."

His mode of commencing an attack also was often singularly effective from its humour and personality: "He was a sly-looking fellow, with a hard, slate-coloured countenance. He set out by blushing, and I may leave any one to guess at the efforts that must be made to get a blush through a skin like his." Again: "Having thus settled the point of controversy, give me leave to ask you, my sweet sleepy-eyed sir!"

The following picture is equal to anything ever sketched by Hogarth, and is called "A Summary of Proceedings of Congress," November, 1794:

"Never was a more ludicrous farce acted to a bursting audience. Madison is a little bow-legged man, at once stiff and slender. His countenance has that sour aspect, that conceited screw, which pride would willingly mould into an expression of disdain, if it did not find the features too skinny and too scanty for its purpose. His thin, sleek air, and the niceness of his garments, are indicative of that economical cleanliness which expostulates with the shoeboy and the washer-woman, which flies from the danger of a gutter, and which boasts of wearing a shirt for three days without rumpling the frill. In short, he has, take him alto-gether, precisely the prim, mean, prig-like look of a corporal mechanic, and were he ushered into your par-lour, you would wonder why he came without his mea-sure and his shears. Such (and with a soul which would disgrace any other tenement than that which contains it) is the mortal who stood upon his legs, con-

fidently predicting the overthrow of the British monarchy, and anticipating the pleasure of feeding its illustrious nobles with his oats."

Again, let us fancy the following sentences, imitating what the gentlemen of the United States call
"stump speaking" delivered with suitable tone and
gesture on the hustings: "The commercial connection
between this country (America) and Great Britain is as
necessary as that between the baker and the miller;
while the connection between America and France may
be compared to that between the baker and the milliner
or toyman. France may furnish us with looking-
glasses, but without the aid of Britain we shall be
ashamed to see ourselves in them; unless the *sans
culottes* can persuade us that threadbare beggary is —
a beauty. France may deck the heads of our wives
and daughters (by the bye, she shan't those of mine)
with ribbons, gauze, and powder; their ears with bobs,
their cheeks with paint, and their heels with gaudy
parti-coloured silk, as rotten as the hearts of the manu-
facturers; but Great Britain must keep warm their limbs
and cover their bodies. When the rain pours down,
and washes the rose from the cheek, when the bleak
north-wester blows through the gauze, then it is that
we know our friends."

Cobbett's talent for fastening his claws into any
thing or any one, by a word or an expression, and
holding them down for scorn or up to horror — a
talent which, throughout this sketch, I have frequently
noticed — was unrivalled. "Prosperity Robinson,"
"Æolus Canning," "The Bloody *Times*," "the pink-
nosed *Liverpool*," "the unbaptized, buttonless black-
guards" (in which way he designated the disciples of

Penn),* were expressions with which he attached ridicule where he could not fix reproach, and it is said that nothing was more teasing to Lord Erskine than being constantly addressed by his second title of "Baron Clackmannan."

VII.

I have alluded, at the commencement of this sketch, to the fact that if the life of Mackintosh was in contradiction to his instincts, and forced to adapt itself to his wishes or ideas, that of Cobbett was ruled by his instincts, to which all ideas and wishes were subordinate. His inclinations were for bustle and strife, and he passed his whole life in strife and bustle. This is why the sap and marrow of his genius show themselves in every line he sent to the press. But at the same time his career warns us how little talents of the highest order, even when accompanied by the most unflagging industry, will do for a man, if those talents and that industry are not disciplined by steadfast principles and

* Of this sect, by the way, he elsewhere speaks in these eulogistic terms:

"Here am I amongst the thick of the Quakers, whose houses and families pleased me so much formerly, and which pleasure is now revived. Here all is ease, plenty, and cheerfulness. These people are never giggling, and never in low spirits. Their minds, like their dress, are simple and strong. Their kindness is shown more in acts than in words. Let others say what they will, I have uniformly found those whom I have intimately known of this sect sincere and upright men; and I verily believe that all those charges of hypocrisy and craft that we hear against Quakers, arise from a feeling of envy; envy inspired by seeing them possessed of such abundance of all those things which are the fair fruits of care, industry, economy, sobriety, and order; and which are justly forbidden to the drunkard, the prodigal, and the lazy."

concentrated upon noble objects. It is not to be understood, indeed, when I say that a man should follow his
nature, that I mean he should do so without sense or
judgment; your natural character is your force, but it
is a force that you must regulate and keep applied to
the track on which the career it has chosen is to be
honourably run. I would not recommend a man with
military propensities to enter the church; I should say,
"Be a soldier, but do not be a military adventurer.
Enlist under a lawful banner, and fight for a good
cause."

Cobbett acknowledged no banner; and one cannot
say, considering the variety of doctrines he by turns
adopted and discarded, that he espoused any cause.
Nor did he consider himself bound by any tie of private or political friendship. As a beauty feels no gratitude for the homage which she deems due to her
charms, so Cobbett felt no gratitude for the homage
paid to his abilities. His idea of himself was that
which the barbarian entertains of his country. Cobbett
was Cobbett's universe; and as he treated mankind, so
mankind at last treated him. They admired him as a
myth, but they had no affection for him as a person.
His words were realities, his principles fictions.

It may indeed be contended that a predominant
idea ran winding through all the twistings and
twinings of his career, connecting his different inconsistencies together; and that this was "a hatred for
tyranny." "He always took his stand," say his de-
fenders, "with the minority:" and there is something
in this assertion. But there is far less fun and excitement in fighting a minority, with a large majority at

one's back, than in coming out, at the head of a small
and violent minority, to defy and attack a body of
greater power and of larger numbers. It was this fun
and excitement which, if I mistake not, were Cobbett's
main inducements to take the side he took in all the
contests he engaged in, whether against the minister of
the day, or against our favourite daughter of the eighth
Henry, who reigned some centuries before his time.
Still the tendency to combat against odds is always
superior to the tendency to cringe to them, and a weak
cause is not unfrequently made victorious by a bold
assertion.

It must be added also, in his praise, that he is
always a hearty Englishman. He may vary in his
opinions as to doctrines and as to men, but he is ever
for making England great, powerful, and prosperous—
her people healthy, brave, and free. He never falls
into the error of mistaking political economy for the
whole of political science. He does not say, "Be
wealthy, make money, and care about nothing else."
He advocates rural pursuits as invigorating to a population, although less profitable than manufacturing.
He desires to see Englishmen fit for war as well as for
peace. There is none of that puling primness about
him which marks the philosophers who would have a
great nation, like a good boy at a private school, fit
for nothing but obedience and books. To use a slang
phrase, there was "a go" about him which, despite all
his charlatanism, all his eccentricities, kept up the
national spirit, and exhibited in this one of the highest
merits of political writing. The immense number of
all his publications that sold immediately on their appearance, sufficiently proves the wonderful popularity

of his style; and it is but just to admit that many of his writings were as useful as popular.

A paper written in 1804, on the apprehended invasion, and entitled "Important Considerations for the People of this Kingdom," was placed (the author being unknown) in manuscript before Mr. Addington, who caused it to be printed and read from the pulpit in every parish throughout the kingdom. For many years this paper was attributed to other eminent men; and it was only when some one thought of attacking Cobbett as an enemy of his country, that he confessed the authorship of a pamphlet, to the patriotism of which every Englishman had paid homage.

Again, in 1816, the people of the northern and midland counties being in great distress, attributed their calamities to machinery, and great rioting and destruction of property was the consequence. Cobbett came forward to stop these vulgar delusions. But he knew the nature of the public mind. It was necessary, in order to divert it from one idea, to give it another. So, he ridiculed the idea of distress proceeding from machinery, and attributed it to misgovernment. His twopenny pamphlet, called "A Letter to Journeymen and Labourers," sold 30,000 copies in a week, and with such advantage that Lord Brougham, in 1831, asked permission to republish it. Much in his exaggerations and contradictions is likewise to be set down to drollery rather than to any serious design to deceive. I remember the late Lady Holland once asking me if I did not think she sometimes said ill-natured things; and on my acquiescing, she rejoined: "I don't mean to burn any one, but merely to poke the fire." Cobbett liked to poke the fire, to make a blaze; but in general

— I will not say always — he thought more of sport than of mischief.

At all events, this very spirit of change, of criticism, of combativeness, is the spirit of journalism; and Cobbett was not only this spirit embodied, but — and this renders his life so remarkable in our history — he represented journalism, and fought the fight of journalism against authority, when it was still a doubt which would gain the day.

Let us not, indeed, forget the blind and uncalculating intolerance with which the law struggled against opinion from 1809 to 1822. Writers during this period were transported, imprisoned, and fined, without limit or conscience; and just when government became more gentle to legitimate newspapers, it engaged in a new conflict with unstamped ones. No less than 500 vendors of these were imprisoned within six years. The contest was one of life and death. Amidst the general din of the battle, but high above all shouts more confused, was heard Cobbett's bold, bitter, scornful voice, cheering on the small but determined band, which defied tyranny without employing force. The failure of the last prosecution against the *Register* was the general failure of prosecutions against the Press, and may be said to have closed the contest in which government lost power every time that it made victims.

Such was Cobbett — such his career! I have only to add that, in his family relations, this contentious man was kind and gentle. An incomparable husband, an excellent father; and his sons — profiting by an excellent education, and inheriting, not, perhaps, the marvellous energies, but a great portion of the ability, of their father — carry on with credit and respectabi-

lity the name of a man, who, whatever his faults, must
be considered by every Englishman who loves our
literature, or studies our history, as one of the most remarkable illustrations of his very remarkable time.

———

CANNING,

THE BRILLIANT MAN.

PART I.

Proper time for writing a biography. — Mr. Canning born (1770). — Education at Eton and Oxford. — Early literary performances. — Brought into Parliament by Mr. Pitt. — Politics he espoused. — His commencement as a speaker. — Writes for the *Anti-Jacobin*. — Quits office with Mr. Pitt. — Opposes Mr. Addington. — Returns to office with Mr. Pitt. — Distinguishes himself in opposition to "All the Talents." — Becomes Minister of Foreign Affairs on their fall. — Foreign policy. — Quarrel with Lord Castlereagh, and duel.

CANNING,

THE BRILLIANT MAN.

—— ——

PART I.

I.

THERE is no period at which an eminent person is so little considered, so much forgotten and disregarded, as during the few years succeeding his decease. His name, no longer noised above that of others by the busy zeal of his partisans, or the still more clamorous energies of his opponents, drops away suddenly, as it were, from the mouths of men. To his contemporaries he has ceased to be of importance — the most paltry pretender to his place is of more; — while posterity does not exist for him, until the dead are distinctly separated from the living; until the times in which he lived, and the scenes in which he acted, have become as a distant prospect from which the eye can at once single out from amidst the mass of ordinary objects, those which were the memorials of their epoch, and are to become the beacons of after-generations.

The French, who are as fond of putting philosophy into action as we are coy of connecting theory with practice, marked out, at one moment, a kind of intermediate space between the past and the present, the tomb and the pantheon; but the interval of ten years, which they assigned for separating the one from the other, is hardly sufficient for the purpose.

We are, however, now arrived at the period that permits our considering the subject of this memoir as a character in history which it is well to describe without further procrastination. Every day, indeed, leaves us fewer of those who remember the clearly-'chiselled countenance which the slouched hat only slightly concealed, — the lip satirically curled, — the penetrating eye, peering along the Opposition benches, — of the old parliamentary leader in the House of Commons. It is but here and there that we find a survivor of the old day, to speak to us of the singularly mellifluous and sonorous voice, the classical language — now pointed into epigram, now elevated into poesy, now burning with passion, now rich with humour — which curbed into still attention a willing and long-broken audience.

The great changes of the last half century have, moreover, created such a new order of ideas and of society, that the years preceding 1830 appear as belonging to an antecedent century; and the fear now is — not that we are too near, but that we are gliding away too far from the events of that biography which I propose to sketch. And yet, he who undertakes the task of biographical delineation, should not be wholly without the scope of the influences which coloured the career he desires to sketch. The artist can hardly give the likeness of the face he never saw, nor the writer speak vividly of events which are merely known to him by tradition.

II.

It is with this feeling that I attempt to say something of a man, the most eminent of a period at which the government of England was passing, imperceptibly perhaps, but not slowly, from the hands of an exclusive but enlightened aristocracy, into those of a middle class, of which the mind, the energy, and the ambition had been gradually developed, under the mixed influences of a war, which had called forth the resources, and a peace which had tried the prosperity, of our country; — a middle class which was growing up with an improved and extended education, amidst stirring debates as to the height to which the voice of public opinion should be allowed to raise itself, and the latitude that should be given, in a singularly mixed constitution, to its more democratic parts.

Mr. Canning was born on the 11th of April, 1770, and belonged to an old and respectable family originally resident in Warwickshire. A branch of it, obtaining a grant of the manor of Garvagh, settled in Ireland in the reign of James I., and from this branch Mr. Canning descended; but the misfortunes of his parents placed him in a situation below that which might have been expected from his birth.

His father, the eldest of three sons — George, Paul, and Stratford — was disinherited for marrying a young lady (Miss Costello) without fortune; and having some taste for literature, but doing nothing at the bar, he died amidst the difficulties incidental to idle habits and elegant tastes.

Mrs. Canning, left without resources, attempted the

stage, but she had no great talents for the theatrical
profession, and never rose above the rank of a mid-
dling actress.   Her son thus fell under the care of his
uncle, Mr. Stratford Canning, a highly respectable
merchant, and an old Whig, much in the confidence of
the leaders of the Whig party and possessing considerable influence with them. A small inheritance of £200
or £300 a year sufficed for the expenses of a liberal
education, and after passing through the regular ordeal
of a private school, young Canning was sent to Eton,
and subsequently to Christ Church, Oxford.   At Eton
no boy ever left behind him so many brilliant recollections.   Gay and high-spirited as a companion, clever
and laborious as a student, he obtained a following
from his character, and a reputation from his various
successes.   This reputation was the greater from the
schoolboy's triumphs not being merely those of school.
Known and distinguished as "George Canning," he
was yet more known and distinguished as the correspondent of "Gregory Griffin;" — such being the
name adopted by the fictitious editor of the *Microcosm*,
a publication in the style of the *Spectator*, and carried
on solely by Eton lads. In this publication, the graver
prose of the young orator was incorrect and inferior to
that of one or two other juvenile contributors, but some
of his lighter productions were singularly graceful, and
it would be difficult to find anything of its kind superior
to a satirical commentary upon the epic merits of an
old ballad:

> " The queen of hearts
> She made some tarts
> *All on a summer's day*," &c. *

* See "Microcosm."

"I cannot leave this line," says the witty commentator, "without remarking, that one of the Scribleri, a descendant of the famous Martinus, has expressed his suspicions of the text being corrupted here, and proposes, instead of 'All on,' reading 'Alone,' alleging, in favour of this alteration, the effect of solitude in raising the passions. But Hiccius Doctius, a high Dutch commentator, one nevertheless well versed in British literature, in a note of his usual length and learning, has confuted the arguments of Scriblerus. In support of the present reading, he quotes a passage from a poem written about the same period with our author's, by the celebrated Johannes Pastor (most commonly known as Jack Shepherd), entitled, 'An Elegiac Epistle to the Turnkey of Newgate,' wherein the gentleman declares, that rather indeed in compliance with an old custom, than to gratify any particular wish of his own, he is going

> "'*All hanged* for to be
> Upon that fatal Tyburn tree.'

"Now, as nothing throws greater light on an author than the concurrence of a contemporary writer, I am inclined to be of Hiccius's opinion, and to consider the 'All' as an elegant expletive, or, as he more aptly phrases it, 'elegans expletivum.'"

The other articles to which the boyish talent of the lad, destined to be so famous, may lay claim, are designated in the will of the supposed editor, Mr. Griffin (contained in the concluding number of the *Microcosm*), which, amongst special bequests, assigns to "Mr. George Canning, now of the college of Eton, all my papers, essays, &c., signed B."

III.

It is needless to observe that an Eton education is more for the man of the world than for the man of books. It teaches little in the way of science or solid learning, but it excites emulation, encourages and gratifies a love of fame, and prepares the youth for the competitions of manhood. Whatever is dashing and showy gives pre-eminence in that spirited little world from which have issued so many English statesmen. It developed in Canning all his natural propensities. He was the show boy at Montem days with master and student.

"Look, papa, — there, there; — that good-looking fellow is Canning — such a clever chap, but a horrible Whig. By Jupiter, how he gives it to Pitt!"

Nor was this wonderful. The youthful politician spent his holidays with his uncle, who only saw Whigs; and then, what clever boy would not have been charmed by the wit and rhetoric of Sheridan, — by the burning eloquence of Fox?

The same dispositions that had shown themselves at Eton, carried to Oxford, produced the same distinctions. Sedulous at his studies, almost Republican in his principles, the pride of his college, the glory of his spouting club, the intimate associate of the first young men in birth, talents, and prospects, young Canning was thus early known as the brilliant and promising young man of his day, and thought likely to be one of the most distinguished of those intellectual gladiators whom the great parties employed in their struggles for power; struggles which seemed at the moment to disorder the administration of affairs, but which, carried on with eloquence and ability in the face of the nation, kept its attention alive to national interests, and could not fail to diffuse throughout it a lofty spirit, and a sort of political education.

IV.

From the University Canning went to Lincoln's Inn. It does not appear, however, that in taking to the study of the law he had any idea of becoming a Lord Chancellor. There was nothing of severity in his plan of life — he dined out with those who invited him, and his own little room was at times modestly lit up for gatherings together of old friends, who enjoyed new jokes, and amongst whom and for whom were composed squibs, pamphlets, newspaper articles, in steady glorification of school and college opinions, which the Oxonian, on quitting the University, had no doubt the intention to sustain in the great battles of party warfare.

But events were then beginning to make men's convictions tremble under them; and, with the increasing differences amongst veteran statesmen, it was difficult to count on youthful recruits.

At all events, it is about this time that Mr. Canning's political career begins. It must be viewed in relation to the particular state of society and government which then existed.

From the days of Queen Anne there had been a contest going on between the two aristocratic factions, "Whig" and "Tory." The principles professed by either were frequently changed. The Tories, such as Sir William Windham, under the guidance of Boling-broke, often acting as Reformers; and the Whigs, under Walpole, often acting as Conservatives. The being in or out of place was in fact the chief difference between the opposing candidates for office, though the Whigs generally passed for being favourable to popular pre-tensions, and the Tories for being favourable to Royal authority.

In the meantime public opinion, except on an occa-sional crisis when the nation made itself heard, was the opinion of certain coteries, and public men were the men of those coteries. It not unfrequently happened that the most distinguished in ability were the most distinguished for birth and fortune. But it was by no means necessary that it should be so. The chiefs of the two conflicting armies sought to obtain everywhere the best soldiers. Each had a certain number of com-missions to give away, or, in other words, of seats in Parliament to dispose of. They who had the govern-ment in their hands, could count from that fact alone on thirty or forty. It matters little how these close boroughs were created. Peers or gentlemen possessed them as simple property, or as the effect of dominant local influence. The Treasury controlled them as an effect of the patronage or employments which office placed in its hands. A certain number were sold or let by their proprietors, and even by the Administra-tion; and in this manner men who had made fortunes in our colonies or trade, and were averse to a public canvass, and without local landed influence, found their way into the great National Council. They paid their £5000 down, or their £1000 a year, and could generally, though not always, find a seat on such terms. But a large portion of these convenient entries into the House of Commons were kept open for distinguished young men, who gave themselves up to public affairs as to a profession. A school or college reputation, an able pamphlet, a club, or county meeting oration, pointed them out. The minister, or great man who wished to be a minister, brought them into Parliament. If they failed, they sank into insignificance; if they succeeded, they worked during a certain time for the great men of the day, and then became great men themselves.

This system had advantages, counterbalanced by defects, and gave to England a set of trained and highly educated politicians, generally well informed on all national questions, strongly attached to party combinations, connected by the ties of gratitude and patronage with the higher classes, having a certain contempt for the middle: keenly alive to the glory, the power, the greatness of the country, and sympathising little with the habits and wants of the great masses of the people.

They had not a correct knowledge of the feelings and wants of the poor man, they understood and shared the feelings of the gentleman. Bread might be dear or cheap, they cared little about it; a battle gained or lost affected them more deeply. A mob might be massacred without greatly exciting their compassion; but the loss of a great general or a great statesman they felt as a national calamity.

Such were the men who might fairly be called "political adventurers:" a class to which we owe much of our political renown, much of our reputation for

11*

political capacity, but which, in only rare instances, won the public esteem or merited the popular affections. Such were our political adventurers when Mr. Pitt sent for Mr. Canning, a scholar of eminence and a young man of superior and shining abilities, and offered him a seat in the House of Commons.

The following is the simple manner in which this interview is spoken of by a biographer of Mr. Canning: *

"Mr. Pitt, through a private channel, communicated his desire to see Mr. Canning; Mr. Canning of course complied. Mr. Pitt immediately proceeded, on their meeting, to declare to Mr. Canning the object of his requesting an interview with him, which was to state that he had heard of Mr. Canning's reputation as a scholar and a speaker, and that if he concurred in the policy which the Government was then pursuing, arrangements would be made to bring him into Parliament."

The person to whom this offer was made accepted it; nor was this surprising.

I have already said that events were about this period taking place, that made men's convictions tremble under them; and in fact the mob rulers of Paris had in a few months so desecrated the name of Freedom, that half of its ancient worshippers covered their faces with their hands, and shuddered when it was pronounced.

But there were also other circumstances of a more personal nature, which, now that young Canning had seriously to think of his entry into public life, had, I have been assured, an influence on his resolutions.

* In the Life given in the edition of Mr. Canning's Speeches.

The first incident, I was once told by Mr. John Allen, that disinclined Mr. Canning (who had probably already some misgivings), to attach himself irrevocably to the Whig camp, was the following one: Lord Liverpool, then Mr. Jenkinson, had just made his appearance in the House of Commons. His first speech was highly successful. "There is a young friend of mine," said Mr. Sheridan, "whom I soon hope to hear answering the honourable gentleman who has just distinguished himself: a contemporary whom he knows to possess talents not inferior to his own, but whose principles, I trust, are very different from his."

This allusion, however kindly meant, was disagreeable, said Mr. Allen, to the youthful aspirant to public honours. It pledged him, as he thought, prematurely; it brought him forward under the auspices of a man, who, however distinguished as an individual, was not in a position to be a patron. Other reflections, it is added, followed. The party then in opposition possessed almost every man distinguished in public life: a host of formidable competitors in the road to honour and preferment, supposing preferment and honour to be attainable by talent. But this was not all. The Whig party, then, as always, was essentially an exclusive party; its preferments were concentrated on a clique, which regarded all without it, as its subordinates and instruments.

On the other side, the Prime Minister stood almost alone. He had every office to bestow, and few candidates of any merit for official employments. Haughty from temperament, and flushed with power, which he had attained early and long exercised without control,

he had not the pride of rank, nor the aristocratic attachments for which high families linked together are
distinguished. His partisans and friends were his own.
He had elevated them for no other reason than that
they were his. By those to whom he had once shown
favour he had always stood firm; all who had followed
had shared his fortunes; — there can be no better promise to adherents.

These were not explanations that Mr. Canning
could make precisely to the Whig leaders, but he had
an affection for Mr. Sheridan, who had always been
kind to him, and by whom he did not wish to be
thought ungrateful: He sought, then, an interview
with that good-natured and gifted person. Lord Holland, Mr. Canning's contemporary, was present at that
interview and told me that nothing could be more respectful, and unreserved, than the manner in which
the ambitious young man gave his reasons for the
change he was prepared to make, or had made; nothing more warm-hearted, unprejudiced, and frank, than
the experienced politician's reception of his retiring
protégé's confession: nor, indeed, could Mr. Sheridan
help feeling the application, when he was himself cited
as an example of the haughtiness with which "the
Whig Houses" looked down on the lofty aspirations of
mere genius. The conversation thus alluded to took
place a little before Mr. Pitt's proposals were made,
but probably when they were expected. Mr. Canning,
his views fairly stated to the only person to whom he
felt bound to give them, and his seat in Parliament
secured, placed himself in front of his old friend, whom
Colonel Fitz Patrick avenged by the following couplet:

"The turning of coats so common is grown,
  That no one would think to attack it;
But no case until now was so flagrantly known
  Of a schoolboy turning his jacket."

V.

There was little justice in Colonel Fitz Patrick's satire. Nine-tenths of Mr. Fox's partisans, old and young, were deserting his standard when Mr. Canning quitted him. The cultivated mind of England was, as it has been said in two or three of these sketches, against the line which the Whig leader persisted to take with respect to the French Revolution — even after its excesses; and it is easy to conceive that the cause of Liberty and Fraternity should have become unfashionable when these weird sisters were seen brandishing the knife, and dancing round the guillotine. Admitting, however, the legitimacy of the horror with which the assassins of the Committee of Public Safety inspired the greater portion of educated Englishmen, it is still a question whether England should have provoked their hostility; for, after the recall of our ambassador and our undisguised intention of making war, the Republic's declaration of it was a matter of course.

"Where could be the morality," said Mr. Pitt's opponents, "of bringing fresh calamities upon a land which so many calamities already desolated? Where the policy of concentrating and consolidating so formidable an internal system by an act of foreign aggression? And if the struggle we then engaged in was in itself inhuman and impolitic, what was to be said as to the time at which we entered upon it?

"The natural motives that might have suggested

war, were — the wish to save an unhappy monarch from an unjust and violent death; the desire to subdue the arrogance of a set of miscreants who, before they were prepared to execute the menace, threatened to overrun the world with their principles and their arms. If these were our motives, why not draw the sword before the Sovereign whose life we wished to protect had perished? Why defer our conflict with the French army until, flushed with victory and threatened with execution in the event of defeat, raw recruits were changed into disciplined and desperate soldiers? Why reserve our defence of the unhappy Louis till he had perished on the scaffold — our war against the French Republic until the fear of the executioner and the love of glory had made a nation unanimous in its defence? Success was possible when Prussia first entered on the contest: it was impossible when we subsidized her to continue it."

The antagonists of the First Minister urged these arguments with plausibility. His friends replied, "that Mr. Pitt had been originally against all interference in French affairs, that the conflict was not of his seeking, that the conduct of the French government and the feelings of the English people had at last forced him into it; that he had not wished to anticipate its necessity; but that if he had, the minister of a free country cannot go to war at precisely the moment he would select; he cannot guard against evils which the public itself does not foresee. He must go with the public, or after it; and the public mind in England had, like that of the Minister, only become convinced by degrees that peace was impossible.

"As to neutrality, if it could be observed when the

objects at stake were material, it could not be maintained when those objects were moral, social, and religious.

"When new ideas were everywhere abroad, inflaming, agitating men's minds, these ideas were sure to find everywhere partisans or opponents, and to attempt to moderate the zeal of one party merely gave power to the violence of the other.

"It was necessary to excite the English people against France, in order to prevent French principles, as they were then called, from spreading and fixing themselves in England."

Such was the language and such the opinions of many eminent men with whom Mr. Canning was now associated, when, after a year's preliminary silence, he made his first speech in the House of Commons.

VI.

This first speech (January 31, 1794), like many first speeches of men who have become eminent orators, was more or less a failure. The subject was a subsidy to Sardinia, and the new member began with a scoff at the idea of looking with a mere mercantile eye at the goodness or badness of the bargain we were making. Such a scoff at economy, uttered in an assembly, which is the especial guardian of the public purse, was injudicious. But the whole speech was bad; it possessed in an eminent degree all the ordinary faults of the declamations of clever young men. Its arguments were much too refined: its arrangement much too systematic: cold, tedious, and unparliamentary, it would have been twice as good if it had attempted half as much; for the great art in speaking, as in writing, consists in knowing what should not be said or written.

This instance of ill success did not, however, alienate the Premier; for Mr. Pitt, haughty in all things, cared little for opinions which he did not dictate. In 1795, therefore, the unsubdued favourite was charged with the seconding of the address, and acquitted himself with some spirit and effect.

The following passage may be quoted both for thought and expression:

"The next argument against peace is its insecurity; it would be the mere name of peace, not a wholesome and refreshing repose, but a feverish and troubled slumber, from which we should soon be roused to fresh horrors and insults. What are the blessings of peace which make it so desirable? What, but that it implies tranquil and secure enjoyment of our homes? What, but that it will restore our seamen and our soldiers, who have been fighting to preserve those homes, to a share of that tranquillity and security? What, but that it will lessen the expenses and alleviate the burdens of the people? What, but that it explores some new channel of commercial intercourse, or reopens such as war had destroyed? What, but that it renews some broken link of amity, or forms some new attachment between nations, and softens the asperities of hostility and hatred into kindness and conciliation and reciprocal goodwill? And which of all these blessings can we hope to obtain by a peace, under the present circumstances, with France? Can we venture to restore to the loom or to the plough the brave men who have

fought our battles? Who can say how soon some fresh
government may not start up in France, which may
feel it their inclination or their interest to renew hosti-
lities? The utmost we can hope for is a short, delusive,
and suspicious interval of armistice, without any material diminution of expenditure; without security at
home, or a chance of purchasing it by exertions
abroad; without any of the essential blessings of peace,
or any of the possible advantages of war: a state of
doubt and preparation such as will retain in itself all
the causes of jealousy to other states which, in the
usual course of things, produce remonstrances and (if
these are answered unsatisfactorily) war."

VII.

In 1796, Parliament was dissolved, and Mr. Canning was returned to Parliament this time for Wendover.
He had just been named Under-Secretary of State for
Foreign Affairs; and it has been usual to refer to this
appointment as a proof of his early parliamentary success. He owed the promotion, however, entirely to
the Prime Minister's favour; for though his late speech,
better than the preceding one, had procured him some
credit, there was still a careless impertinence in his
manner, and a classical pedantry in his style, which
were unsuitable to the taste of the House of Commons.
Indeed, so much had he to reform in his manner, that
be now remained, as it is said, by Mr. Pitt's advice,
silent for three years, endeavouring during this time
to correct his faults and allow them to be forgotten.

It does not follow that he was idle. The *Anti-Jacobin*,

started in 1797, under the editorship of Mr. Gifford, for the purpose which its title indicates, was commenced at the instigation and with the support of the old contributor to the *Microcosm*, and did more than any parliamentary eloquence could have done in favour of the anti-Jacobin cause.

"Must wit," says Mr. Canning, who had now to contend against the most accomplished humorists of his day, "be found alone on falsehood's side?" and having established himself as the champion of "Truth," he brought, no doubt, very useful and very brilliant arms to her service. The verses of "New Morality," spirited, exaggerated, polished, and virulent, satisfied the hatred without offending the taste (which does not seem to have been at that time very refined) of those classes who looked upon our neighbours with almost as much hatred and disgust as were displayed in the verses of the young poet; while the "Friend of Humanity and the Knife-grinder" — almost too trite to be quoted, and yet too excellent to be omitted — will long remain one of the happiest efforts of satire in our language:

"IMITATION SAPPHICS.

"THE FRIEND OF HUMANITY AND THE KNIFE-GRINDER.

"Friend of Humanity:

"Needy Knife-grinder, whither are you going?
Rough is the road, — your wheel is out of order;
Bleak blows the blast, — your hat has got a hole in't,
      So have your breeches.

"Weary Knife-grinder, little think the proud ones,
Who in their coaches roll along the turnpike
Road, what hard work 'tis crying all day, 'Knives and
      Scissors to grind, O!'

"Tell me, Knife-grinder, how came you to grind knives?
Did some rich man tyranically use you?
Was it the squire, or parson of the parish,
    Or the attorney?

"Was it the squire, for killing of his game? or
Covetous parson, for his tithes distraining?
Or roguish lawyer, made you lose your little
    All in a lawsuit?

"Have you not read the 'Rights of Man,' by Tom Paine?
Drops of compassion tremble on my eyelids,
Ready to fall as soon as you have told your
    Pitiful story.

"Knife-grinder:

"Story! God bless you, I have none to tell, sir;
Only last night, a-drinking at the 'Chequers,'
These poor old hat and breeches, as you see, were
    Torn in a scuffle.

"Constables came up for to take me into
Custody; they took me before the justice:
Justice Aldmixon put me in the parish
    Stocks for a vagrant.

"I should be glad to drink your honour's health in
A pot of beer, if you will give me sixpence;
But, for my part, I never love to meddle
    With politics, sir.

"Friend of Humanity:

"I give thee sixpence? I'll see thee damn'd first.
Wretch, whom no sense of wrong can rouse to vengeance!
Sordid, unfeeling, reprobate, degraded,
    Spiritless outcast!"

                    [*Exit, kicking over the wheel, in a
                    fit of universal philanthropy.*]

An instance of the readiness of Mr. Canning's Muse
may be here related.

When Frere had completed the first part of the
"Loves of the Triangles," he exultingly read over the

following lines to Canning, and defied him to improve
upon them:

> "Lo! where the chimney's sooty tube ascends,
> The fair Trochais from the corner bends!
> Her coal-black eyes upturned, incessant mark
> The eddying smoke, quick flame, and volant spark;
> Mark with quick ken, where flashing in between,
> Her much-loved *smoke-jack* glimmers thro' the scene;
> Mark how his various parts together tend,
> Point to one purpose, — in one object end;
> The spiral grooves in smooth meanders flow,
> Drags the long chain, the polished axles glow,
> While slowly circumvolves the piece of beef below."

Canning took the pen, and added:

> "The conscious fire with bickering radiance burns,
> Eyes the rich joint, and roasts it as it turns."

These two lines are now blended with the original
text, and constitute, it is said, the only flaw in Frere's
title to the sole authorship of the first part of the poem
from which I have been quoting: the second and third
parts were both by Canning.

In prose I cite the report of a peroration by Mr.
Erskine, whose egotism could hardly be caricatured, at
a meeting of the Friends of Freedom.

"Mr. Erskine concluded by recapitulating, in a
strain of agonizing and impressive eloquence, the
several more prominent heads of his speech: He had
been a soldier, and a sailor, and had a son at Winchester School; he had been called by special retainers,
during the summer, into many different and distant
parts of the country, travelling chiefly in post-chaises;
he felt himself called upon to declare that his poor
faculties were at the service of his country — of the
free and enlightened part of it, at least. He stood

here as a màn; he stood in the eye, indeed in the hand, of God — to whom (in the presence of the company, and waiters) he solemnly appealed; he was of noble, perhaps royal blood; he had a house at Hampstead; was convinced of the necessity of a thorough and radical reform; his pamphlet had gone through thirty editions, skipping alternately the odd and even numbers; he loved the Constitution, to which he would cling and grapple; and he was clothed with the infirmities of man's nature; he would apply to the present French rulers (particularly *Barras* and *Reubel*) the words of the poet:

> "'Be to their faults a little blind;
> Be to their virtues ever kind,
> Let all their ways be unconfined,
> And clap the padlock on their mind!'

and for these reasons, thanking the gentlemen who had done him the honour to drink his health, he should propose '*Merlin*, the late Minister of Justice, under the Directory, and Trial by Jury.'"

I refer those who wish to know more of the literary merits of Mr. Canning to an article, July 1858, in the "Edinburgh Review," in which article the accomplished writer has exhausted the subject he undertook to treat.

Nor was Mr. Canning's reputation for wit, at this time, gained solely by his pen. Living with few, though much the fashion, who could be more charming in his own accomplished circle — when, the pleasant thought lighting up his eye, playing about his mouth, and giving an indescribable charm to his handsome countenance, he planned some practical joke, or quizzed some incorrigible bore, or related some humorous anec-

dote? No one's society was so much prized by associates; no one's talents so highly estimated by friends;
his fame in the drawing-room, or at the dining-table,
was at least as brilliant as that which he subsequently
acquired in the senate.

This, indeed, was the epoch in his life at which
perhaps he had the most real enjoyment; for though
he felt conscious that his success in Parliament had not
yet been complete, the feeling of certainty that it
would become so, began to dawn upon him, and the
triumphs that his ardent nature anticipated went probably even beyond those which his maturer career accomplished.

VIII.

On the 11th of December, 1798, Mr. Tierney
made a motion respecting peace with the French Republic. The negotiations at Lisle, never cordially
entered into, were at this time broken off. We had
formed an alliance with Russia and the Porte, and
were about to carry on the struggle with new energies,
though certainly not under very encouraging auspices.
The coalition of 1792—3 was completely broken up.
Prussia had for three years been at peace with France;
nor had the Cabinet of Vienna seen any objection to
signing a treaty which, disgracefully to all parties,
sacrificed the remains of Venetian liberty.

France, in the meanwhile, distracted at home, had,
notwithstanding, enlarged her empire by Belgium,
Luxemburg, Nice, Savoy, Piedmont, Genoa, Milan,
and Holland. There were many arguments to use in
favour of abandoning the struggle we had entered

upon: the uncertain friendship of our allies; the increased force of our enemy; and the exhausting drain we were maintaining upon our own resources. In six years we had added one hundred and fifty millions to our debt, by which had been created the necessity of adding to our annual burdens eight millions, a sum equal to the whole of our expenditure when George III. came to the throne.

But the misfortunes which attend an expensive contest, though they necessarily irritate and dissatisfy a people with war, are not always to be considered irrefutable arguments in favour of peace. This formed the substance of Mr. Canning's speech. Defective in argument, it was effective in delivery, and added considerably to his reputation as a speaker.

In the meantime, our sworn enmity to France and to French principles, encouraged an ardent inclination to both in those whom we had offended or misgoverned. The Directory in Paris and the discontented in Ireland had, therefore, formed a natural if not a legitimate league. The result was an Irish rebellion, artfully planned, for a long time unbetrayed, and which, but for late treachery and singular accidents, would not have been easily overcome.

Mr. Pitt, taking advantage of the fears of a separation between Great Britain and the sister kingdom, which this rebellion, notwithstanding its prompt and fortunate suppression, had created, announced, in a message from the Crown, a desire still further to incorporate and consolidate the two kingdoms. Whatever may have been the result of the Irish Union, the promises under which it was passed having been so long denied, so unhappily broken, there was certainly

at this period reason to suppose that it would afford
the means of instituting a fairer and less partial system
of government than that under which Ireland had long
been suffering.

As for the wail which was then set up, and which
has since been re-awakened, for the independent Legislature which was merged into that of Great Britain, the
facility with which it was purchased is the best answer
which can be given as to the assertions made of its
value.

The part, therefore, that Mr. Canning adopted on
this question (if with sincere and honest views of conferring the rights of citizenship on our Irish Catholic
fellow-subjects, and not with the intention, which there
is no reason to presume, of gaining their goodwill and
then betraying their confidence) is one highly honourable to an English statesman. But another question
now arose. That Catholic Emancipation was frequently
promised as the natural result of the Union, has never
been disputed. As such promises were made plainly
and openly in Parliament, the King could not be supposed ignorant of them. Why, then, if his Majesty
had such insuperable objections to their fulfilment, did
he allow of their being made? And, on the other
hand, how could his Ministers compromise their characters by holding out as a lure to a large majority of the
Irish people a benefit which they had no security for
being able to concede? Mr. Canning's language is not
ambiguous:

"Here, then, are two parties in opposition to each
other, who agree in one common opinion; and surely
if any middle term can be found to assuage their animosities, and to heal their discords, and to reconcile their

jarring interests, it should be eagerly and instantly seized and applied. That an union is that middle term, appears the more probable when we recollect that the Popery code took its rise after a proposal for an union, which proposal came from Ireland, but which was rejected by the British government. This rejection produced the Popery code. If *an union were therefore acceded to, the Popery code would be unnecessary.* I say, if it was in consequence of the rejection of an union at a former period that the laws against Popery were enacted, it is fair to conclude that an union would render a similar code unnecessary — that an union would satisfy the friends of the Protestant ascendancy, without passing new laws against the Catholics, and without maintaining those which are yet in force." *

The Union, nevertheless, was carried; the mention of Catholic Emancipation, in spite of the language just quoted, forbidden. Mr. Pitt (in 1801) retired.

IX.

There will always be a mystery hanging over the transactions to which I have just referred, — a mystery difficult to explain in a manner entirely satisfactory to the character of the King and his minister. One can only presume that the King was willing to let the Union be carried, on the strength of the Premier's promises, which he did not think it necessary to gainsay until he was asked to carry them into effect; and that the Minister counted upon the important service he would

* Speech on the King's Message relative to Union with Ireland, January 2, 1799.

have rendered if the great measure he was bringing
forward. became law, for the influence that would be
necessary to make his promises valid. It cannot be
denied that each acted with a certain want of candour
towards the other unbecoming their respective positions,
and that both behaved unfairly towards Ireland. Mr.
Pitt sought to give consistency to his conduct by resigning; but he failed in convincing the public of his
sincerity, because he was supposed to have recommended
Mr. Addington, then Speaker of the House of Commons, and the son of a Doctor Addington, who had
been the King's physician (to which circumstance the
son owed a nickname he could never shake off), as his
successor; and Mr. Addington was only remarkable for
not being remarkable whether for his qualities or for
his defects, being just that staid, sober sort of man
who, respectable in the chair of the House of Commons, would be almost ridiculous in leading its debates.

Thus an appointment which did not seem serious,
perplexed and did not satisfy the public mind; more
especially as the seceding minister engaged himself to
support the new Premier, notwithstanding their difference of opinion on the very question on which the
former had left office. The public did not know then
so clearly as it does now that the King, who through
his whole life seems to have been on the brink of in-
sanity, was then in a state of mind that rendered madness certain, if the question of the Catholics, on which
he had morbid and peculiar notions, was persistingly
pressed upon him; and that Mr. Pitt thus, rightly or
wrongly, thought it was his duty, after sacrificing
office, to stop short of driving the master he had so long

served into the gloom of despair. This, however, was
a motive that could not be avowed, and consequently
every sort of conjecture became current. Was the arrangement made on an understanding with the King,
and would Mr. Pitt shortly resume the place he had
quitted? Did Mr. Pitt, if there were no such arrangement, really mean to retain so incapable a person as
Mr. Addington, at the head of the Government of
England, or was his assistance given merely for the
moment, with the intention of subsequently withdraw-
ing it?

At first the aid offered to the new Premier by the
old one was effective and ostentatious; but a great
portion of the Opposition began also to support Mr. Addington, intending in this way to lure him into an independence which, as they imagined, would irritate his
haughty friend, and separate the *protégé* from the
patron. The device was successful. The Prime Minister soon began to entertain a high opinion of his own
individual importance, Mr. Pitt to feel sore at being
treated as a simple official follower of the Government,
which he had expected unofficially to command, and
ere long he retired almost entirely from Parliament.
He did not, however, acknowledge the least desire to
return to power.

In this state of things, the conduct of Mr. Canning
seemed likely to be the same as Mr. Pitt's, but it was
not so. He did not, even for a moment, affect any
disposition to share the partiality which the late First
Lord of the Treasury began by testifying for the new
one. Sitting in Parliament for a borough for which
he had been elected through government influence, his
conduct for a moment was fettered; but obtaining, at

the earliest opportunity, a new seat (in 1802) by
his own means — that is, by his own money — he
then went without scruple into the most violent opposition.

His constant efforts to induce Achilles to take up
his spear and issue from his tent, are recorded by
Lord Malmesbury, and though not wholly disagreeable
to his discontented chief, were not always pleasing to
him.   He liked, no doubt, to be pointed out as the
only man who could direct successfully the destinies
of England, and enjoyed jokes levelled at the dull
gentleman who had become all at once enamoured of
his own capacity; but he thought his dashing and in-
discreet adherent passed the bounds of good taste and
decorum in his attacks, and he disliked being pressed
to come forward before he himself felt convinced that
the time was ripe for his doing so.   Too strong a show
of reluctance might, he knew, discourage his friends;
too ready an acquiescence compromise his dignity, and
give an advantage to his enemies.

He foresaw, indeed, better than any one, all the
difficulties that lay in his path.   The unwillingness of
the Sovereign to exchange a minister with whom he
was at his ease, for a minister of whom he always
stood in awe; the unbending character of Lord Grenville, with whom he must of necessity associate, if he
formed any government that could last, and who,
nevertheless, rendered every difficulty in a government
more difficult by his uncompromising character, his
stately bearing, and his many personal engagements
and connections. More than all, perhaps, he felt creep-
ing over him what his friends did not see and would
not believe — that premature decrepitude which con-

signed him, in the prime of life, to the infirmities of age. Thus, though he felt restless at being deprived of the only employment to which he was accustomed, he was not very eager as to a prompt reinstatement in it, and preferred waiting until an absolute necessity for his services, and a crisis, on which he always counted, should float him again into Downing Street, over many obstacles against which his bark might otherwise be wrecked.

His real feelings, however, were matter of surmise; many people, not unnaturally, imagined that Mr. Canning represented them; and the energetic partisan, mixing with the world, derived no small importance from his well-known intimacy with the statesman in moody retirement. His marriage, moreover, at this time with Miss Joan Scott, one of the daughters of General Scott, and co-heiress with her sisters, Lady Moray and Lady Titchfield, brought him both wealth and connection, and gave a solidity to his position which it did not previously possess.

X.

In the meantime the Addington administration went on, its policy necessarily partaking of the timid and half-earnest character of the man directing it. Unequal to the burden and the responsibility of war, he had concocted a peace, but a peace of the character which Mr. Canning had previously described: "a peace without security and without honour": a peace which, while it required some firmness to decline, demanded more to maintain, since the country was as certain to be at first pleased with it as to be soon ashamed of it. No administration would have had the boldness to surrender up Malta; few would have been so weak as to promise the cession.

Indeed, almost immediately after concluding this halcyon peace, we find the Secretary of War speaking of "these times of difficulty and danger," and demanding "an increased military establishment." Nor was it long before an additional 10,000 men were also demanded for our naval service. On both these occasions Mr. Canning, supporting the demand of the Minister, attacked the Administration; and after stating his reasons for being in favour of the especial measure proposed, burst out at once into an eloquent exhibition of the reasons for his general opposition:

"I do think that this is a time when the administration of the Government ought to be in the ablest and fittest hands. I do not think the hands in which it is now placed answer to that description. I do not pretend to conceal in what quarter I think that fitness most eminently resides. I do not subscribe to the doctrines which have been advanced, that, in times like the present, the fitness of individuals for their political situations is no part of the consideration to which a Member of Parliament may fairly turn his attention. I know not a more solemn or important duty that a Member of Parliament can have to discharge than by giving, at fit seasons, a free opinion upon the character and qualities of public men. *Away with the cant of measures, not men — the idle supposition that it is the harness, and not the horses, that draw the chariot along.* No, sir; if the comparison must be made — if the distinction must be taken — measures are comparatively nothing, men everything. I speak, sir, of times of difficulty and danger — of times when systems are shaken, when precedents and general rules of conduct fail. Then it is that not to this or that measure, however prudently devised, however blameless in execution, but to the energy and character of individuals a state must be indebted for its salvation. Then it is that kingdoms rise and fall in proportion as they are upheld, not by well-meant endeavours (however laudable these may be), but by commanding, overawing talent — by able men. And what is the nature of the times in which we live? Look at France, and see what we have to cope with, and consider what has made her what she is — a man! You will tell me that she was great, and powerful, and formidable before the date of Bonaparte's government — that he found in her great physical and moral resources — that he had but to turn them to account. True; and he did so. Compare the situation in which he found France with that to which he has raised her. I am no panegyrist of Bonaparte; but I cannot shut my eyes to the superiority of his talents — to the amazing ascendency of his genius. Tell me not of his measures and his policy. It is his genius, his character, that keeps the world in awe. Sir, to meet, to check, to curb, to stand up against him, we want arms of the same kind. I am far from objecting to the large military establishments which are proposed to you. I vote for them with all my heart. But, for the purpose of coping with Bonaparte, one great commanding spirit is worth them all!"*

* Speech on the Army Estimates, Dec. 8, 1802.

Mr. Canning was right. No cant betrays more ignorance than that which affects to undervalue the qualities of public men in the march of public affairs. However circumstances may contribute to make individuals, individuals have as great a share in making circumstances. Had Queen Elizabeth been a weak and timid woman, we might now be speaking Spanish, and have our fates dependent on the struggle between Prim and Narvaez. Had James II. been a wise and prudent man, instead of the present cry against Irish Catholics, our saints of the day would have been spreading charges against the violence and perfidy of some Puritan Protestant — some English, or perhaps Scotch, O'Connell. Strip Mirabeau of his eloquence, endow Louis XVI. with the courage and the genius of Henry IV., and the history of the last eighty years might be obliterated.

Mr. Canning, I repeat, was right; the great necessity in arduous times is a man who inspires other men; and the satirist, in measuring the two rivals for office, was hardly wrong in saying:

"*As London to Paddington,*
So Pitt is to Addington."

XI.

Well adapted ridicule no public man can stand, and there seems to have been something peculiar to Mr. Addington that attracted it. Even Mr. Sheridan, his steady supporter to the last (for the main body of the Whigs, under Mr. Fox, when they saw a prospect of power for themselves, uniting with the Grenvillites, went into violent opposition) — even Mr. Sheridan, in those memorable lines:

"I do not love thee, Doctor Fell,
The reason why I cannot tell;
But this I know, and know full well,
I do not love thee, Doctor Fell":

quoted in defence of the Minister whom so many attacked without saying why they disapproved, furnished a nickname that too well applied to him, and struck the last nail into the coffin that a mingled cohort of friends and enemies bore — a smile on their faces — to the tomb.

Previous to this, the war, which had been suspended by mutual bad faith, was recommenced, each party complaining of the other.

The man to whom Mr. Canning had been so long pointing now came into power, but was not precisely the man, in spite of Mr. Canning's eulogium, for the sort of crisis in which he assumed it. There was, indeed, a singular contrast in the life of Lord Chatham and that of his son. The first Pitt was essentially a war minister; he seemed to require the sound of the clarion and the trumpet and the guns proclaiming victory from the Tower, to call forth the force and instincts of his genius. In peace he became an ordinary person. The second Pitt, on the contrary, was as evidently a peace minister. In quiet times his government had been eminently successful. Orderly, regular, methodical, with a firm and lofty soul, and the purest motives for his guides, he had carried on the business of the country, steadily, prudently, and ably — heedless of the calumnies of envy, or the combinations of factions: but he wanted that imagination which furnishes resources on unexpected occasions. The mighty convulsion which made the world heave under his feet did not terrify him, but it bewildered him; and nothing could be more unfortunate, or even more wavering, than his conduct when he had to deal with extraordinary events. Still, in one thing he resembled his father — he had unbounded confidence in himself. This sufficed for the moment to give confidence to others; and his stately figure, standing in the imagination of the nation, by the side of Britannia, added to the indomitable courage of our mariners, and shed a kindred influence over the heroic genius of their chief. But though Mr. Pitt had in a supreme degree the talent of commanding the respect of his followers and admirers, he had not the genial nature which gives sway over equals; and Mr. Fox had of late won to himself many eminent persons who by their opinions and antecedents were more naturally disposed to join his rival. The Premier felt this difficulty, and being wholly above jealousy, would have coalesced with Mr. Fox, and formed a ministry strong in the abilities which at that critical time were so required. But George III., with a narrowness of mind that made even his qualities defects, said, "Bring me whom you please, Mr. Pitt, except Fox." This exception put an end to the combination in view; for, in spite of Fox's disinterested remonstrances, or, perhaps, in consequence of them, none of his friends would quit his side.

Nevertheless, proud, accustomed to power, careless of responsibility, defying all opponents, inspiring awe by his towering person and sonorous voice, as well as by the lofty tone of his eloquence and the solitary grandeur of his disposition, alone in front of a stronger phalanx of adversaries than ever, perhaps, before or since, were marshalled against a minister, — Mr. Fox, Mr. Sheridan, Mr. Windham, the Grenvilles, Mr. Grey, Mr. Tierney — as daring and undaunted in appearance as in the first flush of his youthful glory, stood this singular personage, honoured even in his present isolation with the public hopes. But Fortune, which in less eventful moments had followed, chose this fatal moment for deserting him. In vain he turned to his most able supporter for assistance: that early friend, more unfortunate than himself, stood disabled, and exposed to a disgraceful impeachment. The struggle was too severe; it wore out a spirit which nothing could bend or appal. On the 23rd of January, 1806, immediately after the fatal battle of Austerlitz, which chilled the remains of life within him, and on the anniversary of the day on which, twenty-five years before, he had been returned to Parliament, Mr. Pitt died.

XII.

Lord Grenville and Mr. Fox (the King's antipathy was this time overborne by necessity) formed the new Ministry, in which Lord Sidmouth (late Mr. Addington), who, Mr. Canning said, "was like the small-pox, since everybody must have him once in their lives," was also included.

During the short time that Mr. Canning had lately held office, his situation as Treasurer of the Navy had invested him with the defence of Lord Melville, a defence which he conducted with much tact and ability, and to this his parliamentary labours had been confined. The employment of "All the Talents" (as the new Administration, comprising men of every party, was called) now left him almost alone amongst the parliamentary debaters in opposition. This position was a fortunate one.

In the most formidable and successful attacks against Lord Ellenborough's seat in the Cabinet, which was indefensible — against Mr. Windham's Limited Service Bill, of which party spirit denied the merits — he led the way. His success on all these occasions was great, and the style of his speaking now began to show the effects of care and experience. A less methodic mode of arguing, a greater readiness in replying, had removed the unprepossessing impression of previous study; while an artful rapidity of style permitted that polish of language which is too apt, when unskilfully employed, to become prolix, monotonous, and languid. It was this peculiar polish, accompanied by a studied though apparently natural rapidity, which, becoming more and more perfect as it became apparently more natural, subsequently formed the essential excellence of Mr. Canning's speaking; for his poetical illustrations required the charm of his delivery, and his jokes, imitated from Mr. Sheridan, were rarely so good as their model; although, even in his manner of introducing and dealing with these, we may trace, as he advanced, a very marked improvement.

The coalition between parties at one time so adverse as those enlisted under the names of Fox, Grenville, and Addington, could only be maintained by the ascendency of that master-spirit which had been so long predominant in the House of Commons. But when Mr. Fox undertook the arduous duties of the Foreign Office, his health (that treasure which statesmen often spend with improvidence, and which he had wasted more than most men) was already beginning to fail, rendering heavy the duties of public life; and in 1806 — while our diplomacy at Paris was making a last attempt to effect that honourable peace which had so long been the object of the worn-out ministers' desires — that great statesman, whose generous and noble heart never deceived him, but whose singular capacity in debate was often marred by a remarkable want of judgment in action, followed his haughty predecessor to an untimely grave.

The Grenville administration, after the death of Mr. Fox, was no more the former Administration of Lord Grenville than the mummy, superstitiously presumed to preserve the spirit of the departed, was the real living body that had been embalmed. It avoided, however, the ignominy of a natural death, by being the first Administration which, according to Mr. Sheridan, "not only ran its head against a wall, but actually built a wall for the purpose of running its head against it." This instrument of suicide was the well-known bill "for securing to all His Majesty's subjects the privilege of serving in the Army and Navy." A measure which, by permitting Irish Catholics to hold a higher military rank than the law at that time allowed them, showed the Whig government to be true to its principles, but without tact or ability in carrying them out;

for this bill, brought forward honourably but unadvisedly, withdrawn weakly, alarming many, and never granting much, dissatisfied the Catholics, angered the Protestants, and gave the King the opportunity of sending a ministry he disliked about their business, on a pretext which there was sufficient bigotry in the nation to render popular. A dissolution amidst the yell of "No Popery!" took place; 'and it was by this cry that the party with which Mr. Canning now consented to act reinstalled itself in power.

XIII.

A person well qualified to know the facts of that time, once told me that, not very long before the dissolution of the Ministry to which he succeeded, at a time certainly when that dissolution was not so apparent, Mr. Canning had privately conveyed to Lord Grenville, who had previously sounded him on the subject, a wish to secede from opposition, and had even received a promise that a suitable place (Mr. Windham's dismissal was at that time arranged) should be reserved for him. Reminded of this when affairs had become more critical, he is said to have observed, "it was too late." Whatever may be the truth as to this story, and such stories are rarely accurate in all their details — one thing is certain — the brilliant abilities of the aspiring orator, though then and afterwards depreciated by the dull mediocrity which affects to think wit and pleasantry incompatible with the higher and more serious attributes of genius, now carried him through every obstacle to the most important political situation in the country.

LIST OF MINISTERS.

	In March, 1807.	In April, 1807.
President of the Council	Lord Sidmouth	Lord Camden.
Lord High Chancellor	Lord Erskine	Lord Eldon.
Lord Privy Seal	Lord Holland	Lord Westmoreland.
First Lord of the Treasury.	Lord Grenville	Duke of Portland.
First Lord of the Admiralty.	Right Hon. T. Grenville	Lord Mulgrave.
Master-General of the Ordnance	Lord Moira	Lord Chatham.
Secretary of State for the Home Office	Lord Spencer	Lord Hawkesbury (Liverpool).
Secretary of State for Foreign Affairs	Lord Howick	Mr. Canning.
Secretary for War and the Colonies	Right Hon. W. Windham	Lord Castlereagh.
Lord Chief Justice	Lord Ellenborough	
Chancellor of the Exchequer	Lord H. Petty (afterwards Marquis of Lansdowne)	Mr. Perceval.
A seat in the Cabinet without office	Lord Fitzwilliam.	

It is remarkable enough that in the Whig or popular cabinet there was only one person (Mr. Windham) —a gentleman of great landed property, as well as remarkable ability — who was not a lord or a lord's son. In the Tory cabinet Mr. Canning formed the only similar exception.

The principles on which the new Government stood in respect to the Irish Catholics were soon put to the test by Mr. Brand, afterwards Lord Dacre, who moved:

"That it is contrary to the first duties of the confidential servants of the Crown to restrain themselves by any pledge, expressed or implied, from offering to the King any advice which the course of circumstances may render necessary for the welfare and security of any part of his Majesty's extensive empire."

This motion was caused by the King having required his late Ministers to pledge themselves not to bring forward any future measure of Catholic relief, and having dismissed them when they refused thus to fetter their judgment.

Mr. Canning rose amidst an unwilling audience. The imputations to which his early change of principles had exposed him were rather vividly confirmed by the recklessness with which he now appeared to be rushing into office amongst colleagues he had lately professed to despise, and in support of opinions to which he was known to be opposed. The House received him coldly, and with cries of "Question," as he commenced an explanation or defence, marked by a more than usual moderation of tone and absence of ornament. The terms on which he had been with the former Administration were to a great degree admitted in the following passage:

"For myself, I confidently aver that on the first intimation' which I received, from authority I believed to be unquestionable, of the strong difference of opinion subsisting between the King and his Ministers, I took the determination of communicating what I had learnt, and I did communicate it without delay to that part of the late Administration with which, in spite of political differences, I had continued, and with which, so far as my own feelings are concerned, I still wish to continue in habits of personal friendship and regard. I communicated it, with the most earnest advice and exhortation, that they should lose no time in coming to such an explanation and accommodation on the subject at issue as should prevent matters from going to extremities."

This statement, it is acknowledged, was perfectly correct; but it leaves untouched the tale to which I have alluded, and which represented the Minister, who was then making his explanations, as having been ready to join a ministry with opinions favourable to the Catholics, almost immediately previous to his joining another ministry avowedly hostile to the Catholic claims. But without denying or vouching for the truth of this tale, (though the authority on which it rests is highly respectable) I may observe that "no coalition can take place without previous compromise or intrigue," and that almost every Administration had, of late years, been formed or supported by coalition. Not a man in public life but had abandoned some opinion which had peculiarly distinguished him in it: not a camp in political warfare which did not contain friends who had been the bitterest opponents.

How had the Administration indeed, which now gave way been originally composed? Of Mr. Windham, the loudest declaimer for war; of Mr. Fox, the most determined advocate of peace; of Lord Sidmouth, the constant subject of ridicule to both Mr. Windham and Mr. Fox. There was Mr. Sheridan, the champion of annual Parliaments; Lord Grenville, opposed to all reform! Besides, it was at that time accepted as an axiom by a large number of the supporters of the Catholics, that the Sovereign's health created a justifiable reason for leaving the Catholic question in abeyance, and that the attempt to push it forward at an untimely moment would not really tend to its success.

Nor did Lord Castlereagh, who had always shown
13*

himself an honest champion of the Catholic cause,
evince more scruples on this matter than the new
Foreign Secretary. But if Mr. Canning's friends made
excuses for him, Mr. Canning himself, always saying
"that a thrust was the best parry," felt more disposed
to attack the enemy than to defend himself; and many
of the political squibs which turned the incapable Administration of "All the Talents" into ridicule, were
attributed to his satirical fancy. From 1807 to 1810,
he remained in office.

XIV.

The period just cited was marked by our interference in Spain, our attack on Copenhagen, and that
expedition to the Scheldt, which hung during two years
over the debates in Parliament, like one of the dull
fogs of that river.

Our foreign policy, though not always fortunate,
could no longer at least be accused of want of vigour.
As to the intervention in Spain, though marked by
the early calamity of Sir John Moore, it was still
memorable for having directed the eye of our nation
to the vulnerable point in that Colossus whom our consistency and perseverance finally brought to the ground.

The Danish enterprise was of a more doubtful
character, and can only be judged of fairly by carrying
our minds back to the moment at which it took place.
That moment was most critical; every step we took
of importance. Before the armies of France, and
the genius of her ruler, lay the vanquished legions
of the north and south of Germany. From the
House of Hapsburg the crown of Charlemagne was

gone; while the throne of the Great Frederick was
only yet preserved in the remote city of König-
berg. In vain Russia protracted an inauspicious
struggle. The battle of Friedland dictated peace.
There remained Sweden, altogether unequal to the
conflict in which she had plunged: Denmark protected
by an evasive neutrality, which it was for the interest
of neither contending party to respect. On the fron-
tiers of Holstein, incapable of defence, hung the armies
of France. Zealand and Funen, indeed, were comparatively secure, but people do not willingly abandon
the most fertile of their possessions, nor defy an enemy
because there are portions of their territory which will
not sink before the first attack.

Ministers laid some stress on their private information, and it is said that Sir R. Wilson, returning, perhaps it may be said escaping, with extraordinary
diligence from Russia, after the Peace of Tilsit, brought
undeniable intelligence as to the immediate intentions
of our new allies. But private information was useless. We do not want to know what a conqueror in-
tends to do, when we know what his character and
interests imperatively direct him to do. It would have
been absurd, indeed, not to foresee that Napoleon could
not rest in neutral neighbourhood on the borders of a
country, the possession of which, whether under the
title of amity or conquest, was eminently essential to
his darling continental system, since through Tonningen
were passed into Germany our manufactures and colonial
produce. Had this, indeed, been disputable before the
famous decree of the 21st of November, * that decree
removed all doubts.

* A virtual declaration of hostility against every neutral power.

Denmark, then, had no escape from the mighty war raging around her, and had only to choose between the tyrant of the Continent or the mistress of the seas. If she declared against us, as it was likely she would do, her navy, joined to that of Russia, and, as it soon would be, to that of Sweden, formed a powerful force — not, indeed, for disputing the empire of the ocean; there we might safely have ventured to meet the world in arms; but for assisting in those various schemes of sudden and furtive invasion which each new continental conquest encouraged and facilitated — encompassed, as we became, on all sides by hostile shores. But if the neutrality of the Danes was impossible, if their fleet, should they become hostile to us, might add materially to our peril, was it wrong to make them enter frankly into our alliance, or to deprive them of their worst means of mischief, if they would not?

What after all did we say to Denmark: "You cannot any longer retain a doubtful position; you must be for us, or we must consider you against us. '*If a friend, you may count on all the energy and resources of Great Britain.*'" The Danish Government had offered to sell a large portion of her marine to Russia, and we offered to purchase it manned. It was required, she said, to defend Zealand; we offered to defend Zealand for her.

But our negotiation failed, and finally we seized, as belonging to a power which was certain to become an enemy, the ships with which she refused to aid us as an ally. A state must be in precisely similar circumstances before it can decide whether it ought to do precisely a similar thing.

Some blamed our conduct as unjust, whilst others praised it as bold. What perhaps may be said is, that if unjust at all, it was not bold enough. War once commenced, Zealand should have been held; the stores and supplies in the merchant docks not left unnoticed; the passage of the Sound kept possession of. In short, our assault on Copenhagen should have been part of a permanent system of warfare, and not suffered to appear a mere temporary act of aggression.

Still it showed three qualities, by no means common. in the Minister who planned and stood responsible for it: secrecy, foresight, and decision.

XV.

But if our conduct towards the Danes admits of defence, luckily for Mr. Canning, the odium of that miserable expedition against Holland — in which

> "Lord Chatham, with his sword undrawn,
> Stood waiting for Sir Richard Strachan;
> Sir Richard, longing to be at 'em,
> Stood waiting for the Earl of Chatham;"

an expedition equally disgraceful to ministers and commanders — fell chiefly on his colleague, who had originated and presided over it, having himself been present at its embarkation.

It is necessary here to say a word or two concerning that statesman, who, though agreeing with Mr. Canning upon the principal question of their time, was never cordially united with him. Lord Castlereagh joined to great boldness in action, — great calm and courtesy of manner, long habits of official routine, and a considerable acquaintance with men collectively and individually. He lived in the world, and was more essentially a man of the world than his eloquent contemporary; but, on the other hand, he was singularly deficient in literary accomplishments, and this deficiency was not easily pardoned in an assembly the leading members of which had received a classical education, and were as intolerant to an ungrammatical phrase as to a political blunder. His language — inelegant, diffuse, and mingling every variety of metaphorical expression — was the ridicule of the scholar. Still the great air with which he rose from the Treasury Bench, threw back his blue coat, and showed his broad chest and white waistcoat, looking defiance on the ranks of the Opposition, won him the hearts of the rank and file of the government adherents. In affairs, he got through details so as to satisfy forms, but not so as to produce results: for if the official men who can manufacture plans on paper are numerous — the statesmen who can give them vitality in action are rare: and Lord Castlereagh was not one of them.

There was never, as I have just said, any great cordiality or intimacy between two persons, each ambitious to be the most conspicuous in their party, and each possessing defects easily perceivable to the other: but they would probably have gone on rising side by side, if they had not now been thrown together and almost identified in common action. The success of most of Mr. Canning's schemes as Minister of Foreign Affairs depended greatly upon the skill with which Lord Castlereagh, as Minister of War, carried them into execution; the personal incapacity of the latter affected the personal vanity of the former. Thus the first difficulty was sure to produce a quarrel. Mr. Canning indeed was constantly complaining that every project that was conceived by the Foreign Office miscarried when it fell under the care of the War Office; that all the gold which he put into his colleague's crucible came out, somehow or other, brass; and these complaints were the bitterer, since, judging that colleague as much with the eye of a man of letters as with that of a man of business, he somewhat underrated his abilities.

Nevertheless, wishing, very probably, to avoid a public scandal, he merely told the head of the Government privately that a change must take place in the Foreign or the War Department, and, after some little hesitation, the removal of Lord Castlereagh was determined on; but some persons from whom, perhaps, that statesman had no right to expect desertion, anxious to keep their abandonment of him concealed as long as possible, requested delay; and the Duke of Portland himself, a man of no resolution, and not daring to consent to the resignation of one of the haughty gentlemen with whom he had to deal, was glad to put off the affront that was intended to the other. Such being the state of things, Mr. Canning was prevailed upon to allow the matter to stand over for awhile, receiving at the same time the most positive assurances as to his request being finally complied with. At the end of the session and the conclusion of the enterprise (against Flushing) already undertaken, some arrangement was to be proposed, "satisfactory, it was hoped, to all parties." Such is the usual hope of temporising politicians. In the meantime, the Cabinet dined, and held council together, as if in the most perfect harmony.

This was not a pleasant state of things to discover in the moment of adversity; when the whole nation felt itself disgraced at the pitiful termination of an enterprise which had been very lavishly prepared and very ostentatiously paraded. Yet such was the moment when Mr. Canning, fatigued at the Premier's procrastination, disgusted by the calamity which he attributed to it, and resolved to escape, if possible, from a charge of incapacity, beneath which the whole Ministry was likely to be crushed, threw up his appointment; and the unfortunate secretary of war learnt, that for months his abilities had been distrusted by the majority of his colleagues, and his situation only provisionally held on the ill-extorted acquiescence of a rival. His irritation vented itself in a letter which produced a duel; a duel that Mr. Canning was not justly called upon to fight; for all that he had done was to postpone a decision he had a perfect right to adopt, and which he deferred expressly in order to spare Lord Castlereagh's feelings, and at the request of Lord Castlereagh's partisans. But the one of these gentlemen was quite as peppery and combative as the other, though it appeared he was not quite so good a shot, for Mr. Canning missed his opponent and received a disagreeable wound though not a dangerous one; the final result of the whole affair being the resignation of the Prime Minister and of the two Secretaries of State, the country paying twenty millions (the cost of the late barren attempt at glory) because the friends of a minister had shrunk from saying anything unpleasant to him until he was prostrate.

CANNING,

THE BRILLIANT MAN.

———

PART II.

Mr. Perceval, Prime Minister. — Lord Wellesley, Minister of Foreign
Affairs. — King's health necessitates regency. — The line taken by Mr.
Canning upon it. — Conduct with respect to Mr. Horner's Finance Committee. — Absurd resolution of Mr. Vansittart. — Lord Wellesley quits
the Ministry. — Mr. Perceval is assassinated. — Mr. Canning and Lord
Wellesley charged to form a new Cabinet, and fail. — Further negotiations
with Lords Grey and Grenville fail. — Lord Liverpool becomes head of
an Administration which Mr. Canning declines to join. — Accepts subsequently embassy to Lisbon, and, in 1816, enters the Ministry. — Supports
coercive and restrictive measures. — Resigns office at home after the
Queen's trial, and accepts the Governor-Generalship of India.

PART II.

I.

A NEW ADMINISTRATION brought Lord Wellesley
to the Foreign Office, and Mr. Perceval to the head of
affairs.

In 1810 the state of the King's health came once
more before the public. Parliament met in November;
the Sovereign was this time insane in earnest. A
commission had been appointed, but there was no
speech with which to address the Houses; no authority to
prorogue them. Mr. Perceval moved certain resolutions.
These resolutions were important, for they furnished a text
for debate, and settled the question so much disputed in
1788-9, deciding (for no one was found to take up the
old and unpopular arguments of Mr. Fox) that Parliament had the disposal of the Regency; and that the
Heir-apparent, without the sanction of the Legislature,
had no more right to it than any other individual.
These first resolutions were followed by others, expressive
of a determination to confer the powers of the Crown
on the Prince of Wales, but not without restrictions.
Here arose a new question, and of this question Mr.
Canning availed himself. Interest and consistency
alike demanded that he should stand fast by Mr. Pitt,

whose name was still the watchword of a considerable party. But Mr. Pitt had alike contended for the right of Parliament to name the Regent, and for the wisdom of fettering the Regency by limitations. Whereas, Mr. Canning though advocating the powers of Parliament to name the Regent was not in favour of limiting the Regent's authority. Through these confronting rocks the wary statesman steered with the skill of a veteran pilot: *

"The rights of the two Houses," said he, "were proclaimed and maintained by Mr. Pitt; that is the point on which his authority is truly valuable. The principles upon which this right was affirmed and exercised are true for all times and all occasions. If they were the principles of the Constitution in 1788, they are equally so in 1811; the lapse of twenty-two years has not impaired, the lapse of centuries could not impair, them. But the mode in which the right so asserted should be exercised, the precise provisions to be framed for the temporary substitution of the executive power — these were necessarily then, as they must be now, matters not of eternal and invariable principle, but of prudence and expediency. In regard to these, therefore, the opinion of any individual, however great and wise and venerable, can be taken only with reference to the circumstances of the time in which he has to act, and are not to be applied without change or modification to other times and circumstances." **

* This is one of the portions from my original sketch, which it would appear that Mr. Bell consulted. See Appendix.
** Speech on Regency Question, Dec. 31, 1810.

II.

Thus all that partisanship could demand in favour of an abstract principle, was religiously accorded to the *manes* of the defunct statesman; and a difference as wide as the living Prince of Wales could desire, established between the theory that no one any longer disputed, and the policy which was the present subject of contention. Here Mr. Canning acted with tact and foresight if he merely acted as a political schemer. The Royal personage on whom power was about to devolve had always expressed the strongest dislike, not to say disgust, at any abridgment of the Regal authority. He was likely to form a new Administration. The Whigs, it is true, were then considered the probable successors to power; but the Whigs would want assistance; and subsequent events showed that a general feeling had begun to prevail in favour of some new combination of men less exclusive than could be found in the ranks of either of the extreme and opposing parties. But it is fair to add that the course which Mr. Canning might have taken for his private interest, he had every motive to take for the public welfare.

Beyond the personal argument of the sick King's convenience, an argument which should hardly guide the policy or affect the destinies of a mighty kingdom, Mr. Perceval had not, for the restrictions he proposed, one reasonable pretext. It might, indeed, be agreeable to George III., if he recovered from his sad condition, to find things and persons as he had left them; and to recognise that all the functions of Government had been palsied since the suspension of his own power

But if ever the hands of a sovereign required to be strongly armed, it was most assuredly in those times. They were no times of ease or peace in which a civilized people may be said to govern themselves; neither were we merely at war. The war we were waging was of life or death; the enemy with whom we were contending concentrated in his own mind, and wielded with his own hand, all the force of Europe. This was not a moment for enfeebling the Government that had to contend against him. The power given to the King or Regent in our country is not, let it be remembered, an individual and irresponsible power. It is a National power devolving on responsible Ministers, who have to account to the Nation for the use they make of it.

"What," said Mr. Canning (having assumed and asserted the right of the two Houses of Parliament to supply the incapacity of the Sovereign), "what is the nature of the business which through incapacity stands still, and which we are to find the means of carrying on? It is the business of a mighty state. It consists in the exercise of functions as large as the mind can conceive — in the regulation and direction of the affairs of a great, a free, and a powerful people: in the care of their internal security and external interests; in the conduct of foreign negotiations; in the decision of the vital questions of peace and war; and in the administration of the Government throughout all the parts, provinces, and dependencies of an empire extending itself into every quarter of the globe. This is the awful office of a king; the temporary execution of which we are now about to devolve upon the Regent. What is it, considering the irresponsibility of the Sovereign as an essential part of the Constitution, —

what is it that affords a security to the people for the faithful exercise of all these important functions? The responsibility of Ministers. What are the means by which these functions operate? They are those which, according to the inherent imperfection of human nature, have at all times been the only motives to human actions, the only control upon them of certain and permanent operation, viz. the punishment of evil, and the reward of merit. Such, then, being the functions of monarchical government, and such being the means of rendering them efficient to the purposes of good government, are we to be told that in providing for its delegation, while it is not possible to curtail those powers which are in their nature harsh and unpopular, it is necessary to abridge those milder, more amiable and endearing prerogatives which bear an aspect of grace and favour towards the subject?"

III.

There was no answer to Mr. Canning, but in the fact that Mr. Perceval thought the King's illness transitory — the Regent's disposition unfavourable to him. In the one case he was securing a personal reward; in the other he was limiting a party mischief. In vain was it urged, "If the powers of a monarch are not necessary now, they are never necessary. In consulting the possible feelings of the sick King, you are injuring the certain interests of kingly authority."

The passions or interests of a faction will ever ride high over its principles; and for a second time within half a century the theory of monarchy received

the greatest practical insult from a high Tory minister.
That the House of Commons thought a new era at
hand was seen by its divisions. On the motion of
Mr. Lamb (afterwards Lord Melbourne) against the
"Restrictions," the majority in favour of Government
was but 224 to 200.

A variety of circumstances, however, to which allusion will presently be made, prevented the general expectation from being realized. The Government remained, but it was not a Government that seemed likely
to be of long duration. On one important question Mr.
Canning almost immediately opposed it.

IV.

The report of a committee, distinguished for its
ability, had attributed the depreciation in the value of
bank-notes to their excessive issue, and recommended
a return, within two years, to cash payments. Mr.
Canning had belonged to this committee, and had
given the subject, however foreign to his ordinary
habits, much attention. The view which he took upon
the sixteen resolutions moved by Mr. Horner, May 8,
1811, was, perhaps, the best. To all those resolutions,
which went to fix as a principle that a real value in
metal should be the proper basis for a currency — a
general landmark, by which legislation should, as far
as it was practicable, be guided — he assented;
that particular resolution, which, under the critical circumstances of the country, went to fetter and prescribe
the moment at which this principle should be resumed,
he opposed.

Such opposition was unavailing; and History instructs us, by the resolution which Mr. Vansittart then proposed, that no absurdity is so glaring as to shock the eye of prejudiced credulity.

"May 13, 1811.

"Resolution III. — '*That it is the opinion of this committee* (a committee of the whole House) *that the promissory notes of the company* (the Bank) *have hitherto been, and are at this time, held in public estimation to be equivalent to the legal coin of the realm, and generally accepted as such.'*"

The Chancellor of the Exchequer thus called upon the House of Commons to assert, that the public esteemed a twenty shilling bank-note as much as twenty shillings; and it had just been necessary to frame a law to prevent persons giving more than £1 and 1 shilling for a guinea, and all the guineas had disappeared from England. It had just been found expedient to raise the value of crown-pieces from 5s. to 5s. 6d. (which was, in fact, to reduce £1 in paper to the value of 18s.), in order to prevent crown-pieces from disappearing also. Persons were in prison for buying guineas at a premium; whilst pamphlets and papers were universally and daily declaring that the notes of the company were not at that time held in public estimation to be equivalent to the legal coin of the realm.

"When Galileo," said Mr. Canning, "first promulgated the doctrine that the earth turned round the sun, and that the sun remained stationary in the centre of the universe, the holy father of the Inquisition took alarm at so daring an innovation, and forthwith declared the first of these propositions to be false and heretical,

14*

and the other to be erroneous in point of faith. The holy office pledged itself to believe that the earth was stationary and the sun moveable. But this pledge had little effect in changing the natural course of things: the sun and the earth continued, in spite of it, to preserve their accustomed relations to each other, just as the coin and the bank-note will, in spite of the right honourable gentleman's resolution."*

But if the opposition had the best of the debate, the minister triumphed in the division; nevertheless, so equivocal a success, whilst lowering the character of Parliament, did not heighten that of the Ministry.

Mr. Perceval, indeed, though endowed with the quick, sharp mind of a lawyer, and the small ready talent of a debater, was without any of those great qualities which enable statesmen to take great views. His very talents as an advocate were defects as a statesman. Lord Wellesley at last revolted at his supremacy, and, quitting the government, observed that "he might serve *with* Mr. Perceval, but could never serve *under* him again."

V.

About this time expired the period during which the Regency restrictions had been imposed; and not long after, the Premier (after being confirmed in office by new and unsuccessful attempts to remodel the Administration) was assassinated by a madman.

The Government, which with Mr. Perceval was weak, without Mr. Perceval seemed impossible; and all persons at the moment were favourable to such a fusion

* Report of Bullion Committee.

of parties as would allow of the formation of a Cabinet, powerful and efficient.

Lord Wellesley, a man who hardly filled the space in these times for which his great abilities qualified him (co-operating with Mr. Canning who was to be leader in the House of Commons), was selected as the statesman through whom such a Cabinet was to be formed. But Lord Liverpool, from personal reasons, at once declined all propositions from Lord Wellesley. Another negotiation was then opened, the basis proposed for a new ministry being that four persons should be returned to the Cabinet by Lord Wellesley and Mr. Canning; four (of whom Lord Erskine and Lord Moira were two) by the Prince Regent; and five by Lords Grey and Grenville, whilst the principles agreed to by all, were to be the vigorous prosecution of the war, and the immediate conciliation of the Catholics. The vigorous maintenance of the war and the conciliation of the Catholics were assented to; nor was it stated that the other conditions were inadmissible, though it was suggested that there would be a great inconvenience in making the Cabinet Council a debating society, and entering it with hostile and rival parties. Lord Wellesley returned to the Regent for further orders. But his Royal Highness deemed it expedient to consider that Lord Wellesley's attempt had been a failure, and the task which had been given to him was transferred to Lord Moira. This nobleman, vain, weak, and honest, undertook the commission, and a new treaty was commenced with Lords Grey and Grenville, whose conduct at this time, it must be added, seems at first sight unintelligible; for they were granted every power they could desire in political matters. But there were various personal and private reasons which rendered all arrangements difficult. In the first place, Lord Grey is said to have despised, and never to have trusted, the Prince, who, as he believed, was merely playing with the Whig party. In the next, Lord Grenville could not make up his mind to resign the auditorship of the exchequer, a certain salary for life, nor to accept a lower office than that of First Lord of the Treasury, while the union of the two offices, the one being a check upon the other, was too evident a job to escape observation; indeed, Mr. Whitbread had positively said that he could never support such a combination.

Thus, a variety of petty interests made any pretext sufficient to interfere with the completion of a scheme which every one was eager to counsel, no one ready to adopt. The most ungracious pretext, that of dictating the Regent's household, was chosen for a rupture; but it happened to chime in with the popular cry, which was loud against the influence of Hertford House; as may be seen by the speeches of the day, and particularly by a speech from Lord Donoughmore, in which he talks of the Marchioness of Hertford, to whose veteran seductions the Regent was then supposed to have fallen a victim, as "a matured enchantress" who had by "potent spells" destroyed all previous prepossessions, and taken complete possession of the Royal understanding.

VI.

There was as much bad taste as impolicy in these attacks; and the long-pending struggle terminated at last in favour of Lord Liverpool, who on June 8, 1812, declared himself Prime Minister. Why did Mr. Canning, who was solicited at the close of the session to join Lord Liverpool's Administration, decline to do so? Not because he was personally hostile to Lord Liverpool: he was warmly attached to that nobleman; not because the Administration was exclusive, and only admitted those who were hostile to the Catholic Question; for he subsequently says (May 18, 1819): "I speak with perfect confidence when I assert that those who gave their support to the present Ministry on its formation, did so on the understanding that every member of it entered into office with the *express stipulation* that he should maintain his own opinion in Parliament on the Catholic Question."

Mr. Stapleton says it was because his friends thought that to the Foreign Office, which he was offered, ought to have been added the lead in the House of Commons, which Lord Liverpool would not withdraw from Lord Castlereagh. But Mr. Canning eventually became a member of the Government whose fate he now declined to share, leaving to Lord Castlereagh the lead in the House of Commons. How, then, are we to account for this difference of conduct at two different epochs?

An explanation may thus be found: During the years 1810 and 1811, our continental policy had still remained unfortunate. True it was that, by the unexpected skill and unexampled energy of our new commander, we gained, during 1811, the possession of Portugal, driving from that country a general who had hitherto been equally conspicuous for his talents and his fortune. But the whole of the Spanish frontier, and the greatest part of Spain itself, was held by the French

armies; while the victory of Wagram, the revolution in
Sweden, the marriage of Napoleon, the birth of the
King of Rome, had greatly added to the weight and
apparent stability of the French empire.

Our differences with the United States had also continually increased; and in 1812, war, which had long
been impending, was declared and justified in an eloquent and able statement by Mr. Madison.

In the meantime Napoleon, surrounded by that
luminous mystery which gave a kind of magic to his
actions, was marching in all the pomp of anticipated
triumph against the remote and solitary state which
alone, on the humbled and subjugated continent, had
yet the means and the courage to dispute his edicts and
defy his power. Up to the 14th of September, when
he entered Moscow, his career was more marvellous,
his glory more dazzling than ever.

VII.

Such was the state of foreign affairs when Mr. Canning and his friends refused to connect themselves with
a feeble and self-mistrusting administration. But the
year following things were strangely altered. The
retreat from Russia had taken place; the battle of
Leipsic had been fought. Russians, Austrians, Saxons,
Swedes, Bavarians, Spaniards, Portuguese, the people
of those various nations, who had formerly to defend
their own territory, were now pouring into France.

   The first gleams of victory shone over the gloomy
struggle of twenty years. An accident yet unexplained
— the burning of a city on the farthest confines of the

civilized world — had changed the whole face of
European affairs. "The mighty deluge," to use Mr.
Canning's poetical language, "by which the Continent
had been so long overwhelmed, began to subside. The
limits of nations were again visible, and the spires and
turrets of ancient establishments began to re-appear from
beneath the subsiding wave."*

From this moment Mr. Canning began to show confidence in a ministry which he had hitherto more or
less despised. The desire of sustaining it in this crisis
of the terrible conflict in which we were engaged, had
no doubt some influence over his conduct; but I venture
to add that there are natures which, without being instigated by low and vulgar motives, have a propensity
to harmonize with success. Mr. Canning's nature was
of this description. It loved the light to shine on its
glittering surface; and he began to feel a sympathy for
the Government, bright with the rays of anticipated
fortune, which in darker moments he had shrunk from
with antipathy and mistrust.

VIII.

Napoleon fell shortly afterwards, and Mr. Huskisson,
the most celebrated of Mr. Canning's followers, was
gazetted as Commissioner of Woods and Forests; Mr.
Canning himself (who at the last general election had
been honoured by the unsolicited representation of
Liverpool) accepting an embassy to Lisbon. His acceptance of this office was one of the actions of his life for
which he was most attacked; it was considered a job;

* Speech on vote of thanks to the Marquis of Wellington, July 7, 1813.

CANNING,

for an able minister (Mr. Sydenham), on a moderate
salary, was recalled, in order to give the eminent orator,
whose support the Government wished to obtain, the
appointment of ambassador on a much larger salary:
and although, when Mr. Lambton (afterwards Lord
Durham) brought forward a motion on the subject, Mr.
Canning made a triumphant reply to the specific charges
brought against his nomination, and although he was
altogether above the accusation of accepting any post
for the mere sake of its emoluments, it was nevertheless
clear that it was because he was going to Lisbon for
the health of his son and that it was more agreeable
to him to go in an official position than as a simple
individual, that he had been employed, and his predecessor removed. It is needless to add he would have
acted more wisely had he not accepted a post in which
little credit was to be gained and much censure was to
be risked.

On his return from Portugal he entered the Cabinet
at the head of the Board of Control. .

During his absence many events had occurred to
characterize the Administration he joined. Peace finally
established on the prostrate armies of France, which at
Waterloo had made their last struggle, left the war
which we had pursued with so lavish an expenditure,
and so desperate a determination, to be estimated by
its results. Whatever the necessity of this war at its
commencement, the cause under which it had been continued for the last fourteen years was sacred.

A military chief at the head of a valorous soldiery,
had during this time trampled on the rights and feelings of almost every people in Europe. The long
established barriers of independent states had been

shifted or pulled down like hurdles, to make them fit
the increasing or diminishing drove of cattle which it
suited the caprices of the French ruler that they should
contain. The inhabitants of such states, treated little
better than mere cattle, had been seized, sold, bartered,
given away. It was no marvel, then, that the conquerors became in the end the conquered; for the
struggle was one which commenced by all the kings
marching against one people, and concluded by every
people marching against one warrior. They invoked
— these new assailants — what is best in philosophy,
morality, policy; they conquered, and what did philosophy, morality, policy gain? Were rights and natural
sympathies respected? Were old landmarks restored?

The peace alluded to was said to be a peace founded on justice, and justice never deserts the weak; yet
Genoa was gone; Venice was no more; Poland remained
partitioned; Saxony had been plundered by Prussia
with as unsparing a hand as that by which she herself
had been despoiled during the conquests of France.
Norway, by a treaty, which Mr. Canning had said, in
1813, when still unshackled by office, "filled him with
shame, regret, and indignation," was become the unwilling recompense to Sweden for the loss of a province
of which a mightier power had taken possession. A
struggle of the fiercest nature had been steadily maintained merely for the sake of restoring things to their
old condition; and no nation not pre-eminent in power
got back its own, except Spain, which recovered the
Inquisition.* Even Holland was not re-invested with
her ancient liberties, her old noble republican name.
Stripped of her glorious history, and weakened by the

* See *Appendix.*

addition of four millions of discontented subjects, the
statesmen of the day fancied her more august and more
secure.   The errors committed at this time were those
of a system; for there were two courses to pursue in
the re-settlement of Europe.   Had it appeared that, after
a conflict of nearly thirty years, during which violence
had held unlimited sway, everything which was dear
to the people it concerned, and which still stood forth
vivid in history, was endowed with a new reality; that
at the overthrow of wrongful power, the right of the
meanest was everywhere weighed, and the right of the
weakest everywhere established: had it appeared that
the mightiest captain of modern times had only been
vanquished by a principle — which, if the general interest could predominate, would regulate the destinies
of the world — then indeed a lesson, of which it is
impossible to calculate the effects, would have been
given to all future ambitious disturbers of mankind:
while the lovers of peace and virtue in every portion
of the globe, even in France, would have seen something holy in the triumph which had been gained, and
gathered round the cause of the allies.   But if this
was one policy, another remained, and that was adopted.

IX.

As Bonaparte had cut up and parcelled out nations
for the purpose of enlarging the boundaries and strength-
ening the dominions of France, so the conquerors of
Bonaparte spoiled and partitioned with equal zeal, in
order to control the boundaries and restrain the dominion
of the warlike people they had defeated.   The limits

imposed by right, justice, antiquity, custom, were all disregarded, and an attempt, by preference, made to throw up against all future schemes of conquest the patchwork barrier of ill-united and discordant populations.

Such had been the termination of affairs in Europe; but our contest with America was also over. We had made a treaty with that Power — a treaty so contrived that it did not settle a single one of those questions for which we had engaged in war. Nor were the circumstances under which this singular arrangement was completed such as compelled us to accede to it. The whole force of the British empire was disengaged; we could no longer say that our fleets were not invincible in one quarter of the world because their strength was exerted in another; whilst, if we meant to keep the dominion of the seas — more important to us than the whole of that continent we had been subsidizing and contending upon — there was every peril to apprehend from leaving unchecked the spirit of a rising rival, who had lately fought and frequently vanquished us on our own element, and who during a long peace would have the opportunity to mature that strength of which she was already conscious and proud. In short, the peace of Europe affected our character for morality, that of America weakened the belief in our power.

Mr. Canning would hardly have joined an Administration which had so mismanaged our foreign affairs, if the glory of our arms had not gilded in some degree the faults of our diplomacy. But the part which that diplomacy had played on the Continent was not without its effect upon things at home. We had become each year more and more alienated from our military allies, who having triumphed by the enthusiasm of their people, seemed disposed to govern by the bayonets of their troops. The Holy Alliance — that singular compact, invented partly by the superstition, partly by the policy of the Emperor Alexander — an alliance by which three sovereigns, at the head of conquering armies, swore in very singular language to govern according to the doctrines of Christian charity, swearing also (which was more important) to lend each other assistance on all occasions, and in all places — this alliance, which no one could clearly understand, and which our Government refused to join, excited all the suspicion and all the apprehension which mystery never fails to produce, and made Englishmen, while they were rejoicing at having subdued an overgrown and despotic tyranny in one quarter of the world, doubt whether they might not have created as dangerous a one in another.

X

Nor was this all. They who begin to be dissatisfied with the fruits of victory, soon grow more and more dissatisfied with what victory has cost. Moreover, this period, from a variety of circumstances, some of them inseparable from the sudden transition from active war to profound peace, was one of great uncertainty and distress; whilst the public mind, no longer excited by military conflict, was the more disposed to political agitation. A demand for diminished imposts, and a demand for political reform, are always to be expected at such moments. Our form of government

led more naturally to these demands, for the theory of
the constitution was at variance with its practice; the
one saying that the English nation should be taxed by
the representatives it elected, the other proving that it
was in many instances taxed by persons chosen by a
powerful patron and not by the people of England.
The evils complained of were exaggerated; there were
exaggerations also as to the remedies for which the
most the clamorous called. But the thoughts of the
nation were directed to economy as a relief from taxation, and to parliamentary reform as a means of economy.
Public meetings in favour of parliamentary reform were
held; resolutions in favour of parliamentary reform were
passed; petitions praying for it were presented; the
energies of a free people, who thought themselves
wronged, were aroused: great excitement prevailed.

XI.

The vessel of the state in these sudden squalls requires that those at the helm should govern it with a
calm heart and a steady hand. Anger and fear are
equally to be avoided, for they lead equally to violent
measures, and the excitement of one party only feeds
the excitement of the other.

Lord Castlereagh, the leading spirit at this time in
the Cabinet, vapid and incorrect as an orator, ineffi-
cient as an administrator, was still, as I have elsewhere said, not without qualities as a statesman — for
he was cool and he was courageous; and, therefore, if
we now see him acting as if under the influence of the
most slavish apprehension, we must look for some rea-

sonable motive for his adopting in appearance a
character so very different from that which he possessed in reality.

Now, the fact is, that he had but two things to do
— to satisfy the discontented as aggrieved, or to rally
the majority of the country against them as disaffected.
The first policy would not keep his party in power;
the second, therefore, was the one he preferred. The
fears of the timid were to be excited; the passions of
the haughty were to be aroused; the designs of the
malcontents were to be darkened, their strength increased — in short, to save the Ministry, it was essential
that the State should be declared in danger. This is
an old course; it has been tried often: it was tried now.

Thus Government opened the Session of 1817 with
a "green bag." This bag, a true Pandora's box, contained threats of every mischief — assassination, incendiarism, insurrection, in their most formidable and
infuriated shapes. One conspiracy, indeed, was a model
that deserves to be set apart for the use of future con-
spirators or — statesmen. It comprehended the storm-
ing of the Bank and the Tower, the firing the different
barracks, the overthrow of everybody and everything,
even the great and massive bridges which cross the
Thames, and which were to be blown up as a matter
of course; but the traitors were pious and brave men,
relying almost wholly on Providence and their courage,
so that only two hundred and fifty pikes and some
powder in an old stocking had been provided to secure
the success of their undertaking.

XII.

Many schemes equally plausible were attributed to, and perhaps entertained by, a few unhappy men in the manufacturing districts; while the well-known doctrines of an enthusiast named Spence* — doctrines which inculcate the necessity of property being held in common, and which under different names have been continually put forward at every period of the world — found amongst the poor and starving, as they will ever find in times of distress and difficulty, a ready reception. "These doctrines," said Lord Castlereagh, "contain in themselves a principle of contradiction;" but he was not willing to trust to this principle alone!

A variety of laws were passed, tending to limit the right of discussion: men were forbidden to co-operate or correspond for the purpose of amending the existing constitution. Public meetings were placed at the disposal of a magistrate, who could refuse or disperse them as he thought proper. Finally, the "Habeas Corpus" Act was suspended.

Nothing could be more wanton or absurd than this last outrage on public freedom. The Ministers who were calling upon the country to defend our institutions, were for sweeping away their very foundations. In vain did Lord Grey, with even more than his usual eloquence, exclaim, "We are warned not to let any anxiety for the security of liberty lead to a compromise of the security of the State; for my part, I cannot separate these two things; the safety of the State can

---

* Spence preached about the period of the French Revolution, and his doctrines were revived now by his follower, Evans.

only be found in the protection of the liberties of the people."

Having entered upon a career of terror, a new violence is daily necessary in order to guard against the consequences of the last; nor was the addition of £3,000,000 of taxes, imposed at the close of 1819, well adapted to soothe popular irritation. In the meantime the meeting at Manchester, foolishly got up, and foolishly and barbarously put down, aroused a cry which only the utmost severity could hope to quell. Such severity was adopted in the Acts which prevented public and parish meetings; which punished offences of the press with transportation; which exposed the houses of peaceable inhabitants to midnight search, and deprived an Englishman of what was once considered his birthright — the right of keeping arms for his own defence. At the same time the bulk of the nation was declared to be sound and loyal, the country prosperous; and as a note which may perhaps be considered somewhat explanatory of these different declarations, came a demand for 10,000 additional troops. It was of no use to argue that the nation was quiet, and resolved only on constitutional means of redress. "Yes, sir," said the figurative seconder of the Address (1819), "yes, sir, there has undoubtedly been an appearance of tranquillity, but it *is the tranquillity of a lion waiting for his prey.* There has been the apparent absence of danger, but it is that of a fire half-smothered by the weight of its own combustible materials." "The meeting at Manchester," argued Lord Lansdowne (Nov. 30, 1819), "if it had not been disturbed by the magistrates, would have gone off quietly." "Perhaps," replied an orator who defended the Government, "that might have been the case; but why? in the contemplation of things to come, the peaceable and quiet demeanour of the disaffected, instead of lessening the danger, ought to aggravate the alarm — *ipsa silentia terrent.*"

XIII.

So because people assembled at a meeting which was likely to disperse peaceably might at some future time (and this was conjecture) act less peaceably, they were to be charged and sabred; while their constitutional conduct neither at this nor at any other period could be of the least avail; heat of language was not even necessary to procure them the treatment of rebels; for if men met and were *silent*, if they met and never uttered a word, their very silence, under the classical authority 'of three Latin words, was to be considered full of awful treason. Jury after jury denounced the conduct of the Government by returning verdicts which were accusations against it. Still the same system was persevered in. Ministers went through the country with a drag net, hauling up — not one or two influential persons (such, indeed, they could not find) — but whole classes of men. Spies also, as it appeared from the different trials, acted as incendiaries, contributing in no small degree to the marvellous plots that they discovered. In one instance, a fellow of the name of Oliver had gone about to all whom he imagined ill disposed, presenting Sir Francis Burdett's compliments; a circumstance the more remarkable, since the only decent colour ever attempted to be given to these notions of insurrection was, that the names of respectable

15*

persons had been used in connection with them. In another case a government creature, by the name of Edwards, actually advanced money to a gentleman who may be considered the arch-traitor of the epoch, since he was the author of that famous conspiracy which included cutting off all the ministers' heads.

This conspiracy — of which Mr. Thistlewood, supported by the aforesaid Mr. Edwards, Mr. Davidson, a man of colour, and Messrs. Tidd and Brunt, two shoemakers, were the leaders — closed the series of those formidable plots for putting an end to King, Lords, and Commons, which for three years alarmed the country; the Ministers affecting to consider the folly of these men whom they delivered to the executioner, as a proof of the wisdom of that policy which gave employment to the Hangman.

Another circumstance is to be remarked in reviewing these times, and attempting to portray their spirit. The Government had not only been tyrannical at home, it had afforded all the assistance in its power to foreign tyrants. First was passed the Alien Bill; a measure which might have been defended in 1793, when France was sending out her revolutionary apostles; which might, with a certain plausibility, have been asked for in 1814, when, if the war were concluded, peace could hardly be considered as established; but which in 1816 could have no other pretext than that of enabling the minister of the day to refuse a refuge to any unhappy exile from the despotism of the Continent.

Shortly afterwards (1819) came the Foreign Enlistment Bill. That which Queen Elizabeth refused to Spain in the height of her power, was conceded to Spain, now fallen into the lowest state of moral as well

as political degradation. It was true that during the
Administration of Sir Robert Walpole, and under the
natural fears of Jacobite armies, formed on foreign
shores, laws had been passed prohibiting British subjects, except upon special permission, from engaging in
foreign service; and the pretext now put forward was
insomuch plausible, that it pretended to place service
in the armies of recognised and unrecognised states on
the same footing — no law existing in respect to the
last. But the law in existence had not been enforced.
Spain, which had been hasty in recognising the independence of the United States, could not ask us to defeat rebellion in her own colonies. Those colonies had,
in fact, been first instigated by us to revolt. The regulation, professing to be impartial, would only operate
in reality against one of the parties; with that party
all our commercial interests were connected. Besides,
this regulation not only regarded Spain and her revolted
subjects, it was in fact an edict against the expression
of British opinion in favour of revolt, however provoked
in any country.

XIV.

It is impossible to look back to these years, and to
consider the conduct of Mr. Canning without deep regret. The most eloquent and plausible defences of the
un-English policy which prevailed were made by him.
In his speech in favour of the Seditious Meetings Bill
(Feb. 24, 1817), may be seen wit supplying the place
of argument; argument rendered attractive by the graces
of rhetoric, and forcible by the appearance of passion.
He had now, indeed, nearly attained the perfection of

his own style, a style which, as it has been said, united
the three excellences of rapidity, polish, and ornament;
and it was the first of these qualities, let it be repeated,
which, though perhaps the least perceivable of his
merits, was the greatest.

"What is the nature of this danger? Why, sir, the
danger to be apprehended is not to be defined in one
word. It is rebellion; it is treason, but not treason
merely; it is confiscation, but not confiscation within
such bounds as have usually been applied to the
changes of dynasties, or the revolution of states; it is
an aggregate of all these evils; it is that dreadful
variety of sorrow and suffering which must invariably
follow the extinction of loyalty, morality, and religion;
the subversion, not only of the constitution of England,
but of the whole frame of society. Such is the nature
and extent of the danger which would attend the success of the projects developed in the report of the committee. But these projects would never have been of
importance, it is affirmed, had they not been brought
into notice by persecution. Persecution! Does this
character belong to the proceedings instituted against
those who set out on their career in opposition to all
law; and who, in their secret cabals, and midnight
counsels, and mid-day harangues, have been voting for
destruction every individual, and every class of individuals, which may stand in their way? But the schemes
of these persons are visionary. I admit it. They have
been laid by these twenty years without being found
to produce mischief. Be it so. Such doctrines when
dormant may be harmless enough, and their intrinsic
absurdity may make it appear incredible that they
should ever be called up into action. But when the

incredible resurrection actually takes place, when the votaries of these doctrines actually go forth armed to exert physical strength in furtherance of them, then it is that I think it time to be on my guard — not against the accomplishment of such plans (that is, I am willing to believe, impracticable), but against the mischief which must attend the attempt to accomplish them by force."

Throughout the whole of this passage it can hardly be said that there is a full stop. However studiously framed, not a period lingers; a rush of sentences gives the audience no time to pause. Abruptly framed, rapidly delivered, the phrases which may have been for hours premeditated in the Cabinet, could not, in the moment of delivery, have the least appearance of art. The oratory of Mr. Canning was also remarkable for a kind of figurative way of stating common-places, which good taste may not approve, but which, nevertheless, is well calculated to strike and inflame a popular assembly.

"The honourable gentleman," Mr. Canning says of Mr. Calcraft (March 14, 1817), "attempts to ridicule these proceedings. He is in truth rather hard to be satisfied on the score of rebellion; to him it is not sufficient that the town had been summoned [N.B. it had been summoned by *one* man], it ought to have been taken; the metropolis should not merely have been attacked, but in flames. He is so difficult in regard to proof that he would continue to doubt until all the mischief was not only certain but irreparable. For my part, however, I am satisfied when I hear the trumpet of rebellion sounded; I do not think it necessary to wait the actual onset before I put myself on my guard.

I am content to take my precautions when I see the
torch of the incendiary lighted, without waiting till the
Bank and the Mansion House are blazing to the sky."

XV.

But if there was much of eloquence, there was more
of sophistry, in these pointed and painted harangues.
The designs on foot were represented as so formidable
that they required the utmost rigour to suppress them;
and yet they were the designs of a few, of a very few,
against whom millions were arrayed. These few were
to be struck down at all hazards and by all means, in
order that the millions might be in security. The
anti-revolutionary statesman was simply borrowing from
the revolutionary apostle. "What are a few aristo-
crats," would Danton say, "to the safety of a nation?
Strike! strike! It is only terror that can save the Republic!" For such principles, destructive of all liberty,
peace, and order, every just man must entertain the
deepest horror; and the dark shadow of hateful recollections still hangs over the party that sanctioned,
and over the career of the statesman who defended the
excesses of those gloomy days.

I do not, however, think that Mr. Canning acted
on the cool systematic calculation by which I do think
Lord Castlereagh might have been guided. Looking
at all affairs with the excitable disposition of the poet
and the orator, and having his attention more called
by his office to the affairs of India than to those at
home, it is not improbable that he allowed himself to
be carried into the belief of dangers which the Govern-

ment he belonged to had in a certain degree created, and in an enormous degree exaggerated; whilst the manner in which even calm and sensible men had their heads confused and their judgment biassed by the alarming reports put in circulation, and the constant arrests that were taking place, reacted upon the Government itself, and made it fancy that the fictions reflected from its fears, were truths established by facts. At all events, whatever were the real opinions and convictions of Mr. Canning, as he was the most eloquent supporter of the policy in vogue, he gathered round himself the greatest portion of the unpopularity that attended it. Nor, though he assumed the air of defying this unpopularity, was he pleased with it.

XVI.

The very bitterness, indeed, which he manifested towards his opponents at this time, shows that he was ill at ease with himself. Linked with a set of men whom in general he despised, and by whom he was in a certain degree mistrusted, and accused, as he well knew, of accepting this alliance merely for the love of "office," which the vulgar made to signify the mere "emoluments of place;" — possessing a mind, which, elevated by education, was inclined to liberality; — careless of the praise of the fanatics of his own party, and careless also of the applause of those timorous spirits amongst the nation with whom he could feel no sympathy; — knowing he was detested by the great masses of the people, whose applause he could not with his temperament refrain from coveting; — knowing

also that though supported by the love and admiration
of a few able friends, he was confided in by no great
political party, and that even if his duties imposed on
him the necessity of struggling against existing difficulties, those difficulties might have been avoided or
palliated by a more conciliatory and prudent policy;
writhing under all these circumstances, and agitated by
all these feelings, — this able, ambitious, and excitable
man may now be seen listening with ears almost greedy
of a quarrel, for reproaches he could retort, and insults he could avenge.   Mr. Hume, not very cautious
in these matters, was called to account: Sir Francis
Burdett, who had spoken disrespectfully, was made to
explain; while to the author of an anonymous libel, in
which the style and invectives of "Junius" were copied
with doubtful success, was sent a note, eminently
characteristic of the galled feelings and gallant spirit
of the writer:

"Sir,
"I received early in the last week the copy of
your pamphlet, which you, I take for granted, had the
attention to have forwarded to me.   Soon after I was
informed, on the authority of your publisher, that you
have withdrawn the whole impression from him, with
the view (as was supposed) of suppressing the publication. I since learn, however, that the pamphlet, though
not sold, is circulated under blank covers.   I learn
this from (among others) the gentleman to whom the
pamphlet is industriously attributed, but who has
voluntarily and absolutely denied to me that he has
any knowledge of it or its author.
"'To you, sir, whoever you may be, I address my-

self thus directly for the purpose of expressing my opinion that *you are a liar and a slanderer, and want courage only to be an assassin.* I have only to add that no man knows of my writing to you, and that I shall maintain the same reserve as long as I have an expectation of hearing from you in your own name." To this letter there was no reply.

XVII.

During the eventful years over which this narrative has been rapidly gliding, the Heiress to the crown, who had already possessed herself of the affections of the British people, had expired (it was in Nov. 1817); and in 1820, as the Ministers, fatigued by its laborious efforts to excite alarm, began to allow the nation to recover its tranquillity, George III. (two years after his young and blooming grandchild) died also. The new King's hatred, and Queen Caroline's temper, each rendering a more decent and moderate course impossible, occasioned the unhappy trial which scandalized Europe.

Nor was the question at issue merely a question involving the Queen's innocence or guilt. The people, comparatively calm, as well on account of the recent improvement in trade, as in consequence of the cessation of that system of conspiracy-making or finding, which had so long kept them in a state of harassed irritation, were still for the main part thoroughly disgusted with the exhibition of fear, feebleness, and violence which, under the name of Lord Liverpool, and through the influence of Lord Castlereagh, had for the last three years been displayed. They detested the

Ministers of the Crown, and they were alienated from
the Crown itself, which had been perpetually arrayed
against them in prosecutions and almost as often stigmatised by defeat.

It was thus that Queen Caroline appeared as a new
victim — as another person to be illegally assailed by
the forms of law, and unjustly dealt with in the name
of justice. Besides, she was a woman, and the daughter
of a Royal house, and the mother of that ill-fated prin-
cess, whose early death the nation still deeply mourned.
The people, then, took up her cause as their own, and
rallied at once round a new banner against their old
enemies.

On the other hand, the Government, urged by the
wounded pride and uncontrollable anger of the Sovereign, consented to bring the unfortunate lady he denounced before a public tribunal, and were thus committed to a desperate career, of which it was impossible
to predict the result.

Mr. Canning had long been the unhappy Queen's
intimate friend; but in adopting her cause, he must, as
we have been showing, have adopted her party — the
party of discontent, the party of reform — a party
against which he had, during the last few years, been
fiercely struggling. Here, as far as the public can
judge from the information before it, lies the only excuse or explanation of his conduct; for it was hardly
sufficient to retire (as he did) from any share in the
proceedings against a friend and a woman, in whose
innocence he said that he believed, when her honour
and life were assailed by the most powerful adversaries,
and on charges of the most degrading character.

He refused, it is true, to be her active accuser; but

neither was he her active defender. He remained silent at home or stayed abroad during the time of the prosecution, and resigned office when, that prosecution being dropped, the Cabinet had to justify its proceedings.

The following letter to a constituent contains the account he thought it necessary to give of his conduct:

"Tuddenham, Norfolk, Dec. 22, 1820.

"MY DEAR SIR,

"I left town on Wednesday, a few minutes after I had written to you, not thinking I should be quite so soon set at liberty to make you the communication promised in my letter of that morning. I had hitherto forborne to make the communication, in order that I might not in any way embarras others by a premature disclosure; and I sincerely expected in return due notice of the time when it might suit them that the disclosure should be made. I have no doubt that the omission of such notice has been a mere oversight. I regret it only as it has prevented me from anticipating with you, and the rest of my friends at Liverpool, the announcement in a newspaper of an event in which I know your kind partiality will induce you to feel a lively interest. The facts stated in the *Courier* of Wednesday evening, are stated in substance correctly. I have resigned my office. My motives for separating myself from the Government (however reluctantly at a conjuncture like the present) is to be found solely in the proceedings and pending discussions respecting the Queen. There is (as the *Courier* justly assumes) but this one point of difference between my colleagues and myself. Those who may have done me the honour to observe my conduct in this unhappy affair from the beginning, will recollect that on the first occasion on which it was brought forward in the House of Commons, I declared my determination to take as little part as possible in any subsequent stage of the proceedings. The declaration was made advisedly. It was made, not only after full communication with my colleagues, but as an alternative suggested on their part for my then retirement from the Administration. So long as there was a hope of amicable adjustment, my continuance in the Administration might possibly be advantageous; that hope was finally extinguished by the failure of Mr. Wilberforce's address. On the same day on which the Queen's answer to that address was received by the House of Commons, I asked an audience of the King, and at that audience (which I obtained the following day) after respectfully repeating to his Majesty the declaration which I had made a fortnight before in the House of Commons, and stating the impossibility of my departing from it, I felt it my duty humbly to lay at his Majesty's feet the tender of my resignation. The King, with a generosity which I can never sufficiently acknowledge, commanded me to remain in his service, abstaining as completely as I might think fit from any share in the proceedings respecting the Queen, and gave me full authority to plead his Majesty's express command for so continuing in office. No occasion subsequently occurred in Parliament (at least no adequate occasion) for availing myself of the use of this authority, and I should have thought myself inexcusable in seeking an occasion for the purpose; but from the moment of my receiving his Majesty's gracious commands, I abstained entirely from all interference on the subject of the Queen's affairs. I did not attend any meetings of the Cabinet upon that subject; I had no share whatever in preparing or approving the Bill of Pains and Penalties. I was (as you know) absent from England during the whole progress of the bill, and returned only after it had been withdrawn.

"The new state in which I found the proceedings upon my return to England, required the most serious consideration; it was one to which I could not conceive the King's command in June to be applicable. For a minister to absent himself altogether from the expected discussions in the House of Commons, intermixed as they were likely to be with the general business of the session, appeared to me to be quite impossible. To be present as a minister, taking no part in these discussions, could only be productive of embarrassment to myself, and of perplexity to my colleagues; to take any part in them was now, as always, out of the question.

"From these difficulties I saw no remedy except in the humble but earnest renewal to my Sovereign of the tender of my resignation, which has been as graciously accepted, as it was in the former instance indulgently declined.

"If some weeks have elapsed since my return to England, before I could arrive at this practical result, the interval has been chiefly employed in reconciling, or endeavouring to reconcile, my colleagues to a step taken by me in a spirit of the most perfect amity, and tending (in my judgment) as much to their relief as to my own.

"It remains for me only to add that having purchased, by the surrender of my office, the liberty of continuing to act in consistency with my original declaration, it is now my intention (but an intention perfectly gratuitous, and one which I hold myself completely free to vary, if I shall at any time see occasion for so doing) to be absent from England again until the agitation of this calamitous affair shall be at an end.

"I am, Sir, &c.,

"George Canning."

Thus, during the years 1821-22 Mr. Canning took little part in the business of the House of Commons, residing occasionally near Bordeaux or in Paris.

He came to England, however, to speak on Mr. Plunkett's motion for a committee to consider the Catholic claims (February 28, 1821), and in 1822 he also made two memorable speeches — one on Lord John Russell's motion for Parliamentary Reform, and another in support of his own proposition to admit Catholic peers into the House of Lords.

These last speeches were made in the expectancy of his speedy departure from England; the Directors of the East India Company, in testimony of the zeal and intelligence with which he had discharged his duties as President of the Board of Control, having selected him as Governor-General of India, a situation which he had accepted.

CANNING,

THE BRILLIANT MAN.

PART III.

Lord Castlereagh's death. — Mr. Canning's appointment. — State of affairs. — Opposition he encountered. — Policy as to Spain and South America. — Commencing popularity in the country, and in the House of Commons. — Affairs of Portugal and Brazil. — Recognition of Brazilian empire. — Constitution taken by Sir Charles Stuart to Portugal. — Defence of Portugal against Spanish treachery and aggression. — Review of policy pursued thus far as a whole.

PART III.

I.

AT this critical moment Lord Castlereagh, who had now the title of Lord Londonderry, worn out by a long continued series of struggles with the popular passions, placed in a false position by the manner in which the great military powers had at Troppau and Laybach announced principles which no English statesman could ever sanction, — too high-spirited to endure defeat, and without the ability requisite for forming and carrying on any policy that might be triumphant, — irritated, over worked, and about to depart for Verona with the intention of remonstrating against acts which he had been unable to prevent, — having lost all that calm and firmness with which his proud but cheerful nature was generally armed, — and overpowered at last by an infamous conspiracy to extort money, with the threat that he should otherwise be charged with a disgraceful and dishonouring offence — put an end to his existence.

Fate looked darkly on the Tory party. Ever since 1817 it had excited one half of the community by fear, as a means of governing the other half by force. But the machinery of this system was now pretty well used up. In the meantime the result of Queen Caroline's trial was a staggering blow to those who had

16*

been its advisers; and though this unhappy and foolish lady did all she could to destroy the prestige which had once surrounded her, and though a timely end at last rescued her from contempt, even her death gave the authorities a new opportunity of injuring themselves by an idle and offensive conflict with her hearse.

In the meantime the affairs in the Peninsula were becoming more and more obscured, whilst through the clouds which seemed everywhere gathering, some thought they could perceive the fatal hour in which a terrible despotism or an ignorant and equally terrible democracy were to dispute for the mastery of the world. In France the Bourbons trembled on their throne, and petty cabals and paltry conflicts amongst themselves rendered their rule at once violent, feeble, and uncertain. The volcanic soil of Italy was covered with ashes from a recent conflagration — some embers might yet be seen alive. Over the whole of Germany reigned a dreamy discontent which any accident might convert into a practical revolution.

II.

What part could the baffled and unpopular Ministers of England take amidst such a state of things as this? To the advocacy of democratic principles they were of course opposed. With the advocates of absolute power they dared not, and perhaps did not feel disposed to, side. Neutrality was their natural wish, since to be neutral required no effort and demanded no declaration of opinion. But it is only the strong

who can be really neutral; and the Government of the
day was too conscious of weakness to hold with confidence the position which, if powerful, it could have
preserved with dignity. Such being the miserable
condition of the British cabinet when Lord Londoñ-
derry was alive, it became yet more contemptible on
losing that statesman's energy and resolution. Mr.
Canning was its evident resource. Yet the wish to
obtain Mr. Canning's services was by no means general
amongst those in power, for the ministry was divided
into two sections: one, hostile to Catholic Emancipation, to any change in, and almost any modification
of, our long-standing system of high duties. and commercial protection, and also to all those efforts in
favour of constitutional liberty which had lately agitated the Continent; another which, though opposed
to any constitutional change that tended to increase
the democratic element in our institutions, was still
favourable to Catholic Emancipation as a means of
conciliating the large majority of the Irish people —
to the development of the principles of Free Trade, as
a means of augmenting our national wealth — and
also to the spread of our political opinions, under the
idea that we should be thus extending our commercial,
moral, and political power.

These two parties, forced to combine under the
common battle-cry of "no parliamentary reform," —
a reform which both opposed (in order to get a parliamentary majority for their united force) — were
nevertheless jealous of each other, and in constant
struggle for the predominant influence. Mr. Canning
out of office, and away in India, there could be no
doubt that the more Conservative section of the Ad-

ministration would occupy the highest ground; Mr. Canning not going to India, and coming into office, the more liberal party, of which he was universally considered the chief, might overtop its rival. Lord Liverpool, however, was himself in a peculiar position. He agreed with Mr. Canning's opponents as to the Catholic emancipation question, but with Mr. Canning on all other questions. His policy, therefore, was to rule a pretty equally balanced cabinet, and not to have one half too strong for the other. With this object he had lately admitted two or three followers of Lord Grenville, who though himself retired from affairs, had still a party favourable to Catholic concessions, and hostile to constitutional innovations. For the same reason he now insisted on the necessity of offering the Secretaryship of Foreign Affairs to Mr. Canning, and impressed his opinions on this subject so strongly on the Duke of Wellington, that the Duke undertook to see his Majesty, and overcome the objections which (having never forgiven the Minister who had deserted him, as he said, at the Queen's trial) he was certain to make to Mr. Canning's appointment. Two or three phrases of the conversation that took place on this occasion have been repeated to me by one who was at that time the confidant of both the King and the Duke.

"Good God! Arthur, you don't mean to propose that fellow to me as Secretary for Foreign Affairs; it is impossible. I said, on my honour as a gentleman, he should never be one of my ministers again. You hear, Arthur, on my honour as a gentleman. I am sure you will agree with me: I can't do what I said on my honour as a gentleman I would not do."

"Pardon me, sir, I don't agree with you at all; your Majesty is not a gentleman."

The King started.

"Your Majesty, I say," continued the imperturbable soldier, "is not a gentleman, but the Sovereign of England, with duties to your people far above any to yourself; and these duties render it imperative that you should at this time employ the abilities of Mr. Canning."

"Well!" drawing a long breath, "if I must, I must," was finally the King's reply.

III.

Mr. Canning thus entered the Cabinet; and under ordinary circumstances his doing so at such a crisis would have been hailed with general satisfaction. It so happened, however, that some time had elapsed between the death of Lord Castlereagh and any offer to his successor; and during this interval, Mr. Canning, then on the verge of departure for the East, made a speech at Liverpool, which from its remarkable moderation, was considered by many as the manifestation of a wish to purchase place by a sacrifice of opinion. The words most objected to were these:

"Gentlemen, if I were remaining in this country, and continuing to take my part in Parliament, I should continue, in respect to the Catholic Question, to walk in the same direction that I have hitherto done. But I think (and as I may not elsewhere have an opportunity of expressing this opinion, I am desirous of expressing it here), I think that after the experience of a fruitless struggle for more than ten years, I should, as an

individual (speaking for none but myself, and not knowing whether I carry any other person's opinion with me)
be induced henceforth, or perhaps after one more
general trial, to seek upon that question a *liberal compromise.*" Thus, when, instead of going to India, the
Governor-General, already named, came into office at
home, it was said at once that he had done so on a
compromise.

The accusation was false, but it was coloured by a
certain plausibility of appearance, and those amongst
the Opposition who believed it were the more furious,
since they thought that if the new Minister had refused to join the administration, they themselves must
ere long have been called to power.

The speeches made against him were consequently
of the bitterest kind. One, by Lord Folkestone, on a
motion for the repeal of the Foreign Enlistment Bill,
delivered with extraordinary vehemence, accused Mr.
Canning of truckling to France.

"Sir," said Mr. Canning, in reply, "I will not
follow the noble lord through a speech of which it
would be impossible to convey the impression by a
mere repetition of language. The Lacedæmonians, with
the desire of deterring their children from the vice of
intoxication, used occasionally to expose their slaves in
a state of disgusting inebriety. But, sir, there is a
moral as well as a physical intoxication; and never
before did I behold so complete a personification of the
character which I have somewhere seen described as
*exhibiting the contortions of the sibyl without her inspira-
tion.* I will not on this occasion reply to the noble
lord's speech, being of opinion that this is not a fit
opportunity for entering into the discussion it would

provoke; but let it not be supposed that I shrink from the noble lord; for he may believe me when I say that however I may have truckled to France, I will never truckle to him."

IV.

This speech was delivered April 16, 1823. On the 17th another important discussion occurred in Parliament: for when Mr. Plunkett, who had joined the Administration with Mr. Canning, brought forward on that day the claims of the Catholics, as a sort of token that he and those who thought with him had not, on taking office, abandoned the question of which they had so long been the most eminent supporters, — Sir Francis Burdett accused both the Attorney-General for Ireland and the Secretary for Foreign Affairs of seeking to make an idle parade of fine sentiments, which they knew would be practically useless. Mr. Canning defended himself, and, as he sat down, Mr. Brougham rose:

"If," said he, "the other ministers had taken example by the single-hearted, plain, manly, and upright conduct of the right honourable Secretary for the Home Department (Mr. Peel), who has always been on the same side on this question, never swerving from his opinions, but standing uniformly up and stating them — who had never taken office on a secret understanding to abandon the question in substance while he contrived to sustain it in words — whose mouth, heart, and conduct have always been in unison; if such had been the conduct of all the friends of emancipation, I should not have found myself in a state of despair with regard to the Catholic claims. Let the conduct of the Attorney-General for Ireland (Mr. Plunkett) have been what it might — let him have deviated from his former professions or not — still, if the Secretary of State for Foreign Affairs had only come forward at this critical moment, when the point was whether he should go to India into honourable exile, or take office in England, and not submit to his sentence of transportation, but be condemned to hard labour in his own country — doomed to the disquiet of a divided council, sitting with his enemies, and pitied by his friends, with his hands chained and tied down on all those lines of operation which his own sentiments and wishes would have led him to adopt — if, at that critical moment, when his fate depended on Lord Chancellor Eldon, and on his sentiments with respect to the Catholic cause — if, at that critical moment, he who said the other night that he would not truckle to a noble lord, but who then exhibited the most incredible specimen of monstrous truckling for the purpose of obtaining office that the whole history of political tergiversation could furnish ..."

At these words, Mr. Canning, labouring to conceal emotion which his countenance had long betrayed, started up, and, in a calm voice, with his eye fixed on Mr. Brougham, said, "Sir, I rise to say that that is false." A dead silence of some minutes ensued; the Speaker interfered; neither party would retract, and both gentlemen were ordered into custody; but at last the matter was arranged through Sir R. Wilson's mediation.

V.

Without going into many details, I have thus said enough to show that Mr. Canning had, in his new post, to contend — first, against the disfavour of the Crown; secondly, against the dislike, jealousy, and suspicion of a large portion of his colleagues; thirdly, against the bitterest hostility of the most able and eloquent amongst his parliamentary opponents.

It is necessary to take into consideration all these difficulties in order to appreciate the rare abilities, the adroit adaptation of means to ends, the clever profiting by times and occasions, the bold bearing-up against powerful antagonists, the conquest over personal antipathies, which in a few years placed England — humbled to the lowest degree when Lord Castlereagh expired — in the highest position she ever occupied since the days of Lord Chatham; and, at the same time ended, by making the most unpopular man with the nation, and the most distasteful minister to the Sovereign, the people's idol and the monarch's favourite.

I have asserted that England was never in a more humbled position than at the death of Lord Castlereagh. I had myself the opportunity of seeing this illustrated in a private and confidential correspondence between Prince Metternich and a distinguished person with whom he was on terms of great intimacy, and to whom he wrote without reserve; — a correspondence in which the Prince, when alluding to our great warrior, who represented England at the Congress of Verona, spoke of him as "the great Baby," and alluded to the power and influence of England as things past and gone.

It was, in fact, too true that all memory of the
long efforts of twenty years, eventually successful in
liberating Europe, had wholly lapsed from the minds
of those military potentates, who having during war
experienced every variety of defeat, appeared at the
conclusion of peace to have recovered unbounded confidence in their arms.

The institutions which had nourished the pride and
valour to which we had owed our victories, were daily
denounced by the sovereigns in whose cause we had
fought; and every new expression of opinion that came
to us from the Continent, manifested more and more
that Waterloo was forgotten by every nation but the
French. Nothing in short, was wanting to complete
our degradation after the false and impudent conduct
of M. de Villele, but its disrespectful avowal; and
painful and humiliating must have been the sentiments
of an English statesman, when he read the speech of
the French minister in the Chamber of Deputies, and
found him boast of having amused our Government
by misrepresenting the force on the Spanish frontier as
merely a *cordon sanitaire*, until it was made to act as
an army of invasion.

VI.

The ground, however, which the sovereigns forming
the Holy Alliance had now chosen for fighting the
battle of principles, was not well selected by them for
the conflict.

During the despotism of Ferdinand, it was never
forgotten in this country that those with whom he filled
his prisons, those whose blood he shed, those of whose

hopeless exile he was the cause, had fought side by
side with our own gallant soldiers; were the zealous
and valiant patriots who had delivered the land from
which they were driven, and re-established the dynasty
which their tyrant disgraced. Many, then, who disapproved of the new Spanish constitution, were disposed
to excuse the excesses of freedom as the almost natural
reaction from the abuses of absolute power.

Nor was this all. There has always been a strong
party in England justly in favour of a good understanding with the French nation. On such an understanding is based that policy of peace which Walpole
and Fox judiciously advocated — the first more fortunately and more opportunely than the last. But as
no policy should ever be carried to the extreme, we
have on the other hand to consider that the only serious
danger menacing to England is the undue aggrandise-
ment of France. Her proximity, her warlike spirit,
her constant thirst for glory and territory, the great
military and naval armaments at her disposal, the
supremacy amongst nations which she is in the habit
of affecting, are all, at certain times, threatening to
our interests and wounding to our pride; and when the
French nation, with the tendency which she has always
manifested to spread her opinions, professes exaggerated
doctrines, whether in favour of democracy or despotism,
the spirit of conquest and proselytism combined with
power makes her equally menacing to our institutions
and to our independence. Her predominance in Spain,
moreover, which unites so many ports to those of
France — ports in which, as we learnt from Napoleon I., armaments can be fitted out, and from which
expeditions can be sent against our possessions in the

Mediterranean, or our empire in the Channel, or against Egypt, on the high road to our Indian dominions, has always been regarded by English statesmen with a rational disquietude, and on various occasions resisted with boldness, perseverance, and success; nor did it matter to us whether it was the white flag or the tri-colour which crossed the Bidassoa, when each was to be considered the symbol of ambition and injustice.

VII.

Thus, Spain became, not inauspiciously, the spot on which a liberal English minister had to confront the despotic governments of the Continent. But for war on account of Spain, England was not prepared; and, indeed, the treachery which we knew existed in the Spanish counsels, rendered war on account of that divided country out of the question. The only remaining means of opposition was protestation, and Mr. Canning at once protested against the act of aggression which France was committing, and against the principles put forth in its justification. The mode of doing this was rendered easy by the speech from the French throne, which was inexplicable, except as a bold asser-tion of the divine rights of kings; and to that slavish doctrine Mr. Canning, who, whichever side he took, was not very guarded in his expressions, roundly stated that "he felt disgust and abhorrence."

The gauntlet of Legitimacy having been thus thrown down, and being in this manner taken up, it only re-mained to conduct the contest.

Caution was necessary in the selection of an opportunity where a stand should be made. Boldness was also necessary in order to make that stand without fear or hesitation, when the fitting occasion arrived.

France, therefore, was permitted to overrun the Spanish territory without resistance. But Mr. Canning declared that, whilst England adopted to this degree, a passive attitude, she could not permit the permanent occupation of Spain, nor any act of aggression against Portugal. At the same time he alluded to the recognition of the revolted provinces in South America, which provinces France was expecting to gain in compensation for her expenses, as an event merely dependent upon time, and protested against any seizure by France, or any cession by Spain of possessions which had *in fact* established their independence. In these expressions were shadowed out the whole of that course subsequently developed. They were little noticed, it is true, at the time, because they did not interfere with the plan of the moment, viz., the destruction of a constitutional government at Madrid; but they became a text to which our Minister could subsequently refer as a proof of the frankness and consistency of the policy that from the commencement of the French campaign he had been pursuing. No one, however, understood better than the statesman who had resolved on this policy, that to be powerful abroad you must be popular at home. Thus at the close of the session in which he had denounced the absolute doctrines of the French Legitimists, we see him passing through the great mercantile and manufacturing towns, and endeavouring to excite amidst the large and intelligent masses of those

towns an enthusiasm for his talents, and that attachment to his person, which genius, when it comes into
contact with the people, rarely fails to inspire.

VIII.

On one of these occasions it was that he delivered
the memorable speech, meant to resound throughout
Europe, and spoken with exquisite propriety in sight
of the docks at Plymouth.

"Our ultimate object, no doubt, is the peace of the
world, but let it not be said that we cultivate it either
because we fear, or because we are unprepared for
war. On the contrary, if eight months ago the Government did not proclaim that this country was prepared
for war, this was from causes far other than those produced by fear; and if war should at last unfortunately
be necessary, every intervening month of peace that
has since passed has but made us so much the more
capable of warlike exertion. The resources created by
peace are indeed the means of war. In cherishing
these resources, we but accumulate these means. Our
present repose is no more a proof of incapability to
act, than the state of inertness and inactivity in which
I have seen those mighty masses that float on the
waters above your town, is a proof that they are
devoid of strength, and incapable of being fitted for
action. *You well know, gentlemen, how soon one of those
stupendous masses, now reposing on their shadows in perfect stillness — how soon upon any call of patriotism or
of necessity, it would assume the likeness of an animated*

thing, instinct with life and motion; how soon it would ruffle, as it were, its swelling plumage; how quickly it would put forth all its beauty and its bravery; collect its scattered elements of strength, and awaken its dormant thunder! Such as is one of those magnificent machines when springing from inaction into a display of its might, such is England herself; while apparently passionless and motionless, she silently concentrates the power to be put forth on an adequate occasion."

Luckily for Mr. Canning, the circumstances of the country in 1824 enabled him to maintain and increase that popularity which he was desirous to acquire. Trade had begun to thrive, the revenue to increase, taxation to diminish; nor were these facts merely valuable in themselves, they were also valuable in affording a facility for entering more freely upon that large and comprehensive system of commerce which was the best adapted to a country that combined great maritime power with great manufacturing capacity.

Besides, by entering frankly upon this system, Mr. Canning was giving strength to one of those links which now began to unite him to the Opposition, and thus to rally round him by degrees nearly the whole liberal force of the House of Commons. Already, indeed, many of his opponents had softened in their tone, and Sir James Mackintosh (June 25, 1824), referring to papers that had been laid before Parliament, passed the highest eulogy on the conduct which the Foreign Secretary was adopting in respect to the South American question.

IX.

The time is now arrived for speaking of that question. From the first moment that the intentions of the French government towards Spain were known, Mr. Canning, as it has been seen, hinted at the recognition of the Spanish colonies, and protested against any proceeding which either directly or indirectly should bring them under the authority of France. A variety of projects, — amongst which that of holding a congress of the Great Powers at Paris, for the purpose of considering how it might be most expedient to assist Spain in adjusting her differences with the revolted colonies, was the most significant, — all tended to show the necessity of some immediate step for placing beyond dispute the condition of those colonies.

By a series of measures, each in advance of the other, none going so far as to excite any burst of resentment, Mr. Canning went on gradually towards the ultimate decision he had in view.

A warning to Spain that unless she forthwith effected an accommodation with her former subjects, their independence would be recognised, was given and repeated; a warning to France that the cession to any other power of the Spanish possessions in America would not be allowed, had also been once given, and was now formally renewed. The project of interfering for their conquest with foreign troops, whatever might be decided by any congress, was boldly forbidden. Consuls had already been appointed to attend to the interests of British commerce in those parts, and commissioners had been sent out to Columbia and Mexico (the emancipation of Buenos Ayres was undisputed) to report on their condition. The memorable declaration of the United States, frequently referred to since — as the Munro Doctrine, — and to which our foreign minister, by his communications with the United States Envoy in London, had in no small degree contributed; — a declaration to the effect that the United States would not see with indifference the attempt of any European power to establish itself on the American continent, was a positive assurance of the only alliance that might be important, should England have to contend by force of arms against a French and Spanish expedition.

At last, strong in popularity at home, having by previous measures, difficult to be opposed, lessened the shock that might have been produced abroad, Mr. Canning put the seal to this portion of his plans, and announced his recognition of three of the most powerful of the new republics.

This recognition, however justifiable on its proper merits, is not merely to be considered on such isolated grounds. It formed a part, and an important part, of European policy; it altered the position in which this country stood towards those powers who had declared their principles to be in opposition to our own. Now it was the turn of Austria, Prussia, and Russia to *remonstrate*, and to have their *remonstrances* treated as those of England had been by them on former occasions. Thus, the part which Great Britain had hitherto played was for the first time reversed; and her character, which at each late congress had been sinking lower and lower in the scale of public opinion, rose at once in the balance. This is the first important epoch in Mr. Canning's foreign administration.

17*

X.

The affairs of Portugal next demand attention.
That country, from the commencement of the new conflict in the Peninsula, had been the scene of French
intrigues for the purpose of destroying English interests;
and of court cabals, with the object of favouring Don
Miguel's pretensions. The Queen, a violent and pro-
fligate old woman, who had never kept any terms with
her passions, countenanced the most desperate schemes;
and King John VI., a weak but not unamiable monarch,
was even obliged on one occasion to seek safety on
board a British frigate. The defeat of the conspiracy
which occasioned this alarm banished Don Miguel; but
M. Subserra, the King's minister and favourite, and a
mere tool in the hands of France, still remained; so
that although the Portuguese government never took
any open part against the Spanish Cortes, the King
would never concede a constitution to his people (this
being very strenuously opposed by the French Government and its allies), nor unite himself cordially with
England, by giving Lord Beresford the command of
his army, and conferring on M. Palmella the chief influence in his cabinet. Our situation in respect to Portugal was moreover complicated by the state of Brazil.
Don Pedro, King John's eldest son, had been left Regent in that colony by his father, when the latter returned to his more ancient dominions. The King's
secret instructions were that the Prince should adopt
any course that circumstances might render necessary,
rather than allow so important a possession to pass
from the family of Braganza. But the spirit of the
Brazilians, who from the long residence of their mon-

arch amongst them had for some time enjoyed the privileges of a Metropolitan State, would not submit to a renewal of their old dependence on the mother country; and the Regent was forced, in obedience to the injunctions just mentioned, to place himself at the head of a revolt, and to become, under the title of "Emperor," sovereign of a new kingdom.

It may be doubtful whether Don Pedro's father was quite pleased at an act of which (whatever might be his commands in the case of a supposed contingency) it might always have been difficult to prove the necessity by formal and unpalatable explanations; but the Portuguese in general were at all events far more violent than their monarch, and would at once have attempted the conquest of their rebellious but distant province if they had possessed any of the means requisite for such an undertaking. Mr. Canning, on the other hand, not only saw that Portugal, for her own sake, should endeavour to enter into some arrangement, admitting a fact which it was impossible to alter; he was also obliged, in consequence of the policy which he was elsewhere pursuing, to endeavour to obtain for Brazil an independent position.

It became desirable, then, on every account, to settle as soon as possible the differences between the colony and the mother country; and, having vainly attempted to do this in other ways, it was resolved at last, as the best and promptest course, to send some superior Diplomatist to Lisbon, who, if he succeeded in obtaining the consent of the Portuguese government to a moderate plan of accommodation, might proceed at once to Rio Janeiro, and urge Don Pedro and his government to accept it. Sir Charles Stuart, (afterwards

Lord Stuart de Rothsay), was selected for the double
mission, and succeeded, after some difficulty, in ac-
complishing its object. He then, however, being in
Brazil, undertook the arrangement of a commercial
treaty between the newly emancipated colony and
Great Britain, and some singular errors into which he
fell delaying the completion of his business, he was
still at Rio when King John died.

XI.

The Emperor of Brazil then became King of Portugal; and having to decide on the relinquishment of
one of these kingdoms, it seeming impossible to keep
them permanently united, he assumed that, in abdicat-
ing the throne of Portugal, he had the right of dictating the method and terms of his abdication. He proposed, then, first, to take upon himself the crown to
which he had succeeded; secondly, in his capacity of
sovereign of Portugal, to give a constitution to the
Portuguese; thirdly, if that constitution were accepted,
and his brother Don Miguel were willing to espouse
his daughter Donna Maria, to place the ancient sceptre
of Portugal in that daughter's hands.

The apparent countenance of Great Britain however obtained, was no doubt of consequence to the success of this project, and Sir Charles Stuart was prevailed upon to accept the title of Portuguese ambassador, and in such capacity to be the bearer of the new
constitutional charter to Portugal. He thus, it is true,
acted without Mr. Canning's authority, for the case was
one which could hardly have been foreseen, and it
may be doubted whether his conduct was well advised;

but still no experienced Diplomatist would have taken upon himself so important a part as Sir Charles Stuart assumed, unless he had pretty fair reasons to suppose that he was doing that which would be agreeable to his chief; and when Mr. Canning gave his subsequent sanction to Sir Charles's conduct, by declaring in a despatch, dated July 12, 1826, that the King entirely approved of the ambassador's having consented (under the peculiar circumstances of his situation in Brazil) to be the bearer of the Emperor's decrees to Lisbon, the world in general considered the whole affair, as in fact it had become, the arrangement of Great Britain.

In this manner did we appear as having recognised the South American Republics, as having arranged the separation and independence of the great Portuguese colony; and, finally, as having carried a constitution into Portugal itself. All the Powers leagued in favour of despotism, protesting at this time against the recognition of any colony, and France being then as their deputed missionary in Spain, for the express purpose of putting down a constitution in that country.

This is the second memorable epoch in Mr. Canning's foreign policy — the second period in that diplomatic war which at Troppau and Verona had been announced, and which when the Duc d'Angoulême crossed the Pyrenees, had been undertaken against Liberal opinions.

XII.

If our government at last stood in a position worthy of the strength and the intellect of the nation it represented, that position was, nevertheless, one that required for its maintenance the nicest tempering of dignity with forbearance; no offence was to be heedlessly given, none timidly submitted to. At the same time, Spain and Portugal, long jealous and hostile, were marshalled under two hostile and jarring opinions. The most powerful, backed by friendly and kindred armies, was likely to invade the weaker; and that weaker we were bound to defend by an indissoluble alliance.

The first step manifesting the feelings of King Ferdinand's government was a refusal to recognise the Portuguese Regency established at King John's death; but matters were certain not to stop here. Portuguese deserters were soon received in Spain, and allowed to arm; nay, were furnished with arms by Spanish authority, for the purpose of being sent back as invaders into their native country. Even Spanish troops, in more than one instance, hostilely entered Portugal, while the Spanish ministry scrupled at no falsehoods that might stretch a flimsy covering over their deceitful assurances and unfriendly designs.

Things were in this state, peace rested upon these hollow and uncertain foundations, when Mr. Canning received at the same time the official news that the rebel troops which had been organised in Spain, were marching upon Lisbon; and the most solemn assurances from Spain herself that these very troops should be dispersed, and their chief arrested. The crisis for action seemed now to have arrived; for England was bound, as I have said, by treaty, to defend Portugal against a foreign power, and a foreign power was in this instance clearly, though meanly, indirectly, and treacherously assailing her. To shrink from the dangerous obligation to which we stood pledged, or even to appear so to

shrink, was to relinquish that hold upon public opinion
which we had at last obtained, and to abandon that
moral power which, if a contest did arise, would be
the main portion of our strength.   On the other hand,
to comply with that request of the Portuguese government for succour (the request was now formally made),
and to send a British force to Portugal was, no doubt,
an event that might be the commencement of a general
war.   Of all policies, a hesitating, shuffling policy
would have been the worst.   Had it been adopted,
Spain, or those who then governed Spain, would have
proceeded to more violent and irremediable acts —
acts which we must have submitted to with the grossest
dishonour, or resented with the smallest chances of success.

XIII.

At this moment, 12th December, 1826, Mr. Canning came down to the House of Commons, his fine eye
kindling with the magnitude of the transactions in
which he was called upon to play so important a part;
and having described the circumstances in which England was placed, and the obligations to which she was
pledged, stated the manner in which the duty of the
English government had been fulfilled:
"I understand, indeed, that in some quarters it has
been imputed to his Majesty's ministers that an extraordinary delay intervened between the taking up the
determination to give assistance to Portugal and the
carrying of that determination into effect.   But how
stands the fact?   On Sunday, the 3rd of this month,
we received from the Portuguese ambassador a direct
and formal demand of assistance against a hostile ag-

gression from Spain. Our answer was, that although rumours had reached us through France of this event, his Majesty's government had not that accurate information — that official and precise intelligence of facts on which it could properly found an application to Parliament. It was only on last Friday night that this precise information arrived — on Saturday his Majesty's confidential servants came to a decision. On Sunday that decision received the sanction of his Majesty; on Monday it was communicated to both Houses of Parliament; and this day, sir, at this hour in which I have the honour of addressing you, the troops are on their march for embarkation."

This exordium possesses all the qualities of oratory, and could hardly have been delivered without exciting a burst of applause. So again, when the Minister, his voice swelling, his arm outstretched, and his face turned towards the benches where sat the representatives of the great monarchs who, but a short time since, derided our power and denounced our principles, said, "We go to plant the standard of England on the *well-known heights* of Lisbon. Where that standard is planted, foreign dominion *shall not come*," a thrill ran through the assembly at these simple but ominous words. But it was perhaps in his reply that the orator rose to his greatest height, when defending the course he had adopted during the recent French expedition, he elevated his hearers to a conception of the grandeur of his views, and the mingled prudence and audacity of his conduct by thus magnificently explaining the conduct he had pursued.

"If France occupied Spain, was it necessary, in order to avoid the consequences of that occupation, that we should blockade Cadiz? No: I looked another way; I sought the materials of occupation in another hemisphere. Contemplating Spain such as her ancestors had known her, I resolved that, if France had Spain, it should not be Spain with the Indies: I called the New World into existence to redress the balance of the old."

XIV.

But the Minister displayed talents far beyond those of the mere orator on this occasion. He took a step which was certain to incur the displeasure and excite the open hostility of a powerful party throughout Europe. Many who might have felt themselves obliged by honour to take this step would have done so with a timid and downcast air, endeavouring by an affectation of humility to deprecate the anger of the high personages they were offending. Such men, exciting no sympathy, creating and maintaining no allies, encouraging the attacks and justifying the insults of all enemies, would have placed their country in a false and pitiful position, where, powerless and compromised, she would have stood before her opponents, exposed by her advance, tempting by her weakness. But the sagacious know that a bold game must be played boldly, and that the great art of moderating opponents consists in gaining friends.

Mr. Canning, then, neither flinched nor faltered. In venturing upon a measure which aroused the anger of so many powerful foes, he made those foes aware that if we were assailed because, in fulfilment of treaties, we marched to the defence of a country which was at-

tacked on account of its liberal institutions, England
would gather beneath her standard all those who loved
liberty throughout Europe. Our country was on the
verge of a contest with the most potent sovereigns.
Our minister neither provoked nor quailed before those
sovereigns, but plainly told them, that if such a contest
did arise, it would be a contest in which many of the
governments eager to provoke it might expect to find,
side by side with our soldiers, not a few of their own
people — a contest in which, were Englishmen forced
to take a part, they would not shrink from taking the
part that befitted the brave and free descendants of
men who had suffered for their religion at the stake,
and adjudged their monarch to the scaffold.

XV.

British troops, then, were at last sent in aid of Portugal; no other troops opposed them; the expedition
was successful; and from that moment Mr. Canning
was pointed to as the first statesman of his time; and
Great Britain — without having excited war or produced revolutions, following a course conformable to
her interests, her history, and her character, backed by
the sympathy of the free, and guarded by the reverence
and affection of the intelligent; having shed no blood,
having exhausted no treasure, having never uttered a
word that our nation did not echo, nor shrunk from
supporting a word that had been uttered — stood before the world in a yet more exalted and noble situation than even at that moment when Napoleon fled
from Waterloo, and the British drum was beating in
the streets of Paris.

This is the third epoch in Mr. Canning's conflict with the crusaders against constitutional principles. I have described the measures by which that conflict had been supported. It would be difficult to point out any stronger measures that a country, placed in similar circumstances, could have taken. But Mr. Canning, acting with force and spirit, had acted without exaggeration. He had not said, like the Conventionalists of France, "I will wage war with certain opinions;" he had not told the sovereigns of Troppau, Laybach, and Verona, "because you chuse to commit aggression and injustice, I will do the same! because you enter into a war against Liberal governments, I will forthwith arm the people of my country against all governments of a despotic nature."

The minister of a state which does not wish to give the law, but which never will receive it, he neither cringed nor threatened. "Publish what doctrines and take what course you may," was the language of England's great statesman, "I will shape my way according to the interests and treaties of my country with equal independence."

With such language the Spanish colonies were recognised, because Spain could be no longer responsible for their conduct; because France maintained herself in Spain under the hope that these colonies would furnish an indemnity for the money she had spent in re-establishing despotism in Spain itself; because England at the head of constitutional governments, found it necessary to check the moral influence of the Holy Alliance, at the head of absolute ones.

Thus the separation of Brazil from Portugal was negotiated, since the struggle between the mother country and her ancient but emancipated possession, was at once uncongenial with British commerce in the Pacific, embarrassing to British influence at Lisbon, and adverse to the general policy it was found expedient to pursue in Spanish America.

Thus British troops were sent even ostentatiously to Lisbon, since Mr. Canning would not for a moment countenance the belief that England would shrink from her engagements to the weakest ally, although the form of government adopted by that ally was contrary to the particular opinions of the most powerful confederacy in the world.

And here it is especially to be remarked that a policy which, regarded as a whole, bears so decided an appearance, and was certain to produce so powerful an effect, offers hardly a single point where the success was doubtful, or the peril great. Developing itself, like that skilful game where the winner advances gradually but surely, each piece protected through a series of moves by a preceding one, our policy had only become conspicuous by the last move which obtained its victory.

Our treaties with Buenos Ayres, with Mexico, and Columbia; guarded as they were by our own previous declarations, and also by the important declaration of the American President, could only expose us to a useless and insignificant exhibition of displeasure.

The severance of Brazil from Portugal, as long as Portugal was a consenting party, could with little decency be objected to by an indifferent power; the concession of a charter to Portugal, coming from the sovereign of Portugal himself, was an act which those who contended for the divine right of kings to do

what they thought proper, could not well oppose: and
finally, the expedition of British troops to Lisbon, —
sent out at the time when the name of "Mr. Canning"
had become the rallying word of England, and "England" herself the rallying word of the free and intelligent throughout the world, demanded also under
circumstances too well known to be disputed, and
authorized by treaties which had always been acknowledged, and to which, from the very commencement of
his administration, Mr. Canning had called attention, —
resolutely as it was announced, gallantly as it was
made, and important as its impression on the public
mind was sure to be, could hardly have been resented
with propriety or advantage. On each occasion the
minister had made his stand at the happiest opportunity
and on the strongest grounds. Abandoning, it is true,
all direct resist nce to France and to the principles
she maintained — where such resistance must have been
made with great peril, and small chance of success —
he had adopted towards both a system of opposition
which successively displayed itself by a variety of acts
little likely to be dangerous, and almost certain to be
effective. In the first place, instead of meeting the
enemy on a ground undermined by factions, and where
a large military force, inconsistent with the nature of
our means, would have been necessary, he carried the
quarrel into a new hemisphere, and placed it on a
question which, mistress of the seas, England had the
undoubted power of deciding. Lastly, when a British
army was sent to the continent, it was sent not on
grounds which might merely be justifiable, but for
reasons which were obligatory; while the people to
whose aid it marched — open to the ocean, animated

by hereditary jealousy against their neighbours, accustomed to British command, and confident in British assistance — were the people whom we were most likely to be allowed to succour with impunity, and most certain, should war ensue, of triumphantly defending.

Something of chance and fortune, no doubt, was mingled in the happy conduct of these events, as is the case in all human affairs; but there is visible a steady and impressive will, tempering and ruling them throughout; the mind and spirit of a man, who was capable of forethought, governed by precaution, and prompt in decision.

CANNING,

THE BRILLIANT MAN.

PART IV.

Mr. Canning's position. — Altered tone of opposition. — Favour of King. — Death of Duke of York and Lord Liverpool. — Struggle for the Premiership. — Nomination of Mr. Canning. — Secession of Duke of Wellington, and Anti-Catholic party. — Junction with Whigs. — Formation of Cabinet. — Effect of Canning on the men of his time, and their effect on a subsequent one. — Eastern affairs. — Treaty concerning Greece with Russia and France. — Sickness. — Death.

PART IV.

FROM THE BEGINNING OF MR. CANNING'S POPULARITY AS FOREIGN
MINISTER TO HIS DEATH.

I.

It is needless to say that a policy which raised
England so high in the world's consideration was
popular with Englishmen; they were proud of their
country and of their minister. The Whig opposition,
moreover, which at first depreciated that minister and
praised his colleagues, soon began to depreciate his
colleagues and to praise him. But Mr. Canning's most
extraordinary and unexpected triumph was at court.
From the most odious man to the King in the King's
cabinet, he had become the King's pet minister, and
one of the most intimate of his chosen circle.

The leader of the House of Commons had one
peculiar mode of obtaining his Majesty's confidence,
and cultivating his intimacy. It was his arduous duty
to send to the Sovereign every night a written account
of that night's proceedings in the assembly to which
he belonged. It is easy to see the advantage which
this established custom may give to a writer who expresses himself with tact and clearness. A minister of
foreign affairs has also more opportunities than any
other minister of captivating the Royal attention.
Foreign politics, which constitute the arena in which
kings are pitted against kings, are the politics which

18*

most interest royal personages.   A monarch there represents before other monarchs the fame, the power,
the character of the nation he rules; he rises as it rises,
he falls as it falls.

George IV., whatever his faults, was not without
talent or ambition.   In early life he wished to · distinguish himself in the military service abroad, and
when, on this being denied him, he entered more
deeply than discreetly into politics at home, it was the
desire for popularity which connected him with the
Opposition.   He still remembered the high position
which after the battle of Waterloo he held, as Regent,
amongst the great potentates of the earth; and though
personally attached to Lord Castlereagh, and unwilling
to sever himself altogether from the sovereigns who
had formerly been his allies, and who now in confound-
ing Liberty with Anarchy came forward as the cham-
pions of Royalty and order, he was still not insensible
to the fact that he had become, little by little, a
nonentity in the councils of his peers, and that his
advice and opinions, even when expressed by the great
warrior who had vanquished Napoleon, were treated
with a disregard which was galling to his pride as a
monarch, and painful to his feelings as an Englishman.
He experienced no small exultation, then, when he
saw this state of things reversed, and that the King of
England was once more a personage whose policy
created hope and alarm.   He had, moreover, a singular
propensity, which was in fact a sort of madness, for
conceiving that he had played a personal part in all
the events which had passed in his reign.   Amongst
other fancies of this kind he believed, or at least
often spoke as if he believed, that he had been on

the great battle-field which had terminated the war in
1815; and I have been told by a person present, that
one day at dinner, after relating his achievements on
this occasion, he turned round to the Iron Duke and
said:

"Was it not so, Duke?"

"I have heard your Majesty often say so," replied
the duke, drily."* It was easy, then, for Mr. Canning
to make George IV. consider Mr. Canning's policy his
policy, Mr. Canning's successes his successes, and indeed Mr. Canning always spoke to his Majesty, when
the popularity of his administration became apparent,
as if he had only followed the inspiration of a prescient
and intelligent master.

I should omit more trifling causes of favour, if I
did not think them necessary to illustrate the character
of the parties, and of the times of which I am speaking, and to show the attention which Mr. Canning,
once engaged in the task of recasting our foreign
policy, gave to the smallest circumstances which might
facilitate it. In the ordinary acceptation of the word,
he was not a courtier, nor a man of the world. Living,
as I have already stated, in the midst of a small clique
of admirers, and little with society at large, he confined his remarkable powers of pleasing to his own set.
He had determined, however, on gaining George IV.'s
goodwill, or, at all events, on vanquishing his dislike, and he saw at once that this was to be done

---

* This story was related by Sir Roundell Palmer in his address to
the jury in the trial of Ryves v. the Attorney General. I do not know
whence Sir Roundell derived the anecdote, but I think it as well to say,
in favour of its authenticity, that I heard it thirty years ago from a person
who was present on the occasion, and that it has been recorded for twenty-
six years in my MS.

rather indirectly than directly, and that it could best be done by gaining the favour of those ladies of the court whom the King saw most frequently, and spoke to most unreservedly. These were Lady Conyngham and Madame de Lieven. For Lady Conyngham George IV. had a sort of chivalric devotion or attachment; Madame de Lieven he liked and appreciated as the lady who had the greatest knack of seizing and understanding his wishes, and making his court agreeable. She was a musician, and he was fond of music; she had correspondents at every capital in Europe; knew all the small gossip as well as the most important affairs that agitated Paris, St. Petersburg, and Vienna, and he was amused by foreign gossip and interested in foreign affairs. Her opinion, moreover, as to the position of any one in the world of fashion was law, and George IV. piqued himself especially on being the man of fashion. Mr. Canning resolved, then, on pleasing this remarkable lady, and completely succeeded. She became, as she afterwards often stated, subjugated by the influence of his natural manner and brilli nt talents; and the favour of Madame de Lieven went the further in this instance with the King, since he had previously a sort of prejudice against Canning, as being too much the man of letters, and not sufficiently the fine gentleman. This prejudice once removed, a man of wit, genius, and information, had no inconsiderable hold on a prince whose youth had been passed in the most brilliant society of his time, and who was still alive to the memory of the sparkling wit of Sheridan and the easy and copious eloquence of Fox. Lady Conyngham's alliance was still more important than that of Madame de Lieven, and one of

Mr. Canning's first acts was to name Lord Francis Conyngham Under Secretary of State, it is said at the King's desire. At all events, Lord Francis's appointment, which was in every respect a good one, pleased the Marchioness, and satisfied his Majesty, who saw in it the willingness of his Minister to bring even the most private acts of his administration under the Royal cognisance.

II.

An anecdote of the time is worth recording, since it connected itself with the recognition of the Spanish colonies, and the subsequent elevation of the minister to whom this important act was due.

Lady Conyngham had been supposed in early life to have greatly admired (there was no scandal, I should say, attached to this admiration) Lord Ponsonby, then the finest gentleman of his day. Lord Ponsonby, who had long been absent from England, returned from the Ionian Islands, where he had held a small office, not a little desirous to get a better place than the one he had quitted. He met Lady Conyngham at Lady Jersey's (so went the story of the day), and Lady Conyngham fainted. So interesting a piece of gossip soon reached the ear of the monarch: the friendship of old men is very often as romantic as the love of young ones. His Majesty took to his bed, declared himself ill, and would see no one. All business was stopped. After waiting some time, Mr. Canning at last obtained an interview. George IV. received him lying on a couch in a darkened room, the light being barely sufficient to read a paper.

"What's the matter? I am very ill, Mr. Canning."

"I shall not occupy your Majesty for more than five minutes. It is very desirable, as your Majesty knows, to send Envoys, without delay, to the States of South America, that are about to be recognised."

The King groaned, and moved impatiently.

"I have been thinking, Sir, it would be most desirable to select a man of rank for one of these posts (another groan), and I thought of proposing Lord Ponsonby to your Majesty for Buenos Ayres."

"Ponsonby!" said the King, rising a little from his reclining position — "a capital appointment! a clever fellow, though an idle one, Mr. Canning. May I ask you to undraw that curtain a little? A very good appointment; is there anything else, Canning, that you wish me to attend to?"

From that moment, said the person who told me this story, Mr. Canning's favour rose more and more rapidly. *

But in mentioning Lady Conyngham and Madame de Lieven, as having been of much use to Mr. Canning, I should also mention Doctor Sir Wm. Knighton. Yet, I would not have it thought that I intend in any way to take from Mr. Canning's character as a great minister by showing that he adopted the small means necessary to rule a court. George IV.'s habits were such that without some aid of this kind no statesman

---

* The correctness of this story has been questioned by a correspondent to the *Times*, who signs "A. W. C." I heard it from a person much in the intimacy of George IV. and Mr. Canning, and noted it when I heard it as curious; but I give it as gossip, which, whether true or false, illustrates the notions of the time, and is not incompatible with what is said by "A. W. C." himself.

could have got current affairs carried on with due re-
gularity, or initiated any policy that required the Royal
support.

III.

The moment was now at hand, when the extent of
this Royal support was to be tested; when, in short, it
was to be decided whether the Canning party or the
Wellington and Eldon party was to be predominant in
the Cabinet. The difference in feeling and opinion
between the two sections was, as I have said, more or
less general; but as the only question on which the
members of the same government were allowed to dis-
agree (according to the principle on which the Cabinet
had been founded) was Catholic Emancipation, so it
was on the Catholic Emancipation question that each
tried its strength against the other. In the preceding
year the Emancipationists had obtained a majority in
the House of Commons, and would have had only a
small majority against them in the House of Lords, but
for the speech of the Duke of York, heir-presumptive
to the throne, who declared that he was, and ever
would be, a determined supporter of the Protestant
principles of exclusion, maintained by his late father.
There is reason to suppose that this declaration was
made on an understanding with the King, who thought
that he should thus fortify his own opinions, which had
become for the last twenty years hostile to the Catholics, and deter Canning and his friends from pushing
forward too eagerly a matter on which they must expect to encounter the opposition of two successive
sovereigns.

On the 5th of January, 1827, however, the Duke
of York died; and though during his illness he strongly
advised his brother to form an anti-Catholic Administration — without which, he said, Catholic Emancipation
must ere long be granted — the counsel, though it had
distressed George IV. considerably, had not decided
him; for his Majesty preferred his ease, as long as he
could enjoy it, to facing difficulties which would disorder the ordinary routine of his social life, as well as
that of public affairs. The Duke of York's influence
on George IV., moreover, was that of personal contact,
of a living man of honest and sterling character, over
a living man of weaker character; it expired, therefore,
when he expired.

Another death soon afterwards occurred. Lord
Liverpool was taken ill in February, 1827, and he
died in March. This left the first situation in the
Government vacant. The moderator between the two
conflicting parties was no more, and a struggle as to
the Premiership became inevitable.

Mr. Canning was at this crisis seriously ill at
Brighton: and we may conceive the agitation of his
restless mind, since Sir Francis Burdett's annual motion on the Catholic claims was just then coming on.
His absence would, he knew, be misinterpreted; and
literally rising from his bed, and under sufferings which
only ambition and duty could have rendered support-
able, appeared to confront his enemies and encourage
his followers in his place in the House of Commons.

The debate was more than warm, and an encounter
between the Master of the Rolls, Sir J. Copley, afterwards Lord Lyndhurst, and the Secretary of State for
Foreign Affairs, was such as might rather be expected

from rival chiefs of hostile factions, than from men belonging to the same government, and professing to
entertain on most subjects the same opinions. Finally,
a majority of four decided against Sir Francis Burdett.

After this trial of strength, it was difficult for the
Minister of Foreign Affairs to insist upon the first
place in a balanced cabinet, with a majority in both
Houses of Parliament against the party which he represented. When, therefore, the King consulted him
subsequently as to a new Administration, he said:

"I should recommend your Majesty to form an Administration wholly composed of persons who entertain,
in respect to the Roman Catholics, your Majesty's own
opinions."

This counsel could not be carried out; but it seemed
disinterested, and forced George IV. to allow, after
making the attempt, that it was impracticable. The
formation of a Cabinet on the old terms of general
comprehension thus became a necessity, and to that
Government Mr. Canning was indispensable. But his
Majesty naturally wished to retain him in a position
that would not offend the rest of his colleagues, and to
place some person opposed to the Catholics in Lord
Liverpool's vacant situation. This Mr. Canning would
not consent to. In serving under Lord Liverpool, he
had served under a nobleman highly distinguished from
his youth, offered, as early as the death of Mr. Pitt,
the first situation in the State, and who, as the head of
a government retaining possession of power for many
years, had enjoyed the good fortune of holding it at
one of the most glorious epochs in British history.
That nobleman left no one behind him entertaining his
own opinions, and on whom his own claims of prece-

dency could be naturally supposed to descend. Besides, he was Mr. Canning's private friend, and agreed with him on almost every question, except the solitary one of Catholic Emancipation.

It was clear, then, that if the successor to Lord Liverpool shared Lord Liverpool's opinions on Catholic Emancipation, but did not share Lord Liverpool's other opinions, and was more or less adverse to Mr. Canning, instead of being particularly attached to him, this would make a great change as to Mr. Canning's position in the Administration, and a great change as to the general character of the Administration itself. Mr. Canning, therefore, could not submit to such a change without damaging his policy and damaging himself. He was to be Cæsar or nobody; the man to lead a party, not the hack of any party that offered him the emoluments of place, without the reality of power.

IV.

But if Mr. Canning was determined to be at the head of the Government, or not to belong to it, his rivals were equally determined not to serve with him if they were to serve under him.

In this dilemma George IV. fixed his eyes on the Duke of Wellington. Few at that period considered the duke fit for the management of civil affairs; but George IV. had great confidence in his general abilities, and thought that with his assistance it might be possible to conciliate a minister whom he was disposed to disappoint, and did not wish to displease. But the Duke of Wellington was the very last man under whom it was Mr. Canning's interest to place himself. That he refused to do so, therefore, is no matter of surprise; his refusal, however, was skilfully framed, and in such terms as were most likely to catch the ear of the nation, "*he could never consent to a military Premier.*" In the meantime, the struggle that had been going on in the Cabinet and the Court, was pretty generally known in the country, and such steps were taken by the two conflicting parties as were most accordant with their several principles and desires. The Duke of Newcastle, on the one hand, claimed the privilege of a Royal audience, and spoke in no measured terms of the parliamentary influence he possessed, and the course he should pursue if Mr. Canning attained his wishes. Mr. Brougham, on the other hand, wrote to Mr. Canning and offered him his unqualified support, saying that that offer was wholly free from any desire for office, which nothing at that moment would tempt him to accept.

V.

A serious contest thus commenced. The different epochs through which this contest was conducted may thus be given. On the 28th of March, the King first spoke to Mr. Canning in a direct and positive manner as to filling up Lord Liverpool's vacancy. Between the 31st of March and the 6th of April affairs remained in suspense. On the 3rd and 4th Mr. Canning and the Duke of Wellington met; and on the 5th, by the desire of the latter, Mr. Canning saw Mr. Peel; the result of these three different interviews being a persuasion on the part of Mr. Canning that it was hoped he would

himself suggest that the Premiership should be offered
to the Duke of Wellington. On the 9th Mr. Peel
again saw Mr. Canning, by the King's desire, and
openly stated that "the Duke of Wellington's appointment would solve all difficulties." On the 10th Mr.
Canning, not having assented to this suggestion, was
empowered to form the new Administration.

The events which followed are well known. On
receiving the King's commands, Mr. Canning immediately requested the services of all his former colleagues, to some of whom his application could only have
been a mere matter of form. For this reason the surprise affected at many of the answers received appears
to me ridiculous. Mr. Canning and his friends would
have retired, if the Duke of Wellington had been made
Premier; and the Duke of Wellington and his friends
retired when Mr. Canning was made Premier.

Nothing was more simple than the tender of those
resignations which were received with such artificial
astonishment; and nothing more absurd than the cant
of abandoning the King, &c. &c., which was applied to
those who tendered them. Nor was the refutation of
such accusations less idle than their propagation. It
might not be true that the seceding Ministers met in a
room, and said, "We will conspire, and you shall send
in your resignation, and I will send in mine." But it
is quite clear that they had common motives of action,
that each understood what those motives were, that as
a body they had long acted in unison, that as a body
they intended to continue so to act. In every representative government men constantly band in this manner together, often denying uselessly that they do so;
and we have only to refer to a memorable instance of

Whig secession, in 1717, in order to find the same accusation as foolishly raised, and the same denial as falsely given.*

But although the resignation of the Duke of Wellington and his friends was almost certain, when the nature of the new arrangement became fully known, the mere fact of Mr. Canning having been commissioned to form a government was not at once taken as the proof that he would possess the power and dignity of Prime Minister.

The Duke of Wellington more particularly seemed determined to consider that nothing as to a Premier was yet decided, and replied to Mr. Canning's announcement that he was charged to form an Administration, by saying:

"I should wish to know who the person is whom you intend to propose to his Majesty as the head of the Government."

To this question Mr. Canning replied at once:

"Foreign Office, April 11, 1827.

"My dear Duke of Wellington,

"I believed it to be so generally understood that the King usually entrusts the formation of an Administration to the individual whom it is his Majesty's

* Lord Townsend being dismissed from the Lord Lieutenancy of Ireland, at the instigation of Lord Sunderland, who had also a party in the Cabinet in 1717, the whole of Lord Townsend's or Walpole's party, including Walpole, resigned. They were attacked in much the same way as the Duke of Wellington, and thought it necessary to defend themselves in the same manner, though there is no doubt that they did resign expressly for the purpose of ousting a government which they thought could not go on without them. In the end they succeeded. — See Coxe's "Memoirs of Sir Robert Walpole," page 107.

gracious pleasure to place at the head of it, that it did not occur to me, when I communicated to your Grace yesterday the commands which I had just received from his Majesty, to add that in the present instance his Majesty does not intend to depart from the usual course of proceeding on such occasions. I am sorry to have delayed some hours the answer to your Grace's letter; but from the nature of the subject, I did not like to forward it, without having previously submitted it (together with your Grace's letter) to his Majesty.

"Ever, my dear Duke of Wellington, your Grace's sincere and faithful servant,

"(Signed)   GEORGE CANNING."

The Duke of Wellington's retirement from office and from the command of the army immediately followed, and now the whole anti-Catholic parti definitely seceded.

VI.

At a cooler moment such an event might have seriously startled George IV., but the pride of the Sovereign overcame the fears and doubts of the politician. "He had not altered his policy; he had merely chosen from amongst his Ministers, a vacancy occurring in the Premiership, a particular individual to be Prime Minister. It was his clear right to select the Prime Minister. Who was to have this nomination? The Duke of Newcastle forsooth!" Thus spoke those of his circle whom Mr. Canning had had the address to gain.

Nor did Mr. Canning himself shrink from his new

situation. His appointment was announced on the very night it took place, and another writ issued for the borough of Harwich, amidst cheers that rang through the House of Commons. Thus he became at once the Minister of the people of England. They anxiously asked themselves whether he could maintain himself in this position?

A circumstance occurred which went far towards settling opinions on this subject. Almost immediately after the official retreat of the anti-Catholic party, Lord Melville, First Lord of the Admiralty, though in favour of the Catholic claims, sent in his resignation, assigning what in the reign of James I. would have been called a good *Scotch reason* for doing so, namely, *he did not think the Government could last.*

The manner of filling up the situation thus vacated might almost have satisfied Lord Melville's scruples. On the 12th his lordship resigned; on the 18th Mr. Canning informed him that the Duke of Clarence, heir-presumptive to the crown, had accepted the office of Lord High Admiral, and would receive Sir George Cockburn and the other Lords of the Admiralty at twelve on the following day. This selection, suggested, it was said, by Mr. Croker, was a decisive blow, and announced the Royal feelings, as far as Mr. Canning was concerned, for two reigns at least. There was still, however, one high appointment most difficult to fill from the Liberal ranks, and there was one member of the new opposition the most formidable, after Mr. Peel (if after him), in the House of Commons. The Lord Chancellorship was the office vacant and difficult to fill. Sir J. Copley, whose recent altercation with the

new Premier on the Catholic question was not forgotten,
was the formidable opponent. But hardly was it known
that the Duke of Clarence was Lord High Admiral,
before it was officially promulgated that Sir J. Copley,
under the title of Lord Lyndhurst, had accepted the
Great Seal. The other appointments immediately made
known were those of Lord Dudley, a Tory who often
voted with Whigs, as Minister of Foreign Affairs; of
Mr. William Lamb, a Whig who often voted with the
Tories, as Secretary for Ireland; of Mr. Sturges Bourne
(a friend of Mr. Canning) as Minister for Home Affairs;
and of Mr. Scarlett, a Whig, as Attorney-General. The
Duke of Portland had accepted the Privy Seal, the
Duke of Devonshire the highest court office, Mr. Robinson, resigning the Chancellorship of the Exchequer
to Mr. Canning, became Lord Goderich, and Leader in
the House of Lords. Lord Palmerston assumed a seat
in the Cabinet. Lord Harrowby, Mr. Wynn, and Mr.
Huskisson retained their former offices.

A private arrangement was also made for admitting
Lord Lansdowne (who was to take the place of Mr.
Sturges Bourne), and also Lord Carlisle and Mr. Tier-
ney, into the Cabinet, at the end of the session.

VII.

In this way commenced that new period in our
history, which finally led to the forming of a large
Liberal party, capable of conducting the affairs of the
country, and to a series of divisions in that Tory party
which had so long governed it. I have said that this
party was already divided before the death of Lord

Castlereagh; for it then contained some influential, well-educated men of Whig opinions, though of Tory alliances, who, whilst opposed to democratic innovations, were dissatisfied with the unpopular resistance to all changes which was the peculiar characteristic of the Lord Chancellor.

Mr. Canning's junction with this section of politicians brought to it a great additional force.

Nor was this all. His genius rallied round him all those in Parliament and the country who had enlightened ideas and generous feelings, and were desirous to see England at the head of civilization, and, whether in her conduct towards foreign nations or at home, exhibiting an interest in the well-being and improvement of mankind. Mr. Canning's feelings on this subject were in no wise disguised by his language.

"Is it not," said he on one occasion, when defending Mr. Huskisson's Free Trade policy, "is it not the same doctrine and spirit now persecuting my right honourable friend which in former times stirred up persecution against the best benefactors of mankind? Is it not the same doctrine and spirit which embittered the life of Turgot? Is it not a doctrine and a spirit such as those which have at all times been at work to stay public advancement and roll back the tide of civilization? A doctrine and a spirit actuating the minds of little men who, incapable of reaching the heights from which alone extended views of human nature can be taken, console and revenge themselves by calumniating and misrepresenting those who have toiled to such heights for the advantage of mankind. Sir, I have not to learn that there is a faction in this country — I mean, not a political faction; I should rather perhaps have said a sect, small in numbers and powerless in might, who think that all advances towards improvement are retrogradations towards Jacobinism. These persons seem to imagine that under no possible circumstances can an honest man endeavour to keep his country upon a line with the progress of political knowledge, and to adapt its course to the varying circumstances of the world. Such an attempt is branded as an indication of mischievous intentions, as evidence of a design to sap the foundations of the greatness of the country."

Again, whilst avowing himself the pupil and disciple of Mr. Pitt, he thus beautifully expresses himself:

"It is singular to observe how ready some people are to admire in a great man the exceptions to the general rule of his conduct rather than the rule itself. Such perverse worship is like the idolatry of barbarous nations, who can see the noonday splendour of the sun without emotion, but who, when he is in eclipse, come forward with hymns and cymbals to adore him. Thus there are those who venerate Mr. Pitt less in the brightness of his meridian glory, than under his partial obscurity, and who gaze on him with the fondest admiration when he has ceased to shine."

In this manner, by his spirit, eloquence, and abilities, he brought public opinion round in such a manner that it even accommodated itself to his personal position, bringing forward into the light his personal views as the popular ones, and throwing those which had formerly been popular, but which he did not support, into the shade. The great constitutional questions hitherto debated were for a time lost sight of, and party spirit, as Mr. Baring stated, leaving its other and more accustomed topics, seemed for the first time to display itself on subjects simply relating to the commerce and mercantile policy of the country.

VIII.

At first the adherents of the Duke of Wellington were like the Royal emigrants from the old French army at the period of the great Revolution. They thought no officers could be found fitted to take their places. But when they saw another government formed, and formed of materials which, if they could be gradually moulded together, would constitute a composition of solid and perhaps permanent endurance, their feelings were marked by that violence and injustice which are almost invariably displayed by men who unexpectedly lose power. Mr. Canning was a renegade for quitting his old political friends to join the Whigs; the Whigs were renegades for abandoning their old political principles to join Mr. Canning. Party rancour had not the candour to acknowledge that if the opinions of Mr. Canning on Catholic Emancipation were sufficient to alienate from him the great bulk of the Conservatives, it was natural that those opinions should attach to him the great bulk of the Liberals. To the attacks of his own party, which he called "the barking of his own turnspits," the new Premier was sufficiently indifferent; but there was one voice lifted up against him, the irony of which pierced his proud heart deeply. Alone and stately, Lord Grey, who had long considered himself the great Whig leader, now stood stripped of his followers, and with little disposition to acknowledge the ascendancy of another chieftain. Contempt was the terrible weapon with which he assailed his brilliant rival, whom from the height of a great aristocratic position and a long and consistent public career, he affected to look down upon as a sort of political adventurer; now carrying out measures the most oppressive to the civil liberties of the people; now spouting liberal phrases which he had no intention to realise; now advocating the claims of the Catholics in glowing words; and now abandoning them when called upon for practical deeds; and finally dressing himself up in borrowed plumes and strutting before the public as the author of a foreign policy the errors of which he cast off upon his colleagues, the merits of which, with equal meanness and unfairness, he took wholly to himself.

If all that Lord Grey said could have been completely justified (which it could not); if all that Lord Grey said, I repeat, had been entirely just (which it was not), the speech which contained it would still have been ill-timed, and impolitic. Mr. Canning represented at that moment those liberal ideas which the public were prepared to entertain. He was encircled by the general popular sympathy, and was therefore in his day, and at the hour I am speaking of, the natural head of the Liberal party. The great necessity of the moment was to save that party from defeat, and give it an advanced position, from which it might march further forward in the natural course of events. If Mr. Canning's party had not obtained power, Lord Grey would never have had a party capable of inheriting it. If Mr. Canning had not become Prime Minister when he did, Lord Grey would not have become Prime Minister three years afterwards.

The public, with that plain common sense which distinguishes most of its judgments, made allowances for the haughty nobleman's anger, but condemned its exhibition. Moreover, the formal charge of Lord Londonderry, who, as his brother's representative, accused Mr. Canning of having forsaken that brother's policy, was more than a counterpoise to Lord Grey's accusation that one Foreign Secretary was no better than the other. Nor did people stop to examine with minute criticism every act of a statesman who had lived in changeful times, and who was then supporting a policy at home favourable to our trade, and carrying out a policy abroad which inspired affection for our name and reverence for our power.

I have as yet purposely confined my observations to those events which were connected with Spain and Portugal, and the struggle we had entered into against the Holy Alliance in regard to those countries; because it was there that Mr. Canning's talents had been most displayed, and that their consequences had been most important. But we are not to limit our review of his conduct merely to these questions.

It was not merely in Spain or in Portugal that England justified her statesman's proud pretension to hold over nations the umpire's sceptre, and to maintain, as the mediatrix between extremes, the peace of the world. Such was the reputation which this statesman had obtained, even amongst those against whom his policy had been directed, that the Emperor Alexander, disgusted with the irresolution of all his other long credited allies, turned at last to Mr. Canning, as the only one capable of taking a manly and decided part in the settlement of a question in which his power was to be guarded against on the one hand, and the feelings of his subjects, and the traditions of his empire, were to be considered on the other.

IX.

The affairs in the East during the last few years require a narrative which, though rapid, may suffice to account for the alliance into which at this time we entered.

In 1821 broke out the Greek insurrection. Suppressed in Moldavia and Wallachia, where it originated, it soon acquired strength in the Greek islands and the Morea. Excesses were natural on both sides, and committed by the conquering race, determined to maintain its power, and the subjugated one, struggling to throw off its chains. The Greek Patriarch was murdered at Constantinople, and a series of savage butcheries succeeded and accompanied this act of slaughter.

By these events Russia was placed in a peculiar and embarrassing position. She could not countenance insurrection; her system of policy just' displayed in Italy could not be reversed in Greece. But the sympathies of religion, and the policy she had long pursued (that of placing herself at the head of the Christian subjects of the Porte by always assuming the air of their protectress), demanded some manifestation of interest in the cause of the rebels. She came forward, then, denouncing the attempt at revolution on the one hand, but protesting on the other against the feelings which this attempt had excited, and the means which had been taken to suppress it. The re-establishment of

the Greek Church, the safe exercise of the Christian
religion, were insisted upon. The indiscriminate mas-
sacre of Christians, and the occupation of Moldavia
and Wallachia by Turkish troops, were loudly condemned. A reply not having been given to the note
in which these remonstrances were expressed within the
time fixed, the Russian Ambassador quitted Constantinople, and war seemed imminent.

But it was the desire of Austria and England especially to prevent war, and their joint representations
finally succeeded in persuading the Sultan to satisfy
the Russian demands; consequently, shortly after Mr.
Canning's accession to office, the Greek churches were
rebuilt, and the Principalities evacuated, while wanton
outrages against the Rayah population were punished
with due justice and severity.

Russia, however, now made new requests; even
these, through the negotiations of the British ambassador at Constantinople, were complied with; and,
finally, after some hesitations and prevarications, the
cabinet of St. Petersburg renewed its diplomatic relations with the Porte.

Still, it was not difficult to perceive that all the
differences hitherto arranged were slight in comparison
with those which must arise if the Greek struggle long
continued unsettled. In ordinary times, indeed, we
shrink before the possibility of a power (whose empire,
however wide, conquest would long keep cemented)
establishing itself across the whole of Europe, and holding on either side, here at the Straits of the Baltic,
there on those of the Mediterranean, the means of carrying on war, or securing safety and peace as it might

seem easy to obtain victory, or advisable to avoid
defeat; a power which, placed in this position, would
demand the constant vigilance of our fleets, establish
an enormous and perpetual drain upon our resources,
and which appeared not unlikely to carry through
Persia (the governor of which would be merely one of
her satraps) disorder and destruction to our Indian
empire. In ordinary times this gigantic vision, when
seen but dimly and at a distance, has more than once
alarmed our government and excited our nation. But
the tardy struggle of that race for independence, to
whose genius and spirit we owe our earliest dreams of
freedom — a struggle in which we were called upon
to side with Greeks fighting for Liberty, with Christians
contending for Christianity, had awakened feelings
which overwhelmed all customary considerations. A
paramount enthusiasm to which a variety of causes,
and especially the verses of Our Poet, were contributing, had seized upon the public mind, and was destined
for awhile to be omnipotent. Guarded by that enthusiasm, Russia might have planted her eagles upon
the walls of Constantinople, if she had appeared as the
champion of that land

— "of gods, and godlike men,"

which had at last "exchanged the slavish sickle for
the sword," and it is doubtful whether an English
Minister could have found a Parliament that would
at that moment have sanctioned his defence of the
Mahometan power.

X.

Mr. Canning, then, only had to chuse between allowing the Russian cabinet to pursue its own plans uncontrolled, or of limiting its action by our co-operation to the particular object it avowed to have in view. The contest, it was evident, after the first successes that had attended the Porte's revolted subjects, would not be allowed to terminate in their subjugation. With the co-operation, or without the co-operation of Great Britain, the Morea was certain to be wrested from the Turks. To stand by neutral, calm spectators of what was certain to take place was to lose our consideration equally with the Ottoman empire and with Christian Europe, and to give to the Government which acted alone in this emergency, as the representative of an universal feeling, an almost universal prestige. But if our interference was expedient, the only question that could arise was as to the time and manner of our interfering.

As early as 1824 Count Nesselrode had had a plan for placing Greece in the situation of the Principalities of the Danube, and the great powers of Europe were invited to consider the subject. Mr. Canning was not averse to this project; but he hoped little from the discordant counsels of the five or six governments called upon to accept it; more especially as both Greece and Turkey, to whom it had become accidentally known, were equally dissatisfied; and he was therefore very properly unwilling to bind his government by a share in conferences which he foresaw were doomed to

be fruitless.   In short, the negotiators met and separated, and the negotiation failed.

But, in the meantime, affairs had been becoming
every day more and more interesting and critical.   On
the one hand the sympathy for the Greeks had been
increased by the unexpected resolution they had displayed; they had a loan, a government, and able and
enterprising foreigners had entered into their service.
So much was encouraging for their cause.   But on the
other hand the Egyptian army of Ibrahim Pasha had
achieved cruel triumphs, and a great part of the Morea,
devastated and depopulated, had submitted to his
arms.

During these events the Czar Alexander died; and
for some little time there was hesitation in the Imperial
counsels.   Alexander's successor, however, soon pursued the policy which his accession to the empire had
interrupted, and propositions (not unlike those formerly
contemplated) were now submitted to our Minister,
propositions in the carrying out of which Great Britain
and Russia were alone to be combined.   The circumstances of the moment showed that the period of action
was arrived, and Mr. Canning no longer shrank from
accepting a part which there appeared some hope of
undertaking with success.

An alliance between two powers, indeed, afforded
a fairer chance of fixing upon a definite course, and
maintaining a common understanding, than the various
counsels amongst which union had previously been
sought.   The Greeks also, who had formerly rejected
all schemes of compromise (May, 1826) now requested
the good offices of England for obtaining a peace upon

conditions which would have recognised the supremacy
of the Sultan, and entailed a tribute upon his former
subjects. Finally, (and this affords an interpretation
to the whole of that policy which prevailed in the
British counsels, from the first to the last moment of
negotiation) the treaty of alliance into which Mr. Canning felt disposed to enter, contained this condition:

"That neither Russia nor Great Britain should obtain any advantage for themselves in the arrangement
of those affairs which they undertook to settle."

France became subsequently a party to this scheme
of intervention, and it was hoped that a confederacy
so powerful would induce the Turks to submit quietly
to the measures which it had been determined, at all
events (by a secret article), if necessary, to enforce.

But whilst these projects were being carried out,
these hopes entertained, that dread King, more potent
than all others, held his hand uplifted over the head of
the triumphant and still ardent statesman.

XI.

On the 2nd of July Parliament had been pro-
rogued; on the 6th the triple alliance was signed. This
celebrated treaty was the last act of Mr. Canning's
official life. The fatigues of the session, short
as it had been, had brought him near the goal to
which the enterprising mind and assiduous labours of
our most eminent men have too often prematurely
conducted them. Of a susceptibility which the slight-
est word of good or evil keenly affected, and of that
sanguine and untiring temperament which would never

suffer him to repose during circumstances in which he
thought his personal honour, his public opinions, and
the welfare of his political friends required his exertions; tortured by every sneer, irritated by every
affront, ready for every toil; in the last few months
in which he had risen to the heights of power and
ambition — such are human objects — was concentrated an age of anxiety, suffering, and endurance. His
countenance became more haggard, his step more feeble,
and his eye more languid. Yet at this moment, jaded,
restless, and worn, he held in the world's eye as high
and enviable a position as any public man ever enjoyed. All his plans had succeeded; all his enemies
had been overthrown. By the people of England he
was cherished as a favourite child; on the Continent he
was beloved as the tutelary guardian of Liberal principles, and respected as the peaceful and fortunate
arbiter between conflicting interests. Abroad, one of
the most formidable alliances ever united against England had been silently defeated by his efforts. At
home, the most powerful coalition that a haughty
aristocracy could form against himself had been successfully defied by his eloquence and good fortune.
The foes of Don Miguel, in Portugal; the enemies of
the Inquisition in Spain; the fervent watchers after
that dawn of civilization, which now opened on the
vast empires of the New World, and which promised
again to shine upon the region it most favoured in
antique times; the American patriot, the Greek freed-
man, and last of all, though not the least interested
(whether we consider the wrongs he had endured, the
rights to which he was justly born, the links which
should have joined him to, and the injustice which

had severed him from, the national prosperity of Great Britain), last of all, the Irish Catholic, dwelt fondly and anxiously on the breath of the aspiring statesman at the head of affairs. His health was too precious, indeed, for any one to believe it to be in danger.

The wound, notwithstanding, was given, which no medicine had the power to cure. On the 1st of August the Prime Minister gave a diplomatic dinner; on the 3rd he was seized with those symptoms which betokened a fatal crisis to be at hand. At this time he was at the Duke of Devonshire's villa at Chiswick, where he had resided since the 20th of July, for the sake of greater quiet and purer air. The room in which he lay, and in which another as proud and generous a spirit, that of Mr. Fox, had passed away, and towards which the eyes of the whole Liberal world were now turned with agonizing suspense for five days, has since become a place of pilgrimage. It is a small low chamber, once a kind of nursery, dark, and opening into a wing of the building, which gives it the appearance of looking into a courtyard. Nothing can be more simple than its furniture or decorations, for it was chosen by Mr. Canning, who had always the greatest horror of cold, on account of its warmth. On one side of the fireplace are a few bookshelves; opposite the foot of the bed is the low chimney-piece, and on it a small bronze clock, to which we may fancy the weary and impatient sufferer often turning his eyes during those bitter moments in which he was passing from the world which he had filled with his name, and was governing with his projects. What a place for repeating those simple and touching lines of Dyer:

> "A little rule, a little sway,
> A sunbeam on a winter's day,
> Is all the proud and mighty have
> Between the cradle and the grave."

After passing some time in a state of insensibility, during which the words "Spain and Portugal" were frequently on his lips, on the 8th of August Mr. Canning succumbed. His remains sleep in Westminster Abbey; a peerage and a pension were granted to his family; and a statue is erected to his memory on the site of his parliamentary triumphs.

The generation amidst which Mr. Canning died, attended his hearse, and crowned his funeral with honours. What is the fame he is entitled to enjoy with after generations of his countrymen?

CANNING,

THE BRILLIANT MAN.

PART V.

One must judge men by a real and not ideal standard of mankind. — Criticisms on Mr. Canning's conduct. — His faults when in a subordinate position. — His better qualities developed in a superior one. — Nature of faculties. — Influence on his own time and the succeeding one. — Foreign policy considered. — Person; manners; specimens of his various abilities; eloquence; art; and turn for drollery and satire. — Style of speaking of despatches. — Always young, and inspiring admiration and affection, even when provoking censure.

PART V.

In estimating the character of public men, the biographer or critic, if he descend from the sublimity of unbounded panegyric, is often apt to elevate himself at the expense of the person of whom he speaks; and to treat with artificial severity any dereliction from that perfection of conduct which he sees nowhere attained. Thanks to this affected severity or paltry envy, we have hardly a great man left to us. Bolingbroke is nothing but a quack; the elder Pitt only a charlatan; Burke himself a declaimer and a renegade; Fox an ambitious politician out of place; all of which things these great men to a certain degree were, being still great men; and deserving the admiration of a posterity which can hardly hope to furnish their equals.

"No one should write history," said Montaigne, "who has not himself served the State in some civil or military capacity." By which this shrewd and impartial observer meant, that no man is fit to judge the conduct of men of action who is not himself a man of action, and can judge it practically, according to what men really are in the world, and not according to any imaginary theory which he may adopt in the obscure nook of his own chimney corner, as to what they might and ought to be.

"We are not," says Cicero, "in the Republic of Plato, but in the mud of Romulus;" and they who

20*

have observed and meditated upon the vicissitudes of
empires, will have seen that such have risen or fallen
according to the number of eminent men, endowed
with lofty intelligences and daring spirits whom they
have produced. And where have such eminent men
existed without defects? Human nature is too imperfect for us to expect to find extraordinary abilities
and energies under the constant control of moderate
virtues.

To those, then, who have read. the preceding
pages, the whole of Mr. Canning's career may be
shortly summed up in the words of Lord Orford (Horace
Walpole), who, speaking of Lord Chatham, says:

"His ambition was to be the most illustrious man
in the first country in the world, and he thought that
the eminence of glory could not be sullied by the
steps to it being passed irregularly" (vol. iv. p. 243).

In the same manner Canning was less scrupulous
than he should have been to obtain power and fame.
But, in the most memorable part of his life, he made
a noble use of the one and well deserved the other.
Desirous of office and distinction, he attached himself,
on entering life, to that minister by whom office and
distinction were most likely to be conferred. The
circumstances of the time afforded him not merely an
apology, but a fair reason for doing this; still, there
seems no injustice in adding that, in ranging himself
under the banner of the great commoner's great son,
he thought of his own personal prospects as well as of
the public interests.

Mr. Pitt died; Mr. Canning was, as he declared
himself, henceforth without a leader. Some of his
opinions inclined him to join his early friends and

recent opponents (the Whigs), who then came into office; and this, it seems, he was on the point of doing, when, by a sudden whirl of Fortune's wheel, the persons he was seceding from were jerked into power, and those he was about to join jerked out of it. A young man, conscious of his abilities, and satisfied in his own mind that, however he might obtain influence, he would use it for the public advantage, he did not refuse a high situation from the party to which he still publicly belonged, in order to follow a party just driven from the Administration, and with which he had but begun to treat.

There are things to say in excuse of this conduct, and I have said them; but no one who wishes that Mr. Canning's life had been without a flaw, can do otherwise than regret that the statesman who made so many subsequent sacrifices for the Catholics, should have joined, at this juncture, a Ministry which rallied its partisans under the cry of "No Popery!"

It is likewise to be regretted that having so frequently expressed his sense of the incapacity of Lord Castlereagh, he should nevertheless have consented first to serve as a subordinate under him when he was mismanaging foreign affairs; and, secondly, to serve as a colleague with him when he was alike lowering us abroad and misgoverning us at home.

During four years he shrunk from the promulgation of no arbitrary edict — from the suppression of no popular right; and though I admit that many liberal and prudent persons (influenced, I cannot but think, by most exaggerated apprehensions) considered that the strongest measures were necessary at that time to control a spirit of insurrection, which the mingled

harshness and incapacity of the ruling Administration
had provoked; still, there is a great difference between
men who sanction bad laws which a bad government,
in which they have had no share, may render momentarily necessary, and men who bring forward bad
laws as the result of a bad government which has been
carried on by themselves.

It is hardly an excuse to say his errors were committed in an inferior situation, with the idea of rising
to a commanding one; but, it is something to observe
that when he had the most power his merits were the
most conspicuous. That he was blamed and praised
with exaggeration was natural; for amidst confronting
arrays he was seen for ever in the first rank with the
most glittering arms, exciting the admiration of friends
and the hatred of foes by his scornful air and ostentatious attitude of defiance.

His talents, by nature showy, were given their
peculiar turn by his early education, and his career
was shaped to the paths which offered to lead him
most easily to distinction. Trained to the juvenile
task of writing a foreign language in polished periods,
he was at times less attentive to following up a sound
argument than to finding an eloquent expression. Not
brought up in communication with the uneducated
classes, he was more keenly alive to the opinion of the
cultivated and refined. Too accommodating as to the
temporary suspension of national freedom at home, he
was constantly anxious and determined to maintain the
power and prestige of the country abroad — throughout
his whole life he exhibited the effects of the public
school and the close borough.

Like most men who have become illustrious, Mr.

Canning owed much to fortune. Lucky in the time of his decease, lucky in the times at which many of those with whom he had hitherto acted deserted him. If he had lived longer, it would have been difficult for him to have kept the station to which he had risen: if he had not been left when he was by a great portion of his party, he would never have obtained the popularity by which his death was hallowed. To few has it happened to be supported by a set of men as long as their support was useful, — to be quitted by them when their alliance would have been injurious. The persons who as friends gave Mr. Canning power, as enemies conferred on him reputation. That reputation was above all others, at the time of his demise, amongst his countrymen and contemporaries; and it still retains its predominance, though the influence which he exercised over our domestic policy, and the events which succeeded his death, are not yet, perhaps, sufficiently recognised. I have already observed that if he had not been Prime Minister in 1827, it is not likely that Lord Grey would have been Premier in 1830. I may add that had not his appointment at the former period brought together all the elements of a great Liberal party, who were allied under the cry of Catholic Emancipation, thus giving a hope and a spirit to the Catholics which they had not previously possessed, the Duke of Wellington would not within a year or two afterwards have been forced to acknowledge that further resistance to them was impossible. Furthermore, if such men as Lord Melbourne, Lord Palmerston, the Grants, and a large party in the country, looking up to these statesmen as safe as well as liberal guides — had not been already connected with the Whigs, and

alienated from the Tories, under the influence of Mr.
Canning in 1827, the Reform Bill would hardly have
been proposed in 1830, and would certainly not have
been carried in 1832. The more minutely, in short,
that we examine the events of the last thirty-six years,
the more we shall perceive how much their quiet development has been owing to Mr. Canning, and to the
class of men whom Mr. Canning formed, and in his
later days represented.

In determining his merits as director of the foreign
policy of Great Britain, I have stood, I confess,
by the old doctrines, and argued upon the assumption
that England is a great state, disposed to maintain
that greatness; that the English people is a proud,
generous, and brave people, prepared to assert its principles and its position, and to assume its part in the
affairs of the world — a nation that takes its share in the
general policy of nations — that feels it has a common
interest in the maintenance of justice, in the limitation
of unscrupulous ambition, in the progress of civilization. I have supposed that the collective wisdom and
experience of past ages, have taught us that human
nature is ever, though under different forms, guided by
the same rules; that the strong, unless they are ade-
quately restrained, insult and oppress, and finally van-
quish the weak; that those who under all circumstances
are determined to be at peace, become eventually the
certain victims of aggression and war; that the spirit
of a people cannot be allowed to droop and languish
with impunity without dimming the brightness of its
genius and losing the force of its character. That a
mere money-making population, which lapped in the
luxury of commercial prosperity, begins to disregard

its nice sense of honour, its admiration for valour and daring, becomes daily weaker against the spoiler, and a greater temptation to spoliation. I have ventured to believe that a noble people has a heart open to noble emotions — that such a heart is not dead to pity for the unfortunate, to sympathy with the brave — to the love of glory inspiring to great deeds, and to the love of power, with the intention to use it for the public good. I do not think it wise to exchange the principles of action derived from these sentiments for a colder, less generous, and, as I feel convinced, a less sound code of political philosophy. The same sentiments which make one man considered and beloved above others, must distinguish the State aspiring to be great and beloved; but it does not follow that if you feel compassion for a drowning man, you are to plunge into the sea to save him if you cannot swim; that if you see two men valiantly struggling against two regiments, you are to rush into the middle of the combat with the certainty of not vanquishing the assailants, and with that of losing your own life. I condemn nations that interfere needlessly with the international affairs of others, as I should the lady who pretended to dictate to her neighbour how she should have her drawing-room swept, or her chimneys cleaned. I condemn governments which threaten heedlessly, and then fail to strike in spite of their threats; but I esteem governments which look carefully after their honour and interests, and do interfere when it is necessary or expedient to do so, in order either to defend that honour, or to maintain those interests; governments cautious to speak, but bold in acting up to their words.

It is with these views that I look upon the foreign

policy of Mr. Canning, — a policy for giving England
a great and proud position, — for giving to Englishmen a glorious and respected name; for safeguarding
our shores by the universal prestige of our bravery
and our power; for limiting the ambition of rival states,
without needlessly provoking their animosity; for showing a wish to conciliate wherever moderation is displayed, and for displaying a resolution to resist when
conciliation is repulsed — a great English policy, with
which the people of England will ever sympathize, and
by which the permanent interests of England will best
be preserved.

There are men who are anxious for civil commotion,
which they think may be more easily brought about
by concentrating the public mind on domestic griev-
ances; there are men who are indifferent to the pride
of country — who would as soon be Portuguese, Mexi-
cans, or Moldo-Wallachians, as Englishmen. There
are men who, though fame and consideration are the
great objects of their countrymen, hold they ought not
to be objects for their country. These will repudiate
my opinion. But every Briton who is justly proud of
his race, who will inquire from a small and despised
state the value of being a great and renowned one,
will, I believe, recognise the foreign policy I have
been describing to be the true policy for maintaining
the dignity and authority, without rashly risking the
peaceful prosperity, of the British empire.

In person Mr. Canning was favoured by nature,
being of a good height, of a strong frame, and of a
regular and remarkably intelligent countenance. The
glance of his eye when excited, and the smile of his

lip when pleased, were often noted by his contemporaries.

> "And on that turtle I saw a rider,
> A goodly man, with an eye so merry,
> I knew 'twas our foreign secretary,
> Who there at his ease did sit and smile
> Like Waterton on his crocodile;
> Cracking such jokes, at every motion,
> As made the turtle squeak with glee,
> And own that they gave him a lively notion
> Of what his own forced-meat balls would be."
>
> *A Dream of a Turtle.* — T. MOORE.

Charming in manner, as I have said, constant in
attachments, it was observed of him at one period,
that he was as dear to his friends as odious to the
public.*

Ever ready to praise his subordinates, and to con-
sult the tastes of his associates, he was honoured as a
chief as much as he was relished as a companion. His
accomplishments were various, and of a kind which
may leave disputes open as to the degree of their excellence, but they were all of that brilliant and genial
description which was sure to attract sympathy and
procure reputation. How many must have chuckled
over the following light and lazy piece of satire:

> "I am like Archimedes for science and skill,
> I am like the young prince who went straight up the hill;
> And to interest the hearts of the fair be it said,
> I am like a young lady just bringing to bed.
> If you ask why the eleventh of June I remember
> So much better than April, or March, or December,
> 'Tis because on that day, as with pride I assure ye,
> My sainted progenitor took to his brewery.
> On that day in the month he began making beer;
> On that night he commenced his connubial career.

* In the Memoirs of Sir J. Mackintosh, in the "Keepsake," 1829.

On that day he died, when had finished his summing,
And the angels all cried here's old Whitbread a coming.
So that day I still hail with a smile and a sigh,
For his beer with an *e* and his bier with an *i*;
And that day every year, in the hottest of weather,
The whole Whitbread family dine altogether.
My Lords, while the beams of the hall shall support
The roof which o'ershades this respectable court
(Where Hastings was tried for oppressing the Hindoos),
While the rays of the sun shall shine in these windows
My name shall shine bright as my ancestor's shines,
Emblazoned on journals as his upon signs."

How many must have felt their minds respond and
their hearts bound at the following argumentative and
spirited declamation:

"When the elective franchise was conceded to the
Catholics of Ireland, that acknowledgment and anticipation, which I now call upon the House formally to
ratify and realize, was, in point of fact, irrevocably
pronounced. To give the latter the elective franchise
was to admit him to political power; for, to make him
an elector and at the same time to render him incapable of being elected, is to attract to our sides the
lowest orders of the community, at the same time that
we repel from us the highest orders of the gentry.
This is not the surest or safest way to bind Ireland to
the rest of the Empire in ties of affection. And what
is there to prevent our union from being wrought more
closely? Is there any moral — is there any physical
obstacle? *Opposuit natura?* No such thing. *We have
already bridged the channel!* Ireland now sits with us
in the Representative Assembly of the Empire; and
when she was allowed to come there, why was she not
also allowed to bring with her some of her Catholic
children? For many years, alas! we have been erecting

a mound, not to assist or improve the inclinations of Providence, but to thwart them. We have raised it high above the waters, and it has stood there frowning hostility and effecting a separation. In the course of time, however, chance and design — the necessities of man and the sure workings of nature — have conspired to break down this mighty structure, till there remains of it only a narrow isthmus standing

> 'between two kindred seas,
> Which mounting view each other from afar,
> And long to meet.'

What, then, shall be our conduct? Shall we attempt to repair the breaches, and fortify the ruins? A hopeless and ungracious undertaking! or shall we leave them to moulder away by time and accident? a sure but distant and thankless consummation! Or shall we not rather cut away at once the isthmus that remains, allow free course to the current which our artificial impediments have constructed, and float upon the mighty waters the ark of our common constitution?"

And we are now to be told that this same man, so playful and jocose, so ornamented and brilliant, was a close arguer, and indefatigable in attendance at his office. But though always ready for business, he would not scruple to introduce a piece of drollery into the most serious affairs. For instance:

The embassy at the Hague is in earnest dispute with the King of Holland; a despatch arrives to Sir Charles Bagot — it is in cypher. The most acute of the attachés set to work to discover the meaning of this particular document; they produce a *rhyme!* they are startled, thrown into confusion; set to work again,

and produce another rhyme. The important paper
(and it was important) contains something like the following doggrel:

> "Dear Bagot, in commerce the fault of the Dutch
> Is giving too little, and asking too much,
> So since on this policy Mynheer seems bent,
> We'll clap on his vessels just 20 per cent."

As a specimen of his more private and trivial plea-
santries may be mentioned his observation to, I believe,
Lord Londonderry, who had been telling a story of
some Dutch picture he had seen, in which all the
animals of antediluvian times were issuing from Noah's
Ark, "and," said Lord Londonderry, "the elephant was
last." "That of course," said Mr. Canning, "he had
been packing up his trunk."

In his celebrated contest with Lord Lyndhurst, that
noble lord having appeared in it with a speech borrowed for the most part from a popular pamphlet,
written by the present Bishop of Exeter, (then Doctor
Phillpotts), he was overthrown amidst shouts of laughter,
by the appropriate recollection of the old song:

> "'Dear Tom, this brown jug that now foams with mild ale,
> Out of which I now drink to sweet Nan of the Vale,' was once
> *Toby Philpot's.*"

Again, who does not remember the celebrated sketch
of Lord Nugent* — who went out to join the Spanish
patriots when their cause was pretty well lost — a
sketch which furnished Mr. Canning's most effective
defence of the neutral policy he had adopted towards
Spain, during the French expedition.

* Lord Nugent was a remarkably large heavy man, with a head even
larger than was required to be in proportion with his body.

"It was about the middle of last July that the heavy Falmouth coach — (here Mr. Canning was interrupted with loud and continued laughter) — that the heavy Falmouth coach was observed travelling to its destination through the roads of Cornwall with more than its wonted gravity (very loud laughter). The coach contained two inside passengers — the one a fair lady of no inconsiderable dimensions, the other a gentleman who was conveying the succour of his person to the struggling patriots of Spain. I am further informed — and this interesting fact, sir, can also be authenticated, that the heavy Falmouth van (which honourable gentlemen, doubtless, are aware is constructed for the conveyance of cumbrous articles) was laden, upon the same memorable occasion, with a box of most portentous magnitude. Now, sir, whether this box, like the flying chest of the conjuror, possessed any supernatural properties of locomotion, is a point which I confess I am quite unable to determine; but of this I am most credibly informed — and I should hesitate long before I stated it to the House, if the statement did not rest upon the most unquestionable authority — that this extraordinary box contained a full uniform of a Spanish general of cavalry, together with a helmet of the most curious workmanship; a helmet, allow me to add, scarcely inferior in size to the celebrated helmet in the castle of Otranto (loud laughter). Though the idea of going to the relief of a fortress, blockaded by sea and besieged by land, in a full suit of light horseman's equipments was, perhaps, not strongly consonant to modern military operations, yet when the gentleman and his box made their appearance, the Cortes, no doubt, were overwhelmed with joy, and rubbed their hands with delight at the approach of the long-promised aid. How the noble lord was received, or what effects he operated on the councils of the Cortes by his arrival, I (Mr. Canning) do not know. Things were at that juncture moving rapidly to their final issue; and how far the noble lord conduced to the termination by throwing his weight into the sinking scale of the Cortes, is too nice a question for me just now to settle."*

Mr. Canning's wit, it is true, was not unfrequently too long and too laboured, and a happy combination of words would almost always seduce him into an indiscretion. The alliteration of "revered and ruptured," as applied to the unfortunate Mr. Ogden, cost him more abuse, and procured him for a time more unpopularity, than the worst of his acts ever deserved. His description of the American navy (in 1812) as "half a dozen fir-frigates, with bits of bunting flying at their heads," excited the American nation more than any actual grievance, and caused in a great measure the bitterness of that contest in which we were so insolent and so unsuccessful. His propensity to jokes made him also many enemies unnecessarily in private life. The late Duke of Bedford told a friend of mine that Mr. Canning, when staying with a party at Lord Carrington's (a few weeks after Lord C. had been made a peer by Mr. Pitt), wrote in chalk, on the outside of the hall-door, the following lines: —

> "One Bobby Smith lives here,
> Billy Pitt made him a peer,
> And took the pen from behind his ear."

* "Annual Register," 1821.

This unnecessary impertinence, I have heard, Lord Carrington never forgave.

In the art of speaking our orator's progress, like that of Pulteney, Fox, and all our great parliamentary debaters, with the exception of the two Pitts, Bolingbroke, and Lord Derby, was slow and gradual; and though I have heard Lord Lansdowne (once known as Henry Petty) observe that he considered Canning in his best days even more effective than Fox or Pitt, he had at an earlier period been often accused, by no mean judges, now of being wordy and tedious, now of being rather elegant than argumentative. To time, practice, a proud spirit, and a continually developing understanding, he owed his triumph over these defects. Then it was that his eloquence approached almost to perfection, as we consider the audience half lounging and sleepy, half serious and awake, to which it was addressed. Quick, easy, and fluent, frequently passionate and sarcastic, now brilliant and ornamented, then again light and playful; or, if he wished it, clear, simple, and incisive; no speaker ever combined a greater variety of qualities, though many have been superior in each of the excellences which he possessed. More usually remarkable for the polish of his language (we have proof, even to the last, of the pains he bestowed upon it), those who knew him well assert that he would sometimes purposely frame his sentences loosely and incorrectly, in order to avoid the appearance of preparation. "Erat memoriâ nulla tamen meditationis suspicio." His action exhibiting when calm an union of grace and dignity, became, as he warmed, unaffectedly fervent; and made natural by its vigour and animation the florid language and figurative decorations in which he rather too fondly indulged. His arguments were not placed in that clear, logical form, which sometimes enchains, but more often wearies, attention; neither did he use those solemn perorations by which it is attempted to instil awe or terror into the mind. His was rather the endeavour to charm the ear, to amuse the fancy, to excite the feelings, to lead and fascinate the judgment; and in these different attributes of his great art he succeeded in the highest degree, insomuch that though he might be said to want depth and sublimity, the faculties he possessed were elevated to such a pitch, that at times he appeared both profound and sublime.

A great merit, which he finally possessed, was that of seizing and speaking the general sense of the popular assembly he addressed. Sir Robert Peel, his distinguished rival, told me one day, in speaking of Mr. Canning, as to this particular, that he would often before rising in his place, make a sort of lounging tour of the House, listening to the tone of the observations which the previous debates had excited, so that at last, when he himself spoke, he seemed to a large part of his audience to be merely giving a striking form to their own thoughts.

Neither were his despatches, though not so elaborately perfect as those of his successor (Lord Dudley), inferior to his orations; possessing precision, spirit, and dignity, they remain what they were justly called by no incompetent authority, models and masterpieces of diplomatic composition.*

---

* Sir J. Mackintosh, in speaking of Mr. Canning's despatches on the South American question, said that "they contained a body of liberal maxims, of policy, and just principles of public law, expressed with a

There are critics who have said that there was something in his character which tended to diminish our respect for his talents, though it softened our censure for his defects. And it is true that the same unstately love for wit — the same light facility for satire — the same imprudent levity of conduct, that involuntarily lowered our estimate of his graver abilities — involuntarily led us to excuse his graver errors. We at one time blame the statesman for being too much the child — at another we pardon the veteran politician in the same humour in which we would forgive the spoiled and high-spirited schoolboy.

Mr. Canning, indeed, was always young. The head of the sixth form at Eton — squibbing "the doctor," as Mr. Addington was called; fighting with Lord Castlereagh; cutting jokes on Lord Nugent; flatly contradicting Lord Brougham; swaggering over the Holy Alliance; he was in perpetual personal quarrels — one of the reasons which created for him so much personal interest during the whole of his parliamentary career. Yet out of those quarrels he nearly always came glorious and victorious — defying his enemies, cheered by his friends — never sinking into an ordinary man, — though not a perfect one.

No imaginative artist, fresh from studying his career, would sit down to paint this minister with the broad and deep forehead — the stern compressed lip — the deep, thoughtful, concentrated air of Napoleon Bonaparte. As little would the idea of his eloquence or ambition call to our recollection the swart and iron

precision, a circumspection, a dignity, which will always render them models and masterpieces of diplomatic composition." — June 15, 1826.

21*

features — the bold and haughty dignity of Strafford. We cannot fancy in his eye the volumed depth of Richelieu's — the volcanic flash of Mirabeau's — the offended majesty of Chatham's. Sketching him from our fancy, it would be as a few still living remember him, with a visage rather marked by humour and intelligence than by meditation or sternness; with something of the petulant mingling in its expression with the proud; with much of the playful overruling the profound. His nature, in short, exhibited more of the genial fancy and the quick irritability of the poet who captivates or inflames an audience, than of the inflexible will of the dictator who puts his foot on a nation's neck, or the fiery passions of the tribune who rouses a people against their oppressors.

Still, Mr. Canning, such as he was, will remain one of the most brilliant and striking personages in our historical annals. As a statesman, the latter passages of his life cannot be too deeply studied; as an orator, his speeches will always be models of their kind; and as a man, there was something so graceful, so fascinating, so spirited in his bearing, that even when we condemn his faults, we cannot avoid feeling affection for his memory, and a sympathetic admiration for his genius.

APPENDIX.

THERE is a circumstance connected with the sketch of
Mr. Canning which I am called upon to notice.

The original MS. — which has since then been but very
slightly altered — was completed twenty-six years ago, and
the greatest part in print not very long afterwards. Before,
however, the whole had been sent to the press, I was
called away on diplomatic duty, and left the proof-sheets
in the hands of Mr. Colburn and the printer's, Beaufort
House; abandoning in my own mind the intention of ever
publishing or completing the work. In fact, in the busy
life of Spain it was forgotten. On my return to England,
in 1848, I received a visit from Mr. Bell, then editor of the
Atlas. He sat with me some time, but did not make to me
any particular communication, and it was only some time
afterwards that I conjectured the purport of his visit. I
then by accident, it might have been in America, read his
Life of Mr. Canning, and found it was undeniably based
on my original sketch. Many anecdotes were in it that I
had had from private sources of a particular description,
some of which anecdotes I have now omitted. Whole passages were entirely the same in purport and almost in
expression; in fact, there are parts, the one relating to the
Treaty of Vienna and the partitions which then took place,
for instance, which are almost verbally repeated. I did not

think it worth while to take notice of this; I was rather glad than otherwise that the labour, which I had considered thrown away, as far as any object of my own was concerned, had been useful in the composition of an able work by another; and I only now mention the facts I have been relating, to clear myself from any charge of plagiarism which might otherwise be reasonably made against me. A copy of the old proofs I still retain.

H. B.

END OF VOL. II.

www.ingramcontent.com/pod-product-compliance
Lightning Source LLC
Chambersburg PA
CBHW060523030726
47498CB00004B/1053